HOLLYWOOD SCANDAL

LOUISE BAY

Published by Louise Bay 2017

ISBN – 978-1-910747-47-6

ONE

Lana

As a teenager, I couldn't wait to escape Worthington, Maine, but as I paused to breathe in the last of Mr. Graham's lilacs, I couldn't imagine why. I'd been incredibly lucky to have grown up in such a beautiful place.

My arms were full of groceries, so I half waved to Polly Larch as she crossed Main Street opposite the post office, tugging at her cat's leash. Even though it looked like Polly was in charge, I was pretty sure she was following wherever the cat wandered.

I pushed my sunglasses to the top of my head and climbed the steps to Mrs. Wells' porch. I knocked and headed straight in. "Mrs. Wells, it's Lana." As well as being a self-proclaimed psychic, Mrs. Wells was the oldest resident of Worthington and a number of us took it in turns to drop off her groceries.

The television fell silent as I shut the door behind me.

"Hello, dear." Mrs. Wells turned to wave at me as I smiled before heading to the kitchen.

"I'm just going to unpack these groceries and I'll be right over," I replied. I put the brown paper bag on the counter alongside the canvas tote that bore my newly designed logo for Kelly Jewelry. I grinned as I straightened it out so I could see the raspberry pink set against the duck-egg blue. I'd spent weeks designing it, had commissioned a painted storefront sign and eventually I would recover the seats of the chairs in my shop with the same colors and maybe paint my nails that same shade of pink. Everything was coming together.

I emptied the tote, rolled it up and snapped it shut in my faux-vintage carpet bag.

"*The Young and the Restless?*" I asked, checking to see which soap opera Mrs. Wells was watching.

"No dear, it's yesterday's *General Hospital*. Thank you for dropping off my groceries, now come and sit here." She removed a faded patchwork quilt from the chair beside her and patted the cushion. "I haven't seen you for a few weeks. Tell me what's been going on."

I smoothed down the back of my skirt before taking a seat. "I'm sure you know far more than I do." Mrs. Wells had been born in this town and there was nothing she didn't know about either before it happened or, at the very latest, the moment after. And it had nothing to do with her psychic ability.

"Did you hear about the movie they're making along the coast?" she asked.

"Is that even true?" More than one person had mentioned the movie being filmed just between here and Portland, but there were plenty of beaches in California. Why would they come to Maine?

"Bree Kendall stopped by on her way back from Portland yesterday. She said she saw a hundred trucks trailing through the town." As Mrs. Wells' house sat right at the end of Main Street, and she spent almost as much time on her porch as she did watching TV, she had a bird's-eye view of most of the action that took place in Worthington and passersby told her the news from out of town.

Not that there was much, which was exactly how I liked it.

"I hear the whole of Portland is full of Hollywood types and all the hotels are booked up," she told me.

"Well, that's good for local business," I said, staring at the TV, trying to work out if I'd seen the woman on the screen in something else. I had a terrible memory for names *and* faces. Another reason why staying in the same place I grew up was such a good idea for me. Other than tourists, there were few new people who came to town.

"It might be good for you, too. Perhaps you should take an ad out in the *Portland Press Herald*."

"Maybe." I was pretty sure if a film crew was in Portland, they'd have neither the time nor inclination to visit a jewelry store thirty-five minutes north of where they were staying.

"You should think about it. There are a lot of things happening for you this summer." I could tell by her sure voice that she wasn't just making small talk. She had information. Or at least she thought she did. Although Mrs. Wells had long-since retired from giving readings to passing tourists on the beach, apparently the spirits weren't so keen on her retirement and she still passed on what they told her to any Worthington resident who asked. But I hadn't asked. And I didn't want to know.

She pulled out my yellow silk scarf from where it was lodged beside her. So that was where it had disappeared. I hadn't seen it in weeks. I should have known. "You must have left it when you were last here, my dear."

She was trying to appear nonchalant, but the sparkle in her eyes told me she was busting at the seams to tell me whatever reading she'd got on my scarf.

"I've told you before, Mrs. Wells, I'm not interested in knowing what my future holds. I want to see it for myself." Unfortunately, Mrs. Wells wasn't one of those fortune tellers who just told you the good stuff. When I'd been to see her about college choices, desperate for her to tell me that art school in New York would make all my dreams come true, I'd been devastated that she'd told me the move would only bring me pain. I'd ignored her, assuming her negative reading was just reflective of the fact that she was a small-town woman frightened of the big city.

I hated that she'd been right, and I'd never asked her what the spirits said again. Since I'd been back in Worthington, I'd worked hard to hold things steady, made sure I was in control of my own destiny. I wanted to keep my life just as it was. I was happy.

"You need to prepare yourself, my dear. This summer there's a storm coming your way. Lots of change."

My stomach flipped over. I didn't do storms. There was no way my world could be thrown off balance—I'd made sure of it. I shook my head. "Well, I've storm-proofed my life." My jewelry shop was turning a small profit, I'd set up an online storefront, and had made more from the last three months of internet sales than I had in the whole of last year. I had my cottage on the beach and good friends and neighbors. There was nothing that could alter any of that.

"It's impossible to avoid. It's your destiny. You can withstand what comes but things will change. Storms can be destructive but they can clear the air, ready for a fresh start. A new beginning," she said, looking at me intently.

"Please, Mrs. Wells. I really don't want to hear any more." I twirled the yellow scarf around my fingers. I'd worked really hard for calm seas these last few years, and I didn't want to think about anything disturbing that. And I didn't need a new beginning. I'd thought that about college and where had that gotten me?

She patted my hand. "Have you rented out your next-door cottage for the summer?"

I was grateful she'd changed the subject. "Actually, it was booked months ago for six weeks. A family from Boston arrived yesterday. I haven't met them yet, but their car is in the driveway." My best friend Ruby and I rented out a house we jointly owned that was a carbon copy of my cottage. When my father died, I couldn't bring myself to live in my childhood home, so I'd decided to sell that house and reinvest in two clapboard cottages next door to each other on the beach less than a ten-minute walk from where I'd grown up. My father would have approved. He'd always been a big believer in brick-and-mortar-based income.

"That's great news, dear. See, there will be lots of good in with the turmoil."

I sighed. I wished she'd drop it. My life wasn't *in turmoil*, and I'd make sure it never would be. And it was no surprise about the rental cottage. Fact was, the house was popular and rented well year-round, but six weeks was a nice long period of time, especially for the money Ruby had managed to secure. She dealt with bookings from her home in New York, and I handled the things on the ground— welcome basket, weekly maid service and generally organizing any necessary maintenance. Often, I never even met the renters. Most people spent their days out exploring the coast.

"Well, I'm looking forward to a great summer for all of us," I said as I stood and straightened out my skirt.

"With all that's coming into your life, it's going to get interesting for you. That's for sure. It won't all be bad. But you're going to have to listen to your heart."

"Mrs. Wells!" I scolded, trying not to stamp my foot like a three-year-old. I couldn't have been clearer that I didn't want to hear her predictions. And I knew full well that listening to my heart was the last thing I needed to do. *That* got me nothing but trouble. "I've told you before that I'm perfectly happy with my life as it is. I don't do turmoil. And I don't want to hear any more."

She clearly couldn't resist. "I'm sorry," she said, pressing her palm to her chest. "I want you to find someone who will love you just like Mr. Wells loved me. And when I got that message from your scarf about the handsome man in your future, I just couldn't hold it in."

"A man?" Her prediction had gotten worse. The very last thing I wanted was a *man*. I'd learned that I couldn't trust men. And I couldn't trust *my judgment* of men. It was an easy solution—I just avoided them. Not that there were many single men under thirty-five in Worthington. Which was exactly why this place was so perfect.

I loved my life here—the lilacs, the thunderstorms and the ocean that I saw every time I looked out of the window. It was home—a harbor of happiness, familiarity and shelter. I might have been a little lonely every now and then on a Saturday night, but Netflix and the sound of the waves crashing against the beach just beyond my cottage plugged most of the gap. I had what I needed. Life was good.

"Okay, Mrs. Wells, I need to get back to the shop." I

stood up again. I'd put the closed sign up while I delivered Mrs. Wells' groceries, and I didn't want to miss people on their way home from work.

"Very well, but make sure you've got an umbrella. It's going to rain."

I frowned. "It's a beautiful day, Mrs. Wells. I don't need an umbrella." I picked up my purse and headed out.

If she couldn't even get the weather right, hopefully Mrs. Wells was losing her touch. I needed my life to remain as it was. Handsome men had never worked out well for me.

TWO

Matt

It had been twenty-seven hours, ten minutes and roughly forty-five seconds since I'd arrived in Worthington, Maine, from LA. Which meant it had been twenty-seven hours, ten minutes and roughly fifty-five seconds since I'd last been recognized.

My heart rate was 132 and the muscles in my thighs had begun to burn but I kept running, taking in the fresh sea air. I couldn't remember the last time I'd run outside. Most of the time it was just too goddamn hot in Los Angeles, though the freaking heat was the least of my problems. Being chased by fans, or worse, the paparazzi, was the bigger issue. But, apparently nobody in Maine went to the movies.

I should have been grateful. After all, fame was simply a byproduct of being a successful Hollywood actor, although some stars *loved* the attention. They kept the paparazzi on speed dial and let them know whenever they were stepping out for a hike. For me, the fame came with the territory and

I put up with it because the upside outweighed the down. I liked that I could run here, but anonymity wasn't worth giving up on success. Fame was a price I was willing to pay.

I shivered as a huge gray cloud slid across the sky like the alien aircraft straight out of Independence Day. Fuck. That seemed ominous.

I'd marked out a route before I left, so I crossed the street and headed toward the park I knew was a shortcut back to my rental. As I passed the entrance gate, my cell vibrated in my pocket. Shit, my agent. I slowed to a walk and answered.

"Hey, Brian," I said, the crack of thunder from above nearly drowning me out.

"Where the fuck are you?" Brian asked.

Big, fat drops of rain began to splatter the path leading through the park. I was about to get drenched. "In a thunderstorm. What's up?"

I scanned the park and spotted a small white gazebo. I headed toward it, hoping I'd be able to finish the conversation without my cell getting waterlogged.

"So, I got a call from Anthony Scott. He loved you in *Vanity Fair*. Wanted to know what your schedule looked like eighteen months from now."

Wow. Anthony Scott had a way of turning things into box office gold. I couldn't say I loved his movies, but an Anthony Scott film would be the next step up—a well-respected director, a sure-fire hit. "What project is he thinking about?"

"Who the fuck cares? If Anthony Scott wants you, that's all you need to know. This is proof that your reputation is beginning to bounce back from your past indiscretions and that you're on track."

Indiscretions. Right. Nice of Brian to put it so delicately, when we both knew I'd lost sight of my goal when I wrapped my third leading role and cashed the corresponding huge paycheck. I'd partied way too hard. Drunk too much, *known* far too many women. It was almost as if I'd forgotten who I was and where I'd come from.

My dad and Brian had pulled me back just before I'd managed to ruin a bright career and future. The last eighteen months I'd rediscovered my focus and worked nonstop. I'd had two hit movies and a cover of *Vanity Fair*. Everything was coming together. My *indiscretions*, as Brian discreetly called that dark period, had been a bump in the road that *I knew* I was over, though I was still having to convince everyone else that I wasn't about to go back there again.

"This might be your shot at a franchise," Brian said. "You never know how these things are going to go."

Franchise—the two syllables sent a shiver down my spine. The Hollywood Holy Grail. Bagging one would show that I hadn't fucked up completely and that I'd *arrived*. Finally. I could practically feel my hands sinking into the wet cement outside Grauman's Chinese Theater. A series of hit, big budget, studio movies would mean multiple contracts, which spelled job security and, most importantly, a big payday. I would never have to worry about money again. And neither would my family. I would have achieved all I wanted to when I left Gary, Indiana, ten years ago, determined to make it. My parents and my brothers would be able to have the lives they'd always dreamed of, rather than the ones that had been dished out at birth. Money bought freedom for me and my family.

"Did you hear me, Matt?"

"I heard you." Climbing the steps of the bandstand, I glanced out over the ocean. The sky covered in clouds, the water looked darker than I'd seen it before. More dangerous. "That's great news."

"Are you sure everything's alright? What are you doing out so early in the morning?"

"I'm out for a run."

Brian was still suspicious that I was about to go off the rails again at any moment. It wasn't going to happen. I'd learned my lesson. He'd been in talks with a big producer on my behalf who ended up pulling their offer once they heard about my arriving on set drunk. I'd lost out on a potential blockbuster as well as nearly being fired from the film I was shooting. But what was worse was my dad turning up to visit in the middle of it all. The shame had been unbearable. Catching the look of disappointment in my dad's eyes was all it took. I'd cleaned up my act. And I'd never go back. Ever. "I'm just heading back. Stop worrying. There's no temptation in this town."

"Okay, if you say so."

I put my finger in my ear to tune out the sound of someone shouting in the distance.

"I do. So, is Anthony going to send over a script or a treatment or something?"

"I don't know. It's opening discussions only. But I told him you'd free up your schedule to work with him."

The yelling got louder.

"Sounds good." I turned to find a woman marching toward me. So much for not being recognized. I pushed my damp hair out of my face and took a breath, ready to smile sweetly when asked for an autograph.

As she got closer, her damp clothes showed off the body of a fifties movie star—all small waist and great legs. Her shirt, weighed down with rain, accentuated her dangerously tempting breasts. Long, dark, wet hair clung against alabaster skin. Her soaked-through skirt treated me to a view of firm thighs and the lacy outline of her panties.

Fuck, it was like the weather *wanted* me to see her pussy.

I didn't fuck fans—it was my number one rule. But at the moment, I wasn't fucking anyone. My current girlfriend was a PR stunt and ever since Brian had made me hire a publicist—Sinclair Evans—to clean up my image, I'd been making do with my fist and an occasional *old friend* from New York. There were two ex-lovers I still saw. I was sure I could trust them and my publicist had them sign non-disclosures for an extra layer of security.

No fans. No more random models. No more ill-advised one-night stands.

But my fist just wasn't scratching the itch, and the woman in front of me was temptation on a stick.

Maybe I could get away with indulging with a fan just this one time? No. Now was not the time to give in to temptation.

"Can you hear me?" Brian asked, but I was too mesmerized by the autograph hunter heading toward me to pay attention, even if he was talking about an Anthony Scott movie.

"Yeah, the line's bad though. I'm not—"

"What are you doing, you crazy asshole?" the brown-eyed girl yelled, stomping up the wooden stairs of the bandstand.

"What?" Brian shouted over the drone of thunder.

Before I could figure out what was happening, the girl had gripped my wrist with her fingers and was trying to drag me out into the rain.

"Brian, I'll call you back."

"Are you the dumbest person on the planet?" she

screamed, jerking me down the steps of the bandstand before finally letting me go.

Had I landed a stalker? If so, fucking her definitely didn't seem like such a good idea. "Look, babe, if you've got a pen, I'll give you an autograph, but I'm not posing for a selfie in this weather."

She paused, a scowl seizing her face. "Are you an *idiot*? Who the hell shelters in a bandstand with a metal roof, on a hill, in the middle of a lightning storm?"

I swept my hand through my hair and shrugged. "Sorry."

She rolled her eyes and turned on her heel. "Unbelievable," she muttered. "Don't shelter under the trees, either." She began to walk away. "We don't need some dumb-assed tourist getting struck by lightning and screwing up our visitor season."

Well, whoever the girl was, she wasn't some stalker who'd followed me from Los Angeles. She hadn't even seemed to recognize me.

She didn't look back, but she did grace me with the most delectable view of her ass as she sashayed away.

God, I wanted to sink my teeth into that ass. I hadn't had a woman speak to me like that since high school. They were too busy giggling, gasping or flirting. As I watched the drenched woman walk away from me, I realized the easy conquest had gotten kinda old.

I stuffed my phone back into my pocket and began to stroll back toward the rental cottage. Maybe I'd take a detour through the park again tomorrow. I wouldn't mind being accosted by that brown-eyed beauty again.

THREE

Lana

I stepped out of the water into a bathroom full of steam. After pulling the towel off the rail, I wrapped myself up in fluffy cotton. I'd been dreaming about my shower all afternoon. Mrs. Wells had been right about the rain. I'd gotten drenched. Luckily, I had a change of clothes at the shop, but I'd felt sticky and cold for the rest of the day. If that crazy tourist hadn't been hiding out in the bandstand, trying to get hit by lightning, I might not have been as wet through to my bones. But no good deed goes unpunished.

I twisted my feet on the soft memory foam mat and sighed. I'd gotten so soaked from the thunderstorm that I'd been tempted to turn back and take the afternoon off, but I'd had a ton of orders to fill and a few tourists came by, so it was just as well I hadn't bailed on the day.

I wrapped my hair up in a towel, padded into my bedroom and sprawled like a starfish on the bed. It was still early enough for me to do a couple of hours on the new jewelry collection I'd been working on if I got my ass into gear.

I dried myself off, slung on some yoga pants and a slouchy tee and began to towel dry my hair as I sat on the edge of the bed facing the window. Next door, a car was parked in the driveway. It had that squashed look of a fancy, expensive sports car. Seemed kinda strange for a family car, but maybe they'd brought two?

I'd left them a welcome package with my number if they had a problem. I didn't usually tell guests I lived right next door. After the first few renters, I'd learned that if I did, I'd have a constant stream of "What's the Wi-Fi code again?" or "Where's good for dinner?"

I discarded my towel and started brushing through my tangles.

The light was on in the kitchen next door; someone's silhouette displayed like a shadow puppet through the white voile blinds. It looked like someone was dancing. A guy. The dad, maybe? Except that it didn't look like dad dancing. He could move. I laughed, then covered my mouth. I shouldn't be laughing. He was paying rent. And I certainly shouldn't be staring.

The blind rippled and two hands dipped beneath the voile and began to fiddle with the catch. I shuffled down my bed. I was pretty sure he wouldn't be able to see me. I was away from the window and my lights weren't switched on, but I didn't want to take any chances. The blind lifted, revealing a perfect torso—golden skin with clearly defined muscles. This guy was built. The voile was only partially up, so I couldn't see if the face matched the body but, boy, if it did? My new neighbor just might be the most handsome man I'd ever come across.

The abs tensed and relaxed as his large hands found the

catch on the window and he pushed it open. I froze. Somehow, the lack of that pane of glass between us brought me up short. I needed to stop staring.

His wife was one lucky woman.

My cell rang on my nightstand. I grabbed it and answered.

"Hey, Ruby," I said, as I held the phone between my ear and shoulder and drew my curtains. That would stop me from being a voyeur. "How's the Big Apple?" We'd both dreamed of leaving Worthington for the city since we'd been old enough to understand there was a world outside Maine. Together, we'd gone to college in New York. She'd never left. I'd never expected to come back. But here I was.

And I was happy.

"Good, though it would be better if you were here. How's the new collection going?"

I designed all the jewelry in my shop, but I sent it to a manufacturer in Massachusetts for production. It kept costs down and meant I could keep up with orders coming in online. There was no way I could make it all by hand and anyway it would mean it would be too expensive for the tourist market. In fact, I'd not handcrafted anything since college. The new designs I was working on would probably never get made. "The collar I'm designing is really lovely. I'll take a picture and send it to you." The chunky necklace was my favorite of the collection so far. It was designed to be made of gold and took its inspiration from ancient Egypt. I'd drawn it in the shape of a crescent moon, with ribbons of gold filigree layered in an asymmetrical pattern across it. I fingered my collarbone as I spoke.

"You've been working on it for months. You're not done yet?"

Ruby and I had this conversation every time we talked

about my designs. I was always designing new stuff, but my Bastet collection, named after the Egyptian goddess of protection, wasn't something I'd just hand off to be manu-factured in Massachusetts. These pieces were special and needed to be handcrafted.

"It's almost there. But there's no rush."

Silence reigned on the other end of the phone. Ruby had always encouraged me to get back to making jewelry again. But I'd been too busy setting up the shop, designing the stock, finding the manufacturer. There were a thousand things to think about. There had been a time that one-off, exclusive pieces were what I thought I wanted to do, but it was more difficult to do that in Worthington when all the buyers and fashion houses were in New York. So I'd aban-doned that ambition when I left the city, and now I was content with my little shop. I was still in the jewelry busi-ness and that's what mattered. It had been my dream since my dad gave me my mom's jewelry box when I was five years old just after she died.

The jewelry I designed and sold in the shop wasn't cheap, but it wasn't so exclusive that a tourist wouldn't buy a necklace, ring or pair of earrings on impulse. Things were working out pretty well.

"I just think it would be good for you to get back into the workshop. I remember how much you've always loved it."

"I did, but life's busy. The shop takes a lot of my time and then there's the property next door. Speaking of, do you know how old the kids are in this family?" The body on the dad would suggest they were little, but I hadn't heard any yelling or screaming.

"I don't know. Why?"

"No reason, just wondering." I peeked through the edge

of the curtain as I finished brushing my hair. The silver sports car still stood alone on the drive.

"I have the email right here. It's a family?" she asked.

"Uh-huh." The kitchen window was still open, but the abs were gone and the floorshow had ended. I released the curtain and headed to my home office.

"Says here on the form it's a corporate booking—Lakeside Limited," Ruby said.

I paused in the doorway. "I thought you said it was a family?"

"There's the family from Boston who're coming later in the season. Anyway, is there a problem? Their payment went through just fine."

"No problem. I must have gotten confused is all." I'd put gummy bears in their welcome basket. I liked to customize each one so it felt more personal. I guess some corporate guest was getting their sugar fill.

"I have no idea. The booking details don't even say how many guests. As long as it's not a bunch of frat boys, right?"

Perhaps it was just a couple, then? That would explain the sports car. Maybe they were gay. Surely someone with a body as hot as the one I'd seen could never be straight.

"So how's Chas?" I asked as I stood over my desk, laying out the line drawings I'd done of the Bastet collection.

"We had an argument," she replied with an exhale. Ruby fighting with Chas wasn't unusual. I wasn't quite sure why she put up with him. They seemed to fight constantly.

"Surely the good sex isn't worth what he puts you through?"

Ruby paused before she said, "The problem is I don't want anything serious—I just want to be seriously casual."

I chuckled. "You know you make no sense whatsoever, right?" I moved the drawings around, trying to put them in the order I wanted to paint them in watercolor. I'd already started on the collar.

"I do make sense. I don't want a guy I have to see all the time—twice a week works for me. And he doesn't need to declare his undying love or buy me flowers, he just needs to turn up if I've cooked dinner."

I winced. "He didn't show last night?" I'd talked her through my recipe for my shrimp marinade, so I knew she'd put in some effort.

"No. He didn't even call. He showed up an hour ago and told me he'd lost track of time in the Hamptons because he was on a bender with the boys. He didn't even seem sorry."

"He knows he's not in college, right?" We'd been having the same old discussions about Chas since she'd met him. Surely she could find someone more mature. Being on her own had to be better than being with Chas.

"I'm not sure he does. But his friends are the same now as they were back then, so they do the same things. Weekends are Party Central. Now that he's rented this share of the Hamptons house for the summer, it's gotten worse."

"Sounds like you need to move on." I drew a finger along the curved lines of the chandelier earrings I'd started on last night. I decided to work on those, and put the rest of the drawings in a pile on my desk.

"But I love the sex. I really do," she whined.

"No dick is worth putting up with his lack of respect. You're in the city that never sleeps. There must be plenty of penis in that place."

"I'm starting to think you might be right. Maybe I should be like you and let my vagina shrivel up and die."

"Hey, my vagina is still alive and kicking." Her jokes about my desiccating vagina were getting old.

"If you say so. What else is new? Any hot men washed up on the beach?"

I groaned as I remembered Mrs. Wells' prediction. "I saw Mrs. Wells earlier. She told me life was about to get difficult for me, *there's a storm brewing* or something. Apparently, some man is about to appear and cause a bunch of trouble." Was that how she'd phrased it?

"A man?" she asked, the decibels coming down the phone suddenly multiplying by a hundred.

"She's way off. This is Worthington. My life can't slide into turmoil if I don't let it. You know she actually stole my yellow scarf?" Which reminded me I needed to retrieve my sodden carpet bag from where I'd left it to dry off on the porch. "So what are you going to do about Chas?" I headed out and found my bag where I'd left it. I pulled my scarf out and hung it over the wooden railing, and arranged the still-wet bag so it got as much air as possible.

"Mrs. Wells has always been completely on point whenever she's given me a reading," Ruby said.

I wished I hadn't brought it up. I was never going to hear the end of it. And I didn't want to think for a moment that she might be right.

"What else did she say?" Ruby asked.

I glanced across at the rental cottage. The light in the kitchen had gone off. "Nothing. Ruby, we were talking about Chas."

"No we were not. Tell me more about this mystery man. Does he live in Worthington?"

"I doubt it. I know all eight hundred thirty-two people in this town."

"So, she saw travel in your future. Interesting. Maybe you're finally going to get your ass down here for a visit."

I rolled my eyes. I hadn't been back to New York since I

left college early with just enough credit to scrape through graduation. And I had no plans to return. It held too many unpleasant memories. "Seriously. Can we go back to Chas?"

"If you promise to tell me when this man sweeps into town causing chaos."

"Deal." Any storms that hit Worthington, I'd watch from my porch under a blanket. There would be nothing to tell.

FOUR

Matt

I hadn't washed dishes since . . . well I couldn't remember ever doing the dishes. Even when I was in New York starting out, I ate takeout precisely so I *didn't have to*. But I felt pretty good about the results as I folded the dish towel and placed it on the counter. It felt normal. Brian had tried to convince me to bring my assistant to Maine so they could fetch and carry for me. But I was enjoying having some time to myself. Back in Los Angeles, I worked most of the time. Even when I wasn't on set, I read scripts, went to industry parties to network, or strategized with Brian and Sinclair.

Brian and Sinclair hadn't wanted me to stay in Portland with the rest of the cast and crew. They thought it would be too much temptation. And I agreed to their suggestion of me renting somewhere on the coast. But for different reasons. I knew that I was on the right track and focused. There was no going back to my partying days. But I was looking forward to getting away from Los Angeles. It was good to finally get some downtime, to escape all the pressure that came with being in LA and that I put on myself.

The thunderstorm had passed and it was warming up again. Maine was hotter than I expected but there was a nice breeze trailing through the cottage now that I'd managed to get the kitchen window open. I was about to head out to do my daily push-up and crunch routine when my cell rang. I grabbed it from the console table.

"Hey, Audrey." I hadn't been expecting my so-called girlfriend to call.

"Hello, lover," she replied.

I chuckled. "If only I'd been lucky enough to meet you before Peter did."

"I still wouldn't have touched you with a ten-foot pole," she said. "You're far too hot, and that always spells trouble."

"Gee, thanks. Thank God you're my girlfriend or I might be offended. What can I do for you?" Audrey and I rarely spoke on the phone. In the six months since we'd signed contracts and begun our "relationship," we'd been out to dinner, attended award ceremonies and other red carpet events, but we didn't hang out unless someone was watching. Like lots of Hollywood romances, there was nothing remotely sexual between us. Audrey had been dating her boyfriend, Peter, on and off since high school.

"Well, I wanted to talk to you about our contract. My agent doesn't know I'm calling you."

That sounded serious.

"Can we just keep this between ourselves?" she asked.

"Sure," I said, opening the door and heading out onto the porch. This place had a swing and everything.

"I'm sorry. I didn't even ask how filming was going. What's it called? *The Perfect Murder?*"

"*The Perfect Wave*." I took a seat on the swing facing the ocean. "We start Monday, but Maine's beautiful."

"You staying in Portland?" she asked.

"No, the rest of the cast and crew are there, but I'm a little north, in a small town. It's gorgeous but a little crazy. I saw a woman taking her cat for a walk this morning. She had it on a leash, if you can believe it."

"Sounds like something you'd see on Venice Beach."

I chuckled, stretching my legs out in front of me. "Yeah, maybe it's not so far from LA. Anyway, enough stalling, what's up?"

Audrey took a deep breath on the other end of the phone. "I know we have another eleven months to run on our contract, but I was wondering how you'd feel about ending things after the premiere."

We'd shot a film together six months ago and it was due to be released just after filming ended on the movie I was about to start shooting.

"You're dumping me?" I laughed. But it wasn't funny. Things were going well for me, and now Anthony Scott was calling—I didn't want to go backward.

"Oh God, please don't tell my agent we're having this conversation."

"Hey, seriously, this is no big deal." I didn't want her to feel bad. She'd done me a favor. I'd definitely gotten more out of our arrangement than she had. I was getting closer and closer to my dream of a franchise. But her timing sucked. "You think your agent will have a problem?"

Audrey didn't have a reputation to save, unlike me. Her team had said yes to me as my star was on the rise and would provide her with extra column inches. Publicity had been a secondary factor as far as I was concerned.

"Man, neither of our agents are going to like this," she

said. "I thought we could split after the premiere of our film, that way the studio will be okay. A breakup just after release might give the movie a little more publicity anyway."

"Sure, whatever you want."

"Yeah, now you can go back to your man-whoring ways."

"I think Brian would prefer it if I were just castrated."

"Or married," she said.

"Isn't that the same thing?" My parents were the epitome of a happy couple, but they had such a special relationship, there wasn't even any point thinking that I could have something like that. It wasn't who I was. I was all about work and getting to the top.

"I hope not, as that's why I'm calling. Peter proposed, and I don't care if it's bad for my career. I've loved the man since I was sixteen. I'm sick of pretending to be someone I'm not."

"Congratulations," I said, staring out over the ocean. "I'm really so happy for you. I know how much he means to you." I'd met Peter several times before we signed our contract to reassure him I wasn't actually interested in Audrey. He'd seemed like a great guy.

"You've been the best fake boyfriend. I'm sure you'll find yourself another fake girlfriend in no time. Especially as rumor has it Anthony Scott wants you in his next feature."

"You heard about that?" Jesus, it had only been a couple of hours since Brian had called *me* about the opportunity.

"You're hot stuff, hot stuff. Everyone is talking about you in this town. You know how Hollywood is."

"I guess. Nothing's official yet, though." Until contracts were signed, I wasn't cracking open the champagne. "So you want me to tell Brian that I can't stand you a moment longer and I want to break our contract?"

"You'd do that for me?"

"It's no big deal. I'm used to taking heat from my team. And you shouldn't be punished for being in love." Hollywood was a fucking shark tank. And women seemed to get it worse than men. If an actress had done half of what I'd done, her career would have been over.

"That's really sweet of you, but no. I need to put my big-girl panties on and face this myself. Peter deserves that much from me."

"Well if you change your mind, just yell. You're thinking we split in about three months, right?" I knew that as soon as she told her team and they spoke to mine, my publicist would be on me to find someone new. Audrey had been great. Low maintenance and chilled out. But I'd heard of some Hollywood girlfriends causing real problems. An actor I knew had gotten his contracted girlfriend pregnant because he'd been stupid enough to fuck her.

"Yeah, three months sounds about right. And it should give you plenty of time to line up someone else."

I'd need to find someone quickly. I couldn't be single for too long.

"I think that's the way I'll go. I can't imagine I'd get anyone better than you though." I pushed my feet against the ground and began to rock back and forth on the swing.

"Stop, you're making me blush." She laughed. "You never know, Matt, you might get someone who turns into something more than a publicity stunt."

I chuckled. "Yeah, I don't think so, but thanks."

"Okay, well, I'll see you at the start of the junkets."

"Sure. Say hi to Peter for me." I hung up and slung my phone onto the seat next to me. How long would it take until Sinclair started to blow up the resumes of wannabes and starlets on the rise? I'd have to go through secret meetings, then an endless number of dinners.

I sighed and stood. Time for a few crunches. That would take my mind off things. I pulled my t-shirt over my head and hit the porch deck. I'd do whatever it took.

I wanted the career I knew was possible.

I wanted to prove I wasn't another Hollywood fuckup, and I wanted to make my dad proud.

Lana

The rainstorm had cleared, the mugginess had returned, so I'd thrown all the doors and windows of my cottage open to catch any breeze passing through Worthington. I'd decided to work on the earrings of the Bastet collection outside.

I hadn't expected to be so distracted by my temporary next-door neighbor who was also out on his porch.

Exercising in public with your shirt off if you're a guy with a six pack, not that I was counting, really should be outlawed. I was pretty sure he didn't realize he had an audience, or he wouldn't be grunting like an animal.

I squeezed my eyes shut for a moment and tried to reset my brain. I should step inside, turn on the TV, but I kinda liked the outdoor show accompanied by the crash of waves on the beach.

I stared at my pad, trying to keep my eyes on my work. Maybe Ruby had been right and it was time to unpack my tools and set up my workshop. I could remember a time when I'd get lost in my latest project and hours would fly by without me noticing. But since college, I couldn't bear to be alone with my thoughts for long. I just ended up focusing on why I wasn't making the high-end exclusive pieces, why

I wasn't in New York. And that was the last thing I wanted to be thinking about.

"Hey," a man called from my left.

Shit. I knew I should have gone inside when I had the chance. I glanced across to find the sweaty, hard-bodied man I'd been trying to ignore coming toward me, waving. As he got closer, he looked kinda familiar, and as he swept his hand through his damp hair, recognition dawned. It was the crazy idiot from the bandstand.

"I thought that was you," he said.

I dropped my feet from the side table I'd rested them on and stood. I hadn't noticed how hot he was when I'd been shouting at him. Since he was as dumb as sand, I guessed it was only fair that he was handsome. I walked to the halfway step on my porch so I didn't seem rude. "I'm glad you managed to survive the storm without being electrocuted," I said, shielding my eyes from the hazy sun.

"I was hoping we'd run into each other again so I could thank you. I'm a masochist apparently," he replied, flashing a bright white smile.

He clearly thought I was the crazy one. "Sorry for yelling at you earlier." I wasn't that sorry, but it seemed like the right thing to say.

"I THINK I CAN FORGIVE YOU."

I shouldn't care one way or another but for some reason I was pleased he wasn't going to hold a grudge. I placed my palm against my chest. "I'm so relieved."

He chuckled. "And for future reference, you don't need to create such a dramatic excuse to hit on me." He cocked his head as if he were waiting for my reaction.

I really hoped he was joking. As he held my gaze, his

eyebrows pulsed upward, convincing me he was just teasing at the same time as making my stomach flip.

"Right," I said, nodding. "Because swearing at guys is my favorite flirting technique."

He chuckled. "You really think I was in danger?"

"You think I generally scream at strangers?"

"Good to know you singled me out for special attention." His glance slid from my eyes to my mouth and back up.

"You seem pretty good at attracting the wrong sort of attention." I folded my arms.

He shrugged. "I've clearly lived in LA too long and forgotten what real weather is."

Ah, California sounded about right. He had the body and the face for it. He was probably "working on getting into the business," which really meant he was working at getting drunk each night and sleeping all day. I'd dated a guy like that for a few weeks in New York. I really couldn't trust my heart.

"So, you're my neighbor," he said.

"Apparently so. You here on vacation?"

He paused for a second and I couldn't figure out whether it was because he didn't want to tell me the truth, or because he wasn't a sharer. "Business *and* pleasure."

The twinkle in his eye told me everything I needed to know. This man was definitely *not* gay. Not the way he made my insides fizz and pop. His expression made it clear he was used to making girls swoon. I just nodded, praying I wasn't blushing under his attention.

"You didn't tell me your name earlier." He swept his eyes up and down my body and then fixed me with his stare. The way he looked at me made everything he said seem so outrageously flirtatious, as if he were picturing me naked.

"Lana." I tried to sound matter-of-fact, as if his presence wasn't affecting me at all, as if I didn't feel this pull toward him. I wanted to write him off as a pretty boy, but something about him made me want to get a little closer.

"As in Turner? Beautiful," he said, his eyes dazzling. "It suits you."

"Lana Kelly. But thanks." I waited for him to tell me his name, all the while trying not to stare at his hard, golden brown chest.

"Oh," he said when he realized I was waiting. "I'm Matt."

"Well, nice to meet you, Matt. I co-own the cottage you're staying in, so if you need anything, let me know."

He jerked his head back to the house as if he were expecting it to have disappeared since he'd walked over. He turned back to me. "You left me the gummy bears?" he asked with a grin.

I leaned against the banister. "Yeah, sorry. I got mixed up and thought a family was staying."

He smiled as though he was in on some secret he'd not told me about yet. "I don't get the opportunity to eat shit like that very often, so thank you." He stared at me so intensely that I glanced toward the ocean. "That's two things I owe you for."

"So you live here?" he asked, and I faced him again. His eyes fixed on me, pinning me to the spot. He seemed to take up more space than most people, as if he had command of the air around him. Maybe it was just because he seemed so sure of himself.

"Yeah. I've been in Worthington my entire life, but I've had this place a couple of years."

He stuck his hands in his pockets, broke eye contact with me then looked up at me from under his lashes with a stare that made my whole body shiver and my skin tighten.

This man was dangerous.

"Actually, there is something you could do for me." His eyebrows pulsed upward and he gave me a half smile.

God knew what he was imagining I might do. I bet this man flirted with his own mother. "What's that?" I asked, trying to keep my tone neutral. I couldn't decide whether his outrageous self-confidence was annoying or justified. Maybe just annoyingly justified.

"I wanted to get the burner to light, but I couldn't find any matches. Do you have any?"

Didn't men like him normally have stoves magically ignite for them? "I'm sorry. They should have been provided." I turned and climbed the steps back up to the deck. "I'll just go and get them," I called over my shoulder.

The screen door creaked and snapped shut behind me. Why was it when I met a man as handsome and almost-naked as Matt, I was wearing yoga pants and no makeup?

Not that it mattered. I wasn't interested in impressing him anyway. In fact, just the opposite.

I found the matches and headed back out. Matt had made his way up onto the porch and was leaning on the railing, facing the door, his arms folded over his chest. Now that we were on the same level, it was clear just how tall he was. Way above six feet.

The fading light caught in his messy, dirty-blond hair, and I bit the inside of my cheek, trying to stop fireworks igniting inside me. I stepped outside and held out my hand. Without breaking eye contact, he reached out to take the matches.

"Thanks." He paused but it seemed like he had something more to say. "We should have a glass of wine one night," he suggested. "It seems . . . neighborly."

"Does it?" I asked, tilting my head to one side.

"In a town like this? I think so." He pushed himself off the railing and suddenly he was too close for a stranger. "Bring a friend if you like. Boyfriend. Girlfriend. Whatever floats your boat."

I shook my head. Men like him were incorrigible. They just assumed they could have everything they wanted without working for it. I couldn't admit to being single. He'd take that as if I was returning his advances. Which I wasn't.

"Thanks," I said and he moved away, the breeze making me aware of the gap between us. He jogged down the stairs.

"I'm here alone." He nodded. "And relaxing by myself all weekend if you want to drop by."

"I'll bear that in mind." I pressed my lips together, trying not to smile.

I grabbed my tray of art supplies and watched as Matt strode back toward the cottage. Probably for a shower—not that I was imagining that or anything.

I sighed and awkwardly pulled the screen door open with my foot before heading inside. The light was fading and my bed was calling.

A little bit of TV before bed would keep my mind off my neighbor. It was nice to be flirted with. Flattering to be noticed by a man like Matt. It did not mean Mrs. Wells had been right. He'd just rented the cottage next door, and the storm tonight had passed.

FIVE

Matt

Five o'clock in the morning was too fucking early. But I wanted to fit in a run before the car came at six. As I got to the entrance to the park I stared at the bandstand and smirked. Who'd have thought that the beautiful, tempting girl I'd mistaken as a stalker not only didn't seem to have a clue who I was, but would end up being my neighbor while I was in Maine?

This really was a small town.

Lana was gorgeous, no doubt about it, and I'd enjoyed our to and fro out on the deck a little *too* much. She was a woman who could give as good as she got and that was a real turn on. So I'd have to avoid her.

I'd spent the weekend learning lines so I hadn't seen her again. I was biologically programmed to flirt with women as beautiful as Lana. I just couldn't help myself. I might not be in a real relationship with Audrey, but getting caught cheating on her would potentially put my image rehabilita-

tion at risk. A cheating scandal was not the way to show the
studios you were reliable.

As I came out of the other end of the park, I got an uninterrupted view of the ocean. Growing up in Northern Indiana, I'd always enjoyed being a bike ride away from the lake.
When I was around seven years old, I'd come to Maine with
my grandfather. When I saw the ocean for the first time, I'd
been disappointed it didn't feel more different to Lake
Michigan. But being here in Worthington this time around,
it was nice not to feel such a long way from home.

I checked my watch. I had twenty minutes before my
car got here. My shower would have to be quick. I had a
reputation to uphold, after all. I turned up on time, knew
my lines and didn't do drugs. Ever. Even in the short time
I'd been in Hollywood, I'd seen people who were white-hot
stop getting scripts because they started to believe their own
hype and behaved accordingly. I'd nearly been one of them.
In my case it wasn't that I'd believed my own publicity. I'd
just thought I'd arrived and been a little concerned that it
wasn't where I wanted to be. But now I had my eye on the
long game.

I stopped just shy of the steps to the deck of the cottage
and leaned forward, my hands braced against my knees as I
tried to catch my breath.

Lana's screen door slammed and I turned my head to
the side. Damn. She appeared in running gear that fit her
like a second skin. Jesus, she had the body of a real woman.
So many female film stars looked okay when you saw them
in a movie but in person were just a bag of bones. Lana had
the ass of a woman who liked a burger, but worked out, too.
Seemed like the perfect combination to me.

"Hey," I called out.

She snapped her head away from the ocean, waved,

then headed down the steps toward me. Her breasts were pushed up, as if they were trying to escape her top. For a second I imagined myself running my tongue along the line of her cleavage and then erased the image from my brain as I stood. "You're up early," she said, looking up at me. She was a lot shorter than me, which was cute.

"Yeah, I have to leave for work at six and wanted to fit in a run."

She shifted her weight from one leg to another, slightly swaying her hips. I wanted to reach out and pull her toward me. "I should let you go," she said.

She didn't ask me what I was doing, or where I was working. I didn't need her to know I was a movie star. Not really. If she'd have asked, I'd have told her—I wasn't a liar. But I wasn't about to volunteer the information. I liked being just another guy to her. A man who knew as much about her as she did about me.

"You going for a run?" I asked, not ready for her to leave just yet. I knew I'd spend most of my waking hours on set in the coming weeks, and I might not see her again.

Which was a good thing, because I needed to avoid temptation.

"Dressed like this?" She swept a hand down her body. "No, I'm off hunting for bears."

I paused and she broke into a grin. "Of course I'm going for a run."

I chuckled. I really liked this girl. "You need to take that show on tour," I said. "And make sure you wear your running gear. It'll be a sellout."

She rolled her lips together as if she were trying not to smile. "Thanks for the tip."

"Anytime." I smoothed my hand across my chin as I imagined how the soft skin of her inner thighs would feel against my palms. "I didn't see you over the weekend," I said, even though I'd been the one avoiding her. "You and your boyfriend didn't drop by for that glass of wine."

I hadn't seen any evidence of a significant other, but I couldn't imagine a woman like her could be on her own. The corners of her generous mouth twitched—she understood that I was trying to establish whether or not she was single. Most women would have fallen over themselves to let me know they were interested. Not Lana. It made her all the more intriguing.

"I had to work," she said.

"What do you do?" Those legs would look good in a nurses' uniform or a tight black skirt of a sexy office worker. Hell, her legs just looked good, no matter what she did.

"I design jewelry. I have a shop in town." She glanced at the ocean as if she wanted to get on with her run. I was late for my shower, but I wanted our conversation to continue. She held my attention, and not just because she looked so incredible, but because I wanted to know more about her world that she seemed so confident in. It seemed so far away from the life I led.

"So you work for yourself?" I asked. "That sounds awesome."

She gave me a tight smile and nodded. I expected her to ask me what I did, but she didn't. I wasn't sure if it was because she didn't care or because she thought it was rude to pry. "I'm so sorry, but I'm going to have to go if I want to fit in my run," she said.

"No problem. I'll be around tonight, though. Maybe I'll see you then." I wanted to know more about her, get to know someone who hadn't already formed a view on the sort of person I was or what they could get out of a conversation with me.

"Maybe you will." She ran off down the path between our houses toward the beach. I watched her glossy brown ponytail bounce away. She was just stunning. The kind of girl next door they made movies about.

When she disappeared out of sight, I glanced at my watch. Shit. Ten minutes. I sprinted back into the house, discarding my sneakers, shorts and socks in a trail behind me as I headed to the shower.

All I needed to do was get clean and throw on some clothes. On set, hair and makeup would sort out the rest.

The car pulled up as I yanked my jeans on. I scrubbed my hair with the towel and put a comb through it before grabbing a t-shirt. My phone chimed from my bed and Sinclair flashed on the screen. Shit. He'd probably heard from Audrey's publicist about the split. I picked up my wallet and stuffed it in my pocket before I answered my cell.

"Are you on the way to set?" Sinclair asked without even saying hello.

"I'm just heading out to the car."

"You don't want to be late."

I rolled my eyes. "I'm not going to be late. I'm right on time."

"And you're keeping it in your pants. No partying."

I sighed as I locked the front door. I was pretty sure I could have left it wide open and it would be fine in this town.

"My pants are securely on."

"I can arrange to have Catherine fly up for a couple of nights on your next day off, if you like?"

Jesus, did he mean that to sound as sordid as it did? Catherine was one of the two models I saw casually. But we were old friends who fooled around. She wasn't a hooker, and she wasn't on call for me.

Sinclair, like most people in Hollywood, thought that the more famous you were, or the more famous a person you worked for was, the more power you had. And that was how people operated. But not me. I didn't give a shit about fame or money when it came to how I treated people. People were people, no matter what their latest movie grossed.

"Hold on," I said as I pressed the phone against my shoulder and reached a hand to the driver. "I'm Matt. Good to meet you."

He shook my hand with a firm grip, which I appreciated. "Morning, sir. I'm Jed, and it's my pleasure to drive you while you're in Maine."

I slid into the car and Jed closed the door behind me.

"I don't need you to arrange dates for me. Thank you," I said into the phone.

"Well, about that. I think we're going to have to switch things around. Audrey wants to pull out of your deal early, and it's not like we can stop her."

Even if we could have stopped her, there was no way I would. She was doing the right thing. "She called me. I'm fine with it. She doesn't want to split until after the premier."

"Yeah, so by then the studio won't give a shit. And we can hook you up with someone else pretty quickly."

I didn't say anything. I knew another contract girlfriend was the right thing to do for my career, but at some point I'd like a shot at living a normal life and being a thirty-year-old man—meet a new girl, flirt, fuck and repeat.

I just wanted a time out. A fistful of humanity.

I sighed. "Okay, send me some details."

"You don't sound so sure. You're not going soft on me,

are you? This is what you pay me for. These last eighteen months have gone well—true love has saved your soul as far as Hollywood is concerned. All being well, you're going to be signing onto the Anthony Scott feature in the near future, which may turn out to be your first franchise. We need to be scandal free."

"We're not disagreeing." I tipped my head back onto the headrest. He was right. "But things need to loosen up if I sign with Anthony Scott." I paid Sinclair to do what I needed, which was to save my career. But at times he forgot who was in charge.

"I think it will be a lot easier for you to start working your way through Victoria's Secret models when you're signed on to carry a major studio franchise. But generally, if you want to stay successful, you'll keep out of trouble."

I wasn't sure that I wanted to sleep with a conveyor belt of women. But Sinclair had to see that things had changed. I wasn't about to go backward. I just wanted to take some control back in my life. I'd like to run my tongue over Lana's collarbone, fuck her mouth, make her moan as I slid into her. I'd just like the *option*.

"Yeah, I learned my lesson."

"So, I'll send over some resumes tonight. Last night I heard Renee Bromley's contract just came to an end, so I'll call her people."

I rubbed my brow. Renee Bromley? "She's fucked every guy in Hollywood. Can't you find me a closeted lesbian?"

"I thought you might like someone who gave you options."

"Renee Bromley doesn't give me options. She's just a star fucker."

"She's a star. You can't be a star fucker if you're a star.

And a relationship with her would bring you a lot of publicity."

"Surely this is about looking reliable, bankable and scandal free. Publicity is a secondary factor."

"But it's still important," Sinclair said. "It gives you double bang for your buck."

The last thing I wanted was to repeat the Affleck/Lopez debacle. I didn't want tabloid column inches. I wanted my franchise, success and the money and freedom that would bring me. "What about a civilian? Someone who isn't famous."

"No fucking way," Sinclair boomed. "I'll never do that again. We want a woman with as much to lose as you. We need a star on the rise with good management. Someone ambitious who understands the game."

My whole life seemed like a game with everyone else taking a spot on the board. I might bust his balls, but the guy was the best in the business. "Okay. Point taken. Send me what you have, just not Renee."

"Deal. But I want someone signed up before you split with Audrey. We haven't agreed on the story yet, but you can't be seen as weak and heartbroken. You need to move on quickly, just not so quickly you look like an asshole."

"Got it. You better get to work."

"I'm always working. That's why I'm up in the middle of the night to call my favorite client on his first day on a new movie."

I laughed. It was God knew what time in LA. I might bitch about how much I paid him, but if I got this franchise, he'd have earned his money.

"Thanks. Now, go get me my franchise."

I pressed cancel on my phone and stared at the ocean as we continued along the coastal road toward Portland. I caught sight of a brunette beauty running on the sand. There was no way to mistake Lana's tempting body.

It was important to me that Brian and Sinclair didn't have even the slightest concern about me and my reliability. They didn't understand that despite my previous mistakes, there were few actors who had the same drive to succeed that I did. I grabbed onto each rung of the ladder as soon as it came into sight and didn't let go. I'd had a wakeup call. I wouldn't need another.

SIX

Lana

I flipped the sign to open and propped the shop door ajar with a rock I'd found on the beach last summer.

Tourists didn't start showing up until after ten in the morning, but I always changed the sign at nine anyway. Mondays were generally slow, but it was the day I allocated to paperwork and catching up with what happened over the weekend. I employed someone to cover Saturdays and Sundays. But even if I wasn't in the shop, I was usually designing or dealing with online orders. I'd never thought running my own business would take so much time and focus.

I lifted the floor-standing sign and carried it out onto the street.

"Hey, Lana."

I looked up to find Mr. Butcher standing in front of me, carrying his fluffy Pomeranian lapdog. If I bumped into him and Mrs. Wells within a couple of days, I was all caught up on the gossip of not just Worthington, but the whole state.

"Good morning, Mr. Butcher. I see Posey has a new outfit." I tugged at the collar of his Pomeranian's coat.

"She's got an entire new wardrobe for summer," he said.

"She's certainly better dressed than I am."

"Nonsense, my lovely. Your New York style is wasted in a town like this."

"You don't mean that." Mr. Butcher had retired to his hometown after a glamorous career in the New York fashion industry. He loved it here, and we both knew it.

"There are parts of this town I love, but people's style is not one of them. You're the exception, my lovely girl. You and your beautiful jewelry. I just wish you'd let me introduce you to some of my friends. I'd have had you world famous by now if I was still in the industry."

I couldn't think of anything worse than being world famous. A slice of notoriety on my college campus had been a step too far and had sent me running home. I'd never even tried to expand my jewelry line into other people's stores. For me, small and inconspicuous was exactly what I wanted. As long as I could pay my bills and indulge my shoe habit every so often, I was happy. "Well, I told you that online orders were doing well, didn't I? I might just conquer a little bit of the global market after all."

"You're very talented. I'm sure Saks would fall over themselves to see your work."

"You know me, Mr. Butcher. I love what I do, and being in Worthington works for me."

"There's a big world out there—Paris, Rome, London. You don't want to explore? You don't want the biggest stars in the world wearing your designs?"

That had been the dream. Once. Before I could fathom what that kind of success would mean giving up. The privacy, the control, the ability to oversee all the details, ensure the quality. "Some people are happy living small-town dreams."

"Oh well, you must tread your own path. You just have so much potential. Now, tell me. Have you heard about the movie filming nearby?" he asked, his eyes lit up with excitement in an exact imitation of the look his dog gave me every time I brought out a biscuit.

"Mr. Butcher, I'm disappointed. *That* is old news. What has the world come to when you're telling me gossip I've already heard?"

Mr. Butcher's shoulders rose conspiratorially. "Have you spotted anyone in town? Someone saw George Clooney antiquing in Portland over the weekend."

"Well, I doubt anyone will come to Worthington." The town was quaint rather than glamorous.

"Perhaps you'll run into that man Mrs. Wells has said is about to appear in your life."

I straightened out the sign, making sure it was tucked in against the wall to provide a little shelter from the ocean breeze that could whip up around here out of nowhere. "I'm sure there's meant to be something sacrosanct between fortune teller and client. Mrs. Wells shouldn't be spreading such wild rumors."

"Oh, it's just between us. She's so excited for you."

I tried hard not to roll my eyes. "Well, I can assure you, there is absolutely nothing to be excited about. I like my feet firmly on the ground. I have no desire to be swept up in any kind of storm. I keep telling you, I'm happy with my life here."

Mr. Butcher gave Posey a kiss on the nose as if he wasn't listening to a word I was saying, which he probably wasn't.

"I have some paperwork to get on with, so please excuse me, Mr. Butcher."

"Of course, dear. Posey and I are just going for our morning promenade."

"All eyes will be on you both, I'm sure." Dressed in a cream, double-breasted suit and a trilby hat, Mr. Butcher couldn't help but draw the eye. No one was going to miss him. I'd seen him a couple of times posing for pictures with tourists. He loved the attention.

"You are such a charming girl. You're going to conquer the world one of these days."

I leaned forward and gave Posey a kiss between her ears. "Have a good day, you two."

The sun was hot and bright as I watched Mr. Butcher and Posey head down to the sea front. Hopefully, the good weather meant the tourists would be here and ready to shop.

I pulled up the stool to the counter and logged on to my laptop. My first job was always to check sales and place any necessary orders from Massachusetts.

As I began going through the sales, my phone rang.

"Hey," I answered when I saw Ruby's name. "How was your weekend?"

"Chas and I split." Her voice sounded far away as if it was too much effort to speak louder.

I took a breath before I replied. I didn't want to sound as relieved as I was. "Oh God, Ruby. I'm sorry."

"Yeah, he told me he didn't want to be tied down."

"But I thought it was casual?"

She sighed. "I thought so, too. I guess I can't even get casual right."

"Hey, this isn't you. He's a man-child. You need to find yourself a grown-up."

"Or I should just retire my vagina."

I laughed. She was always so dramatic. "Take a breath."

"Can't you come down and spend the weekend in New York? I want a girls' night out. Maybe both of us will meet someone."

"I can't." More importantly, she knew I *wouldn't*. "I have the shop and the house is rented. I have to be here." Images of bare-chested Matt flashed into my head. Did he ever wear a shirt? I supposed with the chest he had, he wanted to show it off. His skin this morning had looked hot, and I'd wanted so badly to reach out and press my fingertip against his shoulder, just to check if it burned.

"You're not in the shop on weekends, and the renter next door doesn't need you to be there."

I pressed print on the list of orders that had come in. "Why don't you come back here for the weekend?"

Ruby sighed. "I need to flirt my way out of misery. Who am I going to flirt with in Worthington? Mr. Butcher?"

I chuckled. "Posey would get jealous."

"What's going on there anyway? Any news about Mrs. Wells' prophecy? Any men washed up on the shore?"

One. Next door. He was too tall. Too handsome. Too close. Usually, renters came and went and I never saw them. For some reason, I kept running into Matt, as if our daily pattern had become entangled.

I pulled the first two sheets of orders from the printer. "You know this place. Same old, same old."

"So come to New York," she pleaded, drawing out the vowels like a five-year-old.

"I can't."

Silence reigned on the other end of the phone.

"It's not like it was in college, you know. There are eight million people in this city, none of whom give a shit about you. Just come back for a visit."

I didn't want to have this conversation. There was no

point in bringing up the past. It was done, and I didn't want to think about my untrustworthy ex-boyfriend and how he'd ruined college for me, sending me home to Worthington, my dreams in pieces. "I have a customer. I'm going to have to go."

"I didn't hear the bell ring."

I smiled. She knew me far too well. "The door is open. Try not to obsess over Chas. I'll talk to you later."

I hung up and stared out toward the ocean. This place was beautiful. Safe. I was surrounded by people who'd known me my whole life and knew who I really was. Why would I ever want to leave?

SEVEN

Matt

If today was anything to go by, *The Perfect Wave* was going to hit it out of the park. The director was a great communicator who seemed to respect his cast and crew. We'd had numerous conversations over the past few months about how I saw this character, and we were totally aligned. He seemed to like what I'd done in preparation and had been obviously relieved when I knew my lines. Luckily for me, my co-star was equally focused and professional. We'd gotten through things faster than I expected, and I was on my way back home by six.

I grinned as I remembered the jokes from the crew, which was always the sign of a happy set. Not that the bitching wouldn't start later, but at least right now there wasn't tension and unhappiness draining all the creativity from the production.

I was psyched. The next six weeks were going to be great.

We pulled up outside my cottage and before Jed had a

chance to open my door, I sprang out. "I'll see you tomorrow at seven." My call time's varied, but there were a lot of early mornings. I slammed the door shut.

"You sure have some fancy rides," a woman called from behind me.

I grinned before I even turned around. "How was your run?" I asked Lana, who was out on the porch, a glass of wine on the table in front of her.

"Good, thanks. You been anywhere nice?" she asked, which surprised me. She hadn't initiated our conversations before. She'd never been rude, just concise with her answers. Had she figured out who I was?

"Yeah, down the coast. For work," I said.

There was no glimmer of recognition on her face, no knowing smile. She just nodded as I slowly climbed the steps to her porch.

A slice of cold air ran down my back as I turned toward the ocean. The sky had turned black. Just a few minutes ago it had been a beautiful afternoon.

"It's going to rain," she said as I reached the top of the steps, accompanied by a rumble of thunder. She raised her eyebrows and grinned, clearly delighted at the prospect.

"I thought you didn't like the rain?"

"No, I don't like dumbass out-of-towners trying to get themselves electrocuted." She smiled and took a sip from her glass. "There's nothing like looking out at a Maine thunderstorm from under a blanket on a porch."

I stared back at the sea that was transforming into molasses as the sky growled again.

"Can I get you some wine?" she asked.

I should say no. Head home, read through tomorrow's lines and go through the resumes of potential new girlfriends. Should. But didn't want to.

"Thanks, but let me. You stay there."

She nodded. "Bottle's on the counter. Glass is in the cabinet above the coffee maker."

The screen door snapped shut behind me as I stepped into Lana's cottage. The layout was the same as my place—airy and open with a breakfast bar forming a barrier between the kitchen and the dining area. There was a built-in window seat by the table and a vase of brightly colored flowers on the counter. Somehow, Lana's place seemed warmer than mine, even though it looked so similar. Even the barstools were the same. Maybe it was all the photographs. They were everywhere—on the walls, the windowsills, the fireplace mantel.

"You find it?" she called from the porch, interrupting my surreptitious snooping.

"Yep, I got it," I replied as I collected a glass, scooped up the bottle and headed out. "It's like my place." I put the glass on the table next to her drink and topped up her wine before pouring some for myself.

She'd shifted slightly up the bench so she wasn't behind the table anymore.

"You all set there? You want me to get some popcorn?" She looked so damn cozy, all snuggled up under a blanket as if she were getting ready to watch a movie instead of looking out at the horizon.

"If I had any, I'd say yes. You can't underestimate the entertainment value of a storm. Far better than anything to come out of Hollywood."

"Oh really?" Maybe she *did* know who I was and was just messing with me.

All of a sudden it was as if someone had set off water cannons and the rain started to fall so hard I thought the roof would cave in.

I took a seat next to Lana and we both stared out across the sea as if it held all the answers we were looking for.

"I can't imagine not seeing the ocean every day," she said after a few moments. "It reminds me how small I am. How nothing much matters."

"I'm not sure if that's really depressing or kinda inspiring."

"It is what it is." She shrugged. "Where are you from, by the way? Did you grow up in California?"

"Indiana. No ocean but on the edge of the lake. My family's house is about a fifteen-minute bike ride to the water. But you had to go further to find the more interesting bits, the places good for fishing."

"You don't strike me as a fisherman."

I turned my head to look at her. "What do I strike you as?" I took a sip of my wine, then set my glass on the bench between us, our arms brushing with the movement.

"A guy with a lot of nice rides."

I chuckled.

"Cars, I mean." She laughed.

"That's what I thought you meant—don't be such a pervert."

A deafening crack of thunder interrupted us.

"Christ, it's like it's aiming for this deck."

"It isn't. You just need to be respectful. And it will mind its business."

"Respectful?" I asked, intrigued.

"Yeah, like don't hang out on the shore, or under a tree or in a bandstand."

I turned to look at her. Her cheeks pinked, letting me know she was aware of my scrutiny. I wanted to shift a little closer so we were thigh to thigh, smooth back the wisps of her hair, feel if she was as warm as she looked.

I took a breath and followed her line of sight. "Oh, we're back to the bandstand debacle. Will you ever forget that?"

"The next time I see something dumber."

"Well, that shouldn't be long from what I've seen of this town. Do you know I actually saw a woman with a cat on a leash the other day?"

"Hey, Polly Larch has had six cats in the last three years. And they have all either disappeared, been run over or died for medical reasons. She's just keeping her cat safe. Nothing stupid about that."

"I wasn't trying to say—"

"There are plenty of eccentric people in this town, that's for sure. And even a few stupid ones. But the stupid factor increases tenfold when the tourists arrive."

"I stand corrected," I said gently. I really didn't mean to be insulting. I liked Worthington. And her. "You know my grandfather brought me to Maine once when I was a kid."

She turned to look at me. "From Indiana?"

"Yeah. To fish. My parents were working and my brothers were older. I got to vacay with my grandad. It felt like I was here the whole summer, but my mom said it was less than two weeks."

"And that's why you wanted to come back?"

"I came back for work. But it's nice. Brings back memories."

"And is it how you remembered it?"

"Yeah. Hotter than I recall. Of course, I don't remember the women being as beautiful." I enjoyed her blush a little more than I should have. But she *was* beautiful and deserved to hear it. Every move she made was graceful, her mouth full and generous, even her quasi suspicion of me was a turn-on. She was funny and confident and nothing like any woman I'd ever come across. And to top it all, she had the face and body that would send a thousand women straight into a Beverly Hills plastic surgeon's office.

I needed to take a step back. But I wanted to know more about her. I had this pull toward her that I'd never known before. "Have you always lived here?"

"I went to college in New York, but found the city wasn't for me." A crackle turned into a rumble then continued straight into a boom. It was as if the storm was building to the ultimate crescendo.

"You have a boyfriend?"

She took another sip of wine and set it back on the table before she replied. "You've half asked that before."

I chuckled. True. Not that I was going to act differently if she told me—either way I needed to keep my distance. I just wanted to meet the man who had managed to land this woman. "And I'm still coming up empty." I glanced at the rise and fall of her creamy breasts, only barely covered by her camisole, and swallowed. Hard. I really should leave.

"See that?" she asked, pointing up over the ocean. "Lightning. And again."

"Wow, that nearly cut the sky in half."

Our eyes locked first in excited, shared understanding and then the connection transformed into something that had nothing to do with the lightning. She looked away first. I would have stayed, my eyes fixed on hers the whole night, if she hadn't. "The air feels charged with something."

"I don't have a boyfriend," she whispered.

It was an invitation, and not one I wanted to turn down. I wanted to touch her, see if her lips were as soft as they looked.

"I want to kiss you," I said, shifting so that she, and not the storm, had all my attention.

The thunder rumbled again.

Despite the noise surrounding us, I could only focus on the sound of her breathing. My pulse jumped under my skin, at my neck, in my wrists, in my dick.

I really shouldn't be doing this.

But it was just a kiss.

And she was so beautiful.

And then it would be over.

I slid my thumb over her bottom lip. "Look at me," I said.

My gaze flickered down as her breasts rose with her breath. It took every ounce of control not to yank her cami down and put my mouth on that warm, soft, pliant flesh.

As I looked at her, our eyes locked, and this time heat passed back and forth between us, growing more scorching with each passing moment.

She wanted me to kiss her. Maybe even strip her naked on this deck and fuck her hard and long until I knew every part of her.

I groaned, blood rushing to my dick, and leaned in to press my lips softly on the corner of her mouth. Her breath was hot and heavy against my cheek. I dropped my hand to her ass and slid her onto my lap.

Wrapping my hands around her silky hair that smelled of the ocean, I pulled, tilting her head back and exposing her neck.

I'd been kidding myself to think this was just a kiss. I wasn't sure if it was because it had been so long since I'd fucked someone new or whether it was the storm or just the way Lana looked at me, but my whole body reverberated with lust. I wanted to touch, hold, possess her.

I trailed my teeth along her jaw and she squirmed in my lap. I slid my palms up her thighs and lifted her so she was straddling me.

Just a kiss. Right.

I wanted her closer, so I wrapped my hand around the back of her neck and brought her mouth to mine in a fractured, desperate connection. With my other hand, I pushed her ass against me. The heat of her covered pussy against my erection made me groan. Sliding my tongue against the seam of her lips, I delved deeper. Fuck, I'd forgotten how hot making out could be. The stuff *before* the fucking. Before my reform, it had been all about release. All about seeing how fast I could have a woman's mouth wrapped around my cock after making eye contact with her.

But not now. Not out here on the porch with Lana. All I could think about was how I *couldn't* fuck her, how I'd never make it that far.

She smelled so damn good. Tasted even better.

She circled her hips and I gasped, breaking our kiss. I was so close it was embarrassing. "You're so fucking sexy," I choked out. I wanted to suggest we take this inside, hell, who cared about inside? I wanted to take this up a level or ten. I wanted to see her tits bounce as she rode me, hear that sweet, sexy mouth swear as she came so hard that she forgot what year we were in.

She braced her hand against my chest as I leaned in to kiss her, then climbed off me, sitting back where she'd been when I arrived. "Let's watch the storm," she said without further explanation.

I couldn't argue. Another second of feeling her writhe against me and I'd have been lost, unable to hold back.

She handed me my wine, then took a sip of her own as if nothing had happened. My hard-on and the fact that my pulse was beating out of my neck told a different story.

We sat in silence for a few minutes until the storm

ebbed away. "I have to be up early," she said, standing slowly.

"I wouldn't want to be the cause of a sleepless night," I said, even though I wanted to keep her awake for the next week. I stood and brushed her jaw with my thumb. "Good night, Lana."

When I got to the top of the stairs on my deck, I looked back. She was still on her porch, staring at me, her hair a little rumpled, her silhouette lit up by the moonlight.

She looked like a goddamn movie star.

EIGHT

Lana

"I made out with someone on Monday night," I said the moment Ruby answered my call. The shop had been quiet all afternoon, which had left me time to remember Matt's breath on my neck, the grip of his hand on my ass. Not that it would have been easy to forget even if I was surrounded by a thousand people.

"What?" she yelled. "Who? Were you drunk? And why the hell has it taken you five days to tell me?"

"Four." Slightly less, actually. Three days, nineteen hours and thirty-six minutes if I wanted to be exact. I ran my finger along the glass cabinet that I had just reorganized, trying not to blush.

"Why did you wait at all? You could have just dialed me up and put me on speaker. I'm your best friend."

"And a pervert, apparently."

"Stop stalling and tell me what's happening. We've spoken every day and you've not mentioned anything."

I wasn't sure why I hadn't told her. Maybe I'd been

waiting to run into him again, to be sure he was real. But I hadn't seen him at all since. His car had stayed in the drive all week, but the only time I'd spotted a light on had been early this morning when I'd gotten up for a glass of water.

"It was just a kiss."

When he'd left on Monday night, I'd been five seconds away from inviting him inside and into my bed. He hadn't pushed when I'd put a stop to things. Thank goodness. I would have given in.

The kiss had been ... more than *just a kiss*. I'd felt it in my bones and it had stayed with me for hours afterward. Perhaps it was just because I hadn't kissed someone for so long. But maybe it was the way he'd held me so firmly, possessed my mouth so entirely, that seemed to elevate it to something more.

"Who with?" she exclaimed, jolting me back to our conversation.

"Oh, the guy next door."

"The corporate rental?" She sounded confused. "How did that happen?"

"We watched a thunderstorm together, and then things just sort of . . . evolved." I hadn't noticed the storm once he'd touched me, hadn't heard anything but his breath on my skin, his moans against my ear.

"I didn't even know you'd met him."

I grinned as I remembered Matt's complete confusion as I'd yelled at him by the bandstand. I must have looked like a total crazy person.

"Yeah, just a couple of times."

"Did you have sex? Are you seeing each other again? Or was it a one-time deal?"

I sighed. I wasn't sure I wanted to think about any of her questions. I liked the memory of that night—the thunder and lightning, the wine, the kissing. But for me, it had started and ended on my porch along with the storm. And I was happy to let things stay that way. Why ruin a perfect evening?

"No sex, and yes, it was a one-time deal."

Silence, which was never good where Ruby was concerned. She was either plotting or thinking up impossible-to-answer questions.

"Okay," she said.

"What do you mean, 'okay'?" It couldn't be that simple.

"I mean, okay."

"You're not going to interrogate me further, overanalyze every detail and completely wear the whole thing out?" Maybe she was still too wrapped up in her breakup.

"Nope."

"Nope?" There was no way I was getting away so lightly.

"I've made a vow to be more patient and anyway, it's obvious."

"What is?"

"He's the man Mrs. Wells said was going to come into your life this summer."

I laughed. "Sorry to disappoint you." He was just passing through town. And it had only been a kiss. "It was hardly a storm he caused."

"But is he tall? And handsome?"

So tall and so, so handsome. The way I'd spread my fingers as I tried to grasp his upper arms, his hard, bronzed chest, his dark, dirty-blond hair. My heart was beating faster just thinking about him. "We're not having this conversation —we're not fourteen anymore."

"So? You never grow out of appreciating a hot guy."

Hot? He was five miles ahead of hot. "I'm not going to

discuss his ranking on the hot-o-meter with you."

"Which means he's hot. I knew it," she said, and I could almost see the fist pump on the other side of the phone. "You're living next door to each other—something else is bound to happen."

"I don't think so." Matt had seemed content to walk away—he wasn't chasing a fleeting hookup. And I wasn't chasing anything.

"Well, aren't you full of news today? I bet you find that kiss sets a fire in your loins. It will happen again soon, trust me."

"Don't say 'loins'." I rolled my eyes. "It's the sort of thing your grandmother would say."

"My grandmother is dead, so she's not saying much to anyone. This might be the start of something, Lana."

It was nice to feel attractive, to have a man's arms around me. But it wasn't like it changed anything.

"You know not every guy is the asshole your ex was. And probably still is."

"I know," I said. "What happened in New York with Bobby was a long time ago."

"Exactly. So be open to new possibilities."

I hated the way Ruby made it sound like I'd not done anything since New York. I'd had my hands full to overflowing. I surveyed my boutique. Sunlight slid through the floor-to-ceiling windows and lit the whole shop, giving the light-pink carpet a glow, and creating an *Alice in Wonderland* feel. This place had taken dedication and focus and although I wasn't selling the high-end, handmade pieces I'd thought I'd end up making in college, I was still designing beautiful jewelry. And people were buying it. I'd accomplished so much. I'd taken advantage of a thousand possibilities.

NINE

Matt

I finished off the last of the grilled cheese, picked up my plate and glass and took it to the sink. More washing up. I was pretty sure Leonardo DiCaprio didn't wash his own dirty dishes, but for now I was still enjoying the novelty of it. It was certainly real and that's what I'd been after when I came to Maine.

Tonight was the first time since the first evening that I'd made it back to my rental before midnight, and considering I was up at five, it made for a long, exhausting week. I needed a break, and thankfully, tomorrow was my first day off.

Acting wasn't hard work, no matter what my over-privileged, work-shy contemporaries might say. I'd seen my dad work thirty-five years in a steel yard. *That* was hard work. Seeing friends die or become disabled because of the risks they took at work—that was fucking real. I knew my gig was a walk in the park, but the long hours on set waiting for shots to be set up, scenes to change and lighting to be right sapped my energy.

I hadn't switched any of the lights on and the only thing that lit my way to the kitchen was the muted television. I turned on the faucet and ran my finger under the water, waiting for the heat, lingering at the sink, I glanced up to see Lana in the window lit up from behind. Even just her blurred edges were beautiful.

Our kiss had been sexy, tempting, and dangerous. Thank God she'd put a stop to it when she had. I wasn't sure I would have been able to hold back. I washed the plate and my coffee cup from this morning, all the while watching Lana as she seemed to draw something on a desk-top easel.

She sat back, raised her hands over her head and stretched and then she stood. She checked something at the other end of the room and then crouched. I lifted up on tiptoes to try to spot her. When she rose, we came face-to-face. I wasn't sure if she could see me until she gave me a little wave.

I tapped two fingers to my forehead in a casual salute and she turned back to her desk.

She looked like she was on her own.

Did she want company?

I pulled my phone from my pocket. It was only just nine, and I liked the idea of hanging out with someone who had nothing to do with the film industry, who didn't even know who I was. Someone who smelled like the summer ocean. I could go over, ask to borrow a cup of sugar. I glanced back up, but her light was off. Damn. So much for that thought.

I grabbed a beer from the fridge and headed to the porch to relax and listen to the waves crash against the beach. The screen door snapped shut behind me and I took a deep breath, the crisp, salty ocean air reminding me of how Lana tasted.

This place sure was beautiful, even when it rained, even after the sun had set.

Smashing glass on Lana's porch caught my attention.

"You okay?" I called.

She jerked up from where she'd bent over. "Yeah, just dropped my wine."

I walked toward the edge of the deck and leaned my palm against the house. "Can I offer you a beer instead?"

She cocked her hip out to the side.

I'd been told since I was four years old that I had a movie-star smile—times like this it came in useful.

After a couple of long seconds, she placed something down on her table. "Sure," she said as she padded down the steps toward me, barefoot.

My breath caught in my throat as she came into focus beneath the yellow porchlight. She was stunning. I wasn't sure why that surprised me.

"Hey," I said, taking in her plump lips, her sharp jaw. The way her t-shirt exposed her collarbone in a defiantly tempting way. Unlike most of the women I knew in Holly-wood, I'd never seen Lana with makeup on or dressed up. She had something more than beauty, more than external, manufactured glamor. Presence. A way of being that made it impossible to take my eyes off her.

"So?" she asked, climbing the steps.

"So?"

"So, are you going to get me that beer?"

"Of course." I waited until she was at the top of the steps, reluctant to look away, before I went inside to grab a beer from the fridge.

"Wanna try out the swing with me?" I asked when I returned.

She gave me a small nod and accepted the bottle I held out to her. I sat at an angle in the deep seat, turning toward her and resting my arm on the back, my fingers an inch from her shoulder. "How was your week?" I asked.

"Not as busy as yours, it seems," she replied.

Was she keeping tabs on me? Interesting.

She blushed as I raised my eyebrows. "I meant I haven't seen the lights on much."

I brushed the back of my index finger over her cheek, wanting to feel the heat of her blush. "This week has been a little crazy." I didn't want to talk about me. I wanted to know more about her, every one of her fantasies, hopes and fears. I didn't ever remember being so interested in what someone had to say. And although the feeling should have sent me running for the hills, I couldn't imagine what would have me move from this spot beside her. I dropped my hand back to the swing, my fingers grazing her shoulder. "How's the jewelry business?"

She tilted her head as if taking my question seriously. "Good. I actually made some solid progress on a few designs I'm doing for a handmade collection."

"I'd love to see them sometime."

"You want to see my etchings?" She looked up at me from under her lashes.

I chuckled. "And anything else you want to show me." I reached across and slid her closer to me so our thighs pressed against each other.

"This is a bad idea," she mumbled, almost echoing what I *should* be thinking.

Except I wasn't. I'd deal with the consequences of this

tomorrow. Something told me that Lana wasn't the kind of girl who was going to go running to the tabloids.

"Cold beer, deep porch swings and unhurried kisses are all *excellent* ideas."

I cupped the back of her neck and pulled her closer to me. Her breath came out in little huffs against my skin. It was all the encouragement I needed. I pressed my mouth against hers. The way her lips met mine—it was like coming home, like finding where I was meant to be.

Without breaking our kiss, I threw my beer over the porch rail, pulled her onto my lap.

The cold press of her beer bottle settled against my shoulder, the temperature contrasting the heat of her mouth. I snaked my tongue past her lips, took the drink from her hands and threw it in the same direction I'd tossed mine. I'd rescue them tomorrow from the grass. Right now, I needed our hands to be free to explore each other.

Tonight a kiss was not going to be enough.

"Matt," she whispered.

Damn, I should have told her who I was. I was going to fuck this woman and she wasn't going to know I was a Hollywood movie star and would ask her to sign an NDA tomorrow morning. For a split second, I felt a little bit shitty about it, but then her fingers trailed up my chest and began to pop open my shirt buttons.

Lana

My fingertips burned as I trailed them down Matt's hard chest. I shouldn't be doing this. But the way he looked at *me*. As if I was the most important person he'd ever come across.

As I got closer to him, his pull grew stronger. He wore no

cologne but he had an earthy, masculine scent that suggested somehow I could trust him. His muscular arms encircled me and it felt like he could protect me from the whole world.

He slid the wide neck of my t-shirt off my shoulder and began to trail kisses along my exposed skin, setting off sparks of heat down my spine to my clit.

I'd known from the moment he'd touched me on the swing that tonight wouldn't end with a kiss. He wanted more. *I* wanted more. We both understood that.

I gripped his shoulders and twisted my hips against his.

"No dry humping. I want your hot, naked body pressed against mine."

He stood, and I wrapped my legs around his waist before I had a chance to think about it. I wanted his fingers on my clit, his cock in my mouth.

I wanted to be consumed by him, used by him, fucked by him.

Our eyes locked and he huffed before pressing my back against the wood of the house and grinding his covered erection between my thighs. He plundered my mouth with his tongue, as though he wanted more, was desperate to squeeze that last bit of nectar from the flower.

Through his open shirt, he pressed his defined chest against mine. I wanted to feel all that toned skin against me. I reached for my t-shirt and pulled it up over my head, interrupting our kiss for a second. The wood against my bare back and the heat from his body heightened every sensation, and my nipples beaded against the lace of my bra.

Being with Matt was the only time sex in a small town could take place without consequence. There would be no storm where he was concerned. He'd be gone soon. It wasn't as if I was about to sleep with the mayor who I'd have to see on Main Street every time I went to buy groceries. And I was in my twenties. One-night stands were okay. I relaxed, giving myself up to the moment.

"Lana," he said, pausing between kisses, "I should tell you something. I don't want you to think I'm hiding anything."

I reached for the screen door. I wanted to take this inside. I could barely focus on what he was saying.

"Lana," he whispered.

"Let's go indoors," I replied.

He caught the door I'd pried open with his foot.

"I'm an actor," he said. "I'm in the area shooting a movie." He pulled back, a little crease appearing between his eyebrows.

I nodded. "Okay." My brain was fuzzy and focused on soothing this ache inside me. Why was he telling me this? "Should I know you?"

He shook his head. "No. I just thought you should know. That I'm Matt Easton," he said as if it were important, as if I needed to listen carefully. As if I should be understanding something I didn't. "I don't want to hide anything, mislead you in any way."

"Mislead me? How?"

He blinked once then twice. "Just by not telling you."

"Okay." Had I heard of him before? Seen him in anything? He was handsome enough to be a movie star and his name did sound familiar, but he could just as easily have been the guy our town librarian praised for mowing her lawn. I trailed my fingertips over his eyebrow. I wasn't sure why he felt he had to tell me. It wasn't as if he was George Clooney and a swarm of paparazzi was gathered on the deck. He was clearly some here today, gone tomorrow actor.

And soon he'd be far away from Worthington. "Does that mean you want to stop?"

He ground his hips toward me and kissed me again. I guess I had my answer. Maybe I'd understand why he'd hit pause for a couple of seconds later, but right now the only thing I wanted was more of his kisses.

"Let's go inside," I said and he pulled me from the wall and led us indoors.

The door clicked shut and darkness enveloped us.

He carried me into the kitchen, set me on the counter-top. "You're beautiful," he said, taking a half step back.

I covered my mouth with my splayed fingers, trying to hide my smile at his compliment. I'd pulled on yoga pants after work, and no one was beautiful wearing an elasticized waist.

His hands dipped into the back of my leggings and panties and somehow, without effort, he stripped me naked so my bare ass was on the counter and I wore nothing but my bra.

"Let me look at you." He stepped back and lifted his chin as if he were proud of the way he'd undressed me. "Your bra—take it off."

He pulled his open shirt out of his pants and stripped it off as I reached behind my back for the clasp.

He deserved to be on display with his face—all cut jaw and soft blue eyes. Masculine and beautiful at the same time. With his body—chiseled and the color of brown sugar.

He was perfect.

I watched as the light coming from the porch lit up his hungry face. "Yeah. That's good," he said as I removed my bra.

The cold marble beneath my hot skin seemed to feed my lust. I opened my legs under his inspection. I wanted his eyes, his fingers, his dick between my thighs. Right. Now.

"You have a beautiful pussy," he said, bringing his gaze from between my legs to my face.

I tilted my head in acknowledgment, in invitation.

Two feet of space separated us, but it felt as if every glance physically touched me.

Slowly, his hands went to his fly, popping open his jeans. His eyes never left mine.

He slid his pants down. I was anxious to see what came next.

I sucked in a breath as he fisted his cock, dragging his hand up, rounding the head before pushing back down.

I couldn't remember a man's dick making my mouth water before.

"Let's mess this pretty pussy up a little, shall we?"

My hips rolled forward, and he didn't torture me any longer as he stepped between my legs.

Watching me, he trailed his fingers over my folds with one hand, his other still on his cock. I bit my lip, fighting back the moan building from the base of my stomach.

"Don't hold back. I want to take what I want. But I want to give you what you need. And I have to see, hear, *feel* what that is."

I gasped.

"Yeah," he said with approval and blinked, slowly, as if lust was stalling his reactions.

His fingers left my sex and he grabbed my nipple, circling then pulling. They were almost painfully swollen with arousal. My breath caught and I braced my arm against his chest.

"Oh yeah. You like that. You like it a little rough." I tensed. I didn't like the thought of being hurt. "Oh no, baby, not pain. But you wanna get fucked right. I get it. I know it. And I'm the man to do it."

He slid his hand down, exploring confidently, showing me he was in charge.

It was *exactly* what I wanted.

He pulled me to the edge of the counter and pushed his cock up my folds. My stomach wound tighter and tighter.

He broke our kiss, and I glanced down to find him positioning a condom over his tip. He didn't wait until it was on before he slid his lips against mine, diving his tongue back in to explore my mouth.

His crown pressed at my entrance and our kiss slowed and deepened, our foreheads touched as I nudged my fingertips against his shoulder, preparing myself. Our mouths open, our lips just a breath apart, he began to push into me, firing off sensation into every atom of my body.

He was so hot, so big, so full. He kept pushing and pushing, his hands holding me in place. I tried to swallow down my cries but then remembered what he'd said and choked out, "Yes."

He groaned as he buried himself in me, stilling, adjusting, giving us both a chance to savor the moment. This couldn't get better, wouldn't last.

"You're so tight. So mother*fucking*—" He ground out the words as if speaking stole the last drops of energy in the universe.

I squeezed and released my muscles, trying to milk his cock, encouraging him to soothe my need for him.

"Holy Jesus." As if he'd been hit by a lightning strike, renewed power coursed through him. He kissed me again, pulling out just a little and then pushing in farther than I thought possible.

I tightened my fingers against his skin, hanging on to the feeling that I might burst with pleasure at any moment.

"More," I cried out. "Please."

The corners of his mouth twitched with a smile. He blinked, then shifted gears and found his rhythm. Every time he pushed in, my breath caught. Every time he pulled out, I whimpered with the loss.

Shifting angles, he pressed me back until I lay flat on the counter. I reached behind my head, fumbled for the edge, and braced myself.

"Christ, you look too perfect." He swept his hand between my breasts and pushed against my lower abdomen as he continued to pump into me. I arched my back in response to the pleasure ratcheting up with each touch.

"I'm going to come," I screamed.

The hair around his face was darkened with sweat and he increased his pace, his breathing heavy and labored. He was like a living sculpture, every carved muscle perfectly crafted, every inch of him in complete proportion.

He glanced between our bodies, staring at the place where his dick slid into me. I followed his gaze, then looked up. Our eyes locked and, the final step toward my climax complete, I screamed out as my orgasm tore through me like a tornado.

The booming in my ears muffled his grunts and moans, and instead of floating down from bliss I continued to climb, my orgasm circling and circling like a stuck vinyl record.

"Yes, yes, yes," he chanted from above me, his fingers moving against my clit. I searched for breath, unsure if I could take any more. "Yeah, come again, baby, show me what my cock does to you."

He pushed harder and faster, tearing another climax from me as he demanded, "Look at me."

I opened my eyes, watching as his own orgasm crashed across his face.

There was nothing but grunts and sighs from us both as we found our breaths and blood began to flow normally around our bodies again.

"Fuck, that was sensational," he said, looking at me as if incredulous. His palms were flat on either side of my head and he dipped to kiss me. We were still joined.

"If you keep squeezing me like that, I'm going to wanna fuck you again."

"Good. I want you to have me again." There was nothing else I would wish for until the end of time other than to be fucked by this man. Again. And again. And again.

A small, confident grin curled his lips. "Yeah, well, let's try to make it to the bedroom for the next round, okay?"

Lana

"It's almost six," I said as Matt dragged me toward him as we lay on our sides, my back to his front.

I'd never had so much sex in one night. Never been fucked so hard. So expertly.

"It's Saturday. You can sleep all day. Right now, I need to fuck you again."

I squeezed my thighs together. How could I want him again? We hadn't slept for a second. At one point, we'd paused for a glass of water, and there had been a few bathroom breaks, one of which ended up with a blistering orgasm in the shower as he went down on me.

He pulled me closer and snaked his fingers between my thighs.

"God, you're always so wet and ready to go," he said.

I laughed as his erection grazed my cheeks. He was one to talk.

A crash sounded in the kitchen. I grabbed his wrist to still his hand then froze. "What was that?" I asked.

He dropped a kiss on my neck. "Nothing. Shhh."

"Matt?" a man called from outside the bedroom.

"What the fuck?" Matt hissed.

The bedroom door flew open and before I had time to think about what was happening, I grabbed a sheet and tried to cover myself.

"What the hell?" A stocky, middle-aged man filled the doorway. His eyes flickered to mine and he shook his head as he turned his attention to Matt. "Jesus, you told me you were keeping it in your pants. I hope she's signed an NDA."

"Get out," Matt bellowed as I moved away from him, not knowing what to do next.

I wanted to disappear, somehow transport myself back to my cottage.

Who the fuck was this guy?

The stranger in the door seemed to feel quite comfortable as he stood, asking Matt questions despite our compromising situation.

"I mean it, if the press catches you cheating on Audrey then the last eighteen months' work is down the drain."

What? The room turned red and began to spin.

Matt had been cheating?

"Get the fuck out!" Matt shouted as I pulled the sheet from the bed, resisting Matt's attempts to keep me in there. Wrapping the bedding around me, I ran for the front door. I wasn't sure if I pushed past the stranger or whether he moved, I just concentrated on getting out of there.

The rough wood of the deck was warmer than I

expected against my bare feet as I leapt down the stairs then bolted across the lawn to my house.

I burst inside, locked the door behind me and pulled down my blinds.

What the *hell* had just happened?

I'd spent the night having the most incredible sex only to be interrupted by a stranger who'd told me Matt was cheating.

This was why I'd not been with anyone since New York.

This was why I avoided turmoil.

Maybe the reason he'd wanted to tell me he was an actor before we kissed again last night was because he knew there would be fallout. Had he expected me to know he was with someone? As if putting me on notice made that okay.

I should have known. Things like last night didn't happen without consequences. There was always a catch whenever things got too good.

I jumped at the sound of fists banging on my back door. I realized I was standing in the middle of my living room, wrapped in a sheet, the scent of Matt and our night together fresh on my skin.

"Lana," he called through the door, but I didn't want to hear from him. I needed to wash him off.

I stumbled into my bathroom and turned the shower on, stepping in while the water was still cold. I didn't feel it.

It made sense Matt wouldn't think twice about taking me to bed despite being involved with someone. He was on location, which to him apparently meant Vegas rules applied to his . . . wife? Girlfriend? Maybe he had both. I didn't care.

I shuddered. It was all so sleazy and that was something I'd left New York to avoid. Worthington was pure and simple and the opposite of everything I'd run away from. Surely I didn't deserve to feel dirty, betrayed, exposed. Again.

After scrubbing myself with every potion and soap I could find, I stepped out of the shower, pulled on a robe and wrapped my hair in a towel. The banging at the door had stopped, but I closed the rest of the blinds in the house before finding my laptop. I sat cross-legged on my bed, brought up Google and entered "Matt Easton Actor." As I waited for the results, a picture of a movie poster flashed across my memory. A comedy. A girl in a red dress. Matt's sexy smile.

As if reading my mind, Google found that exact image.

Shit. He was *that* guy.

Hadn't Ruby screenshotted a cover of him on *Vanity Fair*? I found my phone on my nightstand and scrolled through the images.

Yes. It was from about four weeks ago with a message. *"Am I too old to hang posters of this hottie on my bedroom wall?"*

I'd sent back a laughing emoji.

Was this really the man I'd spent the night with? The guy who kissed like it was his job? The person who'd made me come five, six or seven times?

I scrolled down the screen, then clicked on an article from *Hollywood Reporter* about an Anthony Scott film. I scanned it, then went back to the search results and read headlines that started with words like *Playboy, Scandal, Heartbreaker*.

Finally, something with "girlfriend" in the description beneath the link caught my eye. *Matt Easton Finds Love*, the headline stated. A picture of him and a girl I recognized from a movie Ruby had made me watch the last time she'd visited.

Audrey Tanner. I was sure that the man in Matt's bedroom this morning, the same one who had seen me *naked*, had mentioned Audrey when he'd burst in on us.

Nausea rose from my stomach.

Not only had I slept with someone who attracted attention wherever he went, but he was in a relationship, too.

I pulled the towel from my head and flopped back onto my bed.

The one time I'd been reckless. The one time I'd taken a risk, and this was how the universe paid me back.

My phone buzzed and for a split second I wondered if it was Matt. Silly, I realized. He didn't have my number.

I checked the caller ID. Ruby. My stomach churned.

"Hey, Ruby," I said, trying to keep my voice steady as I answered.

"I'm officially done with men," she announced. I couldn't have said it better myself. "Last night I stayed in and watched *Game of Thrones*, ate ice cream, tried to do some ab exercises and went to bed at midnight. It was the best night I've had in a long time. I'm calling a time out on dating."

Perhaps if she'd made this argument to me last night, I wouldn't have accepted that invitation for a beer.

"Lana?"

"Hi, yes, sorry. I think that's a great plan."

"Are you okay? You sound a bit—"

"You know that actor you were perving at a couple of weeks ago?" I asked her. "The one on the cover of *Vanity Fair*."

"Matt Easton?"

"Yeah."

"Yes. Why—"

"Well, he's the guy living next door. I didn't realize at first." Ruby shrieked, but I ignored her. I needed to get this out. Have her help me assess the fallout. I had to know how bad this was going to be. "He's the one who kissed me on Monday, and . . . and last night I slept with him." I laughed a little hysterically. "Or he fucked me is more accurate, but then this morning some guy burst in on us, talking about Matt's girlfriend and . . ."

My tears over took my words and I rolled onto my side, pulling my legs up, making myself small.

"Hey, breathe, breathe with me," Ruby chanted down the phone. "In two, three, four. Out two, three, four."

Unconsciously I started to follow her pattern and, slowly, my tears stopped.

"What have I done, Ruby?"

"Sounds like you had a good time. Was the sex good, at least?" she asked.

"Epic." My body was still reeling from his touch. "But that's not the *point*."

"So start from the beginning. I can't tell if you're freaking out because you had a one-night stand, because he's famous, or because you got interrupted."

"B and C, obviously, but also because he has a girl-friend!" I screamed, my panic renewing the more I thought about it. "Oh God, I ran across our front yards in a sheet! What if someone saw me? Or worse, got a picture?"

"You need to calm down or you're going to have an aneurysm. Were there photographers outside the house? Is that what you're worried about?"

"I don't know. Maybe. I mean, he's a Hollywood star, right? Like an A-lister."

"Yeah, but you're in Worthington, Maine. Not LA or

New York. I can't imagine the *Portland Press Herald* camped out overnight in front of your house ready to ask Matt if he's sampled the lobster roll yet."

True. I hadn't seen any photographers. In fact, I hadn't heard anyone mention Matt being in town at all. There'd been plenty of talk about the movie being made down the coast and people being spotted in Portland, but nothing about my next-door neighbor. "You think no one knows?"

"That you and Matt fucking Easton had sex? Well I know and he knows. And there's a chance Mrs. Wells knows because she's psychic. But who else is there?"

"What about the guy who interrupted us this morning?"

"Do you know who it was?"

"I have no idea. He said something about Audrey and an NDA."

"Yeah, he's been dating Audrey Tanner for ages. He was a total modelizer and party guy until she came along and tamed him."

I groaned. "What have I done? This is the storm that Mrs. Wells was talking about." I let my arm flop over my face.

"This isn't a storm. This isn't even a light shower. Did he say anything about her before you slept with him?" she asked.

"I didn't know who he was. He told me he was an actor, and thinking back on it, his face *was* familiar but you know what it's like, we get plenty of tourists coming back every year. I just assumed I'd seen him around town."

Ruby chuckled. "Only you could come face-to-face with Matt Easton and not know who he was."

"Ruuuby. This is not helping." It wasn't funny. "I slept with someone's boyfriend."

"But you didn't know he was seeing anyone. You can't be responsible for that."

But I *felt* responsible. If I hadn't fucked an almost-stranger, maybe I would have had a chance to find out his relationship status. "But what happens if she finds out and goes to the tabloids?" I covered my eyes with the palm of my free hand, trying to block out the possibility. "There'd be no escape if that happened. I mean, I just Googled the guy. He's everywhere."

"Yeah, he's Matt Easton. He's the hottest thing in Hollywood. But you don't need to escape—you didn't do anything wrong. You didn't let him take photos, did you?"

I bolted upright. "Of course not. You think I haven't learned my lesson?"

"Yeah, I know. I'm sorry."

The wind from the ocean rattled the windows as Ruby and I sat in silence. That familiar feeling of dread hovered just above my head, ready to rain down on me. I couldn't go through that again.

I'd made the mistake of trusting a man enough to take photos just once. It had been the most humiliating moment of my life. The experience had torn through my understanding of the world, through my understanding of myself. Up until then, I'd always thought that I was a pretty good judge of character and that people were fundamentally decent. I believed that if you worked hard and tried to be kind, life turned out okay for you.

But I'd learned how unfair life could be. How unjust. How in a second your world as you knew it could be over and everything you'd ever wanted ripped to shreds.

Apparently, it was a lesson the universe felt I needed a refresher on.

"Are you okay?" Ruby asked. "It's not the same. No one got pictures. No one is going to know."

"What happens if whoever burst in this morning tells Audrey and she exposes me?"

"Who was this guy? If he felt comfortable enough to interrupt and talk about NDAs, he has to be someone Matt knows—his manager, his dad or something. What did he look like anyway? I'm sure there must be something on the internet."

The click of Ruby's fingers on her keyboard soothed me.

"I'm sending through a picture of his agent, check it out."

I held the phone in the air and swiped to see the image. "No, that's not him. He had curly hair, gray at his temples."

Another image appeared. "What about any of those guys?"

It was a photograph of Matt with his arms around two older men. "Yeah, the one on the right. That's him. Who is it?"

"Oh good, it's just his publicist."

"Are you sure? He seemed really angry."

"Of course he is. Matt and Audrey are the perfect couple, and there's been loads of rumors about how he's slept with the whole of Hollywood."

I chuckled and the black cloud above my head shrank slightly. "Yeah, nothing about last night indicated he lacked experience."

Ruby sighed. "I'm jealous."

"So you think it's going to be okay?" I asked. I needed someone to reassure me.

"I know so."

Trust me to pick a Hollywood superstar to edge back to normality with.

Lana

"Hi, Polly," I said as I passed her with Molly the cat, headed toward the grocery store. The call with Ruby had calmed me and I'd spent most of the day yesterday sleeping. Today seemed brighter. The sun agreed, and when I'd heard Matt's car pull out from the driveway this morning, I decided to go grab some ice cream and broccoli.

Polly stopped abruptly and I turned back. "Did you hear we have a movie star staying in Worthington?"

My stomach churned. The secret was out. "We do? Where'd you hear that?"

"Bob said his daughter spotted someone in there." She pointed in the direction of the grocery store.

I nodded, trying to freeze my face into a neutral expression. "Well, Worthington's a beautiful place. It's bound to attract attention."

"I hear he's very handsome. Tall. Smells good."

"Have you been sniffing strangers again?" I teased.

She shrugged. "Just what I heard. He was polite, too, by all accounts."

"He was just wandering around town?"

"Picking up milk and chips, apparently. He signed a few autographs and took a few pictures with people."

How had I been so dumb? I really was the last to know everything in this place.

"Speaking of, I'm just going to get a few things myself." I waved, then dipped into the store. I grabbed a basket and sped around the three aisles in record time. As I waited in line to be served, a magazine stocked by the register caught my eye.

There he was, smiling out at me from the cover of a popular tabloid. How could I not have noticed him before? I might not have seen his movies, but I must have come across his face a hundred times.

I put my basket on the counter and quickly stuck a copy of the magazine in as well, hoping it would go unnoticed.

"He's staying in town," Jennifer said as she swiped the bar code of the tabloid and placed it in a bag. "He was in here buying milk, chips and gum yesterday. I served him."

"Really?" I asked, trying to sound uninterested.

"Apparently, he picked up some beer at the liquor store." She scanned the other items I had in my basket. "He was very polite, and twice as handsome in real life," she said, nodding at my magazine.

She didn't need to tell me how handsome he was. I shoved some cash at her, desperate to get out of there and find out more about the man I'd slept with. Was he really the kind of guy to sleep with someone when he was getting married? I wanted to get out of there so I could tear those pages open and see what they were saying.

Matt

I strode up the stairs to Lana's porch, still dressed in my running gear, and rapped on the back door. Christ, what a mess. I'd cursed Sinclair out after Lana had left yesterday. He might be responsible for my brand but only because I allowed it. That didn't mean he could burst into my house uninvited and scream at me.

Even if he was right.

Sleeping with Lana hadn't been smart, but it had been unavoidable. There was no way I could have resisted her any longer. When she'd come over for a beer last night without a scrap of makeup on, it had hit me. She wasn't trying to impress me. I couldn't remember the last time that had happened.

I knocked on the door again. She hadn't answered when I'd dropped by yesterday either. No doubt she was embarrassed—Sinclair had chased her out in only a *sheet*. I at least wanted to make sure she was okay. If I had her number I could have messaged her, but I hadn't even had a chance to say good-bye, or thanks for the sex, before she'd run out as if the building was on fire. Not that I could blame her.

Jeez, Sinclair could be such a prick. Lana wasn't some Hollywood girl fucking me to get ahead. She was different. She was cool and confident and not interested in me just because of who I was.

I tried to peer through the kitchen window but the blinds were still closed. Her car was in the drive, so maybe I'd go for a run and try again later. I dropped down the stairs two at a time and almost knocked into Lana as she came toward me, her nose buried in a magazine.

I grinned as she looked up and she froze. Her eyes went from the tabloid to my shoes.

"You're an asshole," she said matter-of-factly as she smacked the magazine against my stomach and tried to move past me.

"Hey," I said, taking the tabloid from where it had hit me in the abs and changing direction to follow her back up her porch steps. "You don't know me well enough yet to know if I'm an asshole."

"I know enough." She stomped toward her front door and jerked it open, nearly hitting me in the face.

"Look," I said, lingering on the threshold, "I'm sorry about Sinclair. He oversteps his boundaries sometimes. But he does have my best interests at heart even if it's difficult to tell."

"Yeah, well it looks like overstepping is catching. You need to go." She unloaded her grocery bag onto the counter and began to put things away.

I grinned. I liked her fired up like this. I could too easily picture pinning her arms behind her back while her warm body struggled against mine before becoming pliant and welcoming. "Hey, I said I'm sorry. He's gone now and I have the rest of the day off."

Scowling, she turned to me. It would have been scary if it hadn't been so damn cute. "Seriously? You expecting a blow job just because your publicist isn't here?" Her eyes flitted to the magazine she'd thrown at me. "I suggest you call your girlfriend, or fiancée or whoever the hell *she* is."

Wow, she was really mad. I held my hands up in surrender. "Hey, slow down for a second. It wasn't my fault Sinclair crashed in yesterday. And this"—I held the tabloid up—"is all bullshit. Obviously." I flung the magazine onto the counter.

"Oh? So it's bullshit that you're engaged?"

"Of course it is."

She rolled her eyes and slammed the freezer door shut. "Oh well, you only cheated on your girlfriend. That's okay then."

I took a step into her house. Before he'd left, Sinclair had given me a confidentiality agreement for Lana to sign, but right at this moment, I didn't give a shit about anything other than making her understand the situation. "Hey, I'm not a cheater. Audrey isn't my girlfriend."

"Are you serious?" she asked, stomping around the counter toward me. "Let me point out the obvious." She flipped the magazine to a double page filled with photographs of me with Audrey on red carpets, in restaurants, even one of us going for a hike.

I really didn't know Lana well enough to explain the details of my and Audrey's relationship, and Sinclair would kill me if I told her the truth without putting an NDA in place. "Audrey and I are friends."

She burst out laughing. "Right. Now, can you get out of my kitchen? I have things to do."

I grabbed her wrist as she walked away. "Look, I want to explain, but to do that I need you to sign a non-disclosure agreement."

"Are you kidding me? It's okay for you to sleep with me but I have to sign an NDA if we're to have a conversation? Well, don't worry. As if I want anyone to know I'd been anywhere near you. I'm not going to say a word."

Her expression hit me like a bullet to the chest. She looked disgusted. Plenty of women were against cheating, but I'd never had to explain myself to any woman. They weren't concerned with my relationship status. But this was exactly why I liked Lana. She wasn't like all those other girls.

"Look, I've been told not to get into this until you sign

the NDA. But Audrey isn't my girlfriend. It's just a Hollywood thing. She has a boyfriend back in her hometown. I've never so much as kissed her."

"So you pretend she's your girlfriend?" she asked, twisting her arm free and turning to face me.

"Yeah. We have a movie coming out and my publicist thought it would be good to create a buzz." I wasn't being entirely honest with her. "And I had kinda a bad rep back there for a little bit. I'm trying to be taken more seriously, so it seemed like a good idea to appear settled down." Sinclair was going to be so *pissed* if he found out that I'd told her this shit without the protection of a confidentiality agreement.

She put her hand on her hip and narrowed her eyes. "You just lie to everyone?"

"It's Hollywood. That's how it works." I took a step closer but she backed away. "I like you. I've—" How could I explain that I hadn't fucked anyone other than a couple of regular girls since I'd signed up to be Audrey's boyfriend? It made me sound like a douchebag. But I *did* like her. I liked the way she was busting my balls rather than falling over herself for a repeat performance. I really liked the way the arrangement I had with Audrey seemed so alien to her, because when anyone thought about it, it was pretty fucking ridiculous. I even liked the way she looked at me as if I was kind of an ass for agreeing to it. "I like you, or I wouldn't have kissed you. I can't tell you how much shit Sinclair gave me for getting intimate without an NDA. But you were worth the risk. I don't think about all that crap when I'm with you."

She rolled her eyes and went back behind the counter. "I'm overwhelmed at the compliment."

She might not know it, but being with her was a big

fucking deal—my reputation, my career, my future was at stake.

"So you won't say anything? If the tabloids find out, they'll make me out to be some kind of cheater."

"When in fact, you're just a liar." She flung open the refrigerator and began to put away the groceries she'd carried in with her, practically throwing things onto the shelves.

"Hey, I'm not a liar." Though I wasn't exactly telling the truth to the whole world, either. "Anyway, my arrangement with Audrey only lasts until we finish publicity for the film. And then she's done. She just got engaged."

"Unbelievable." Lana shook her head. I seemed to be making things worse, not better.

"It's just how it is in Hollywood. Your entire life is a show. It's not like I'm the only one. You know Bradley Bartha? He and that model have a contract."

Her forehead crinkled. "Don't be ridiculous. I just read about them in that magazine." She pointed at the tabloid that had my face on the cover. "They just had a baby."

"He's gayer than a gay thing on a gay day. That kid is not his."

"Well lucky for me, I've never slept with Bradley Bartha, but thanks for the heads-up."

"Lana, come on. Give me a break here—I'd get black-balled if anyone found out what I was telling you."

She shrugged, picked up an apple from the bowl on the counter and headed toward her couch. "So don't tell me and get out of my house."

I sighed. I should just leave. But it wasn't like we could avoid each other. We lived next door, for fuck's sake. Besides, I'd like to get to know her a bit more. Our night together had been so much better than I'd thought it would be —Lana was funny, sexy and knew what she wanted. And I hadn't quite got enough of her when this morning had been cut short.

"I'm having beers on my balcony later. I'd really like you to join me."

She fell back onto the sofa. "Ask your girlfriend."

"Fuck, Lana. I told you she's not my girlfriend." I ran my fingers through my hair. She wasn't listening to me at all.

"Why would I believe a word that comes out of your mouth? You've lied about everything." She turned the TV on with the remote, blatantly ignoring me.

"No, I really haven't. Audrey isn't my girlfriend—"

"Even if that's true," she said, turning to me, her eyes lit with indignation, "and I find that very difficult to believe, given what I've read about the two of you, you still didn't tell me that you were famous."

"I told you I was an actor. If you don't go to the movies or open a fucking magazine, why am I the asshole?" And yeah, I'd found it hot that she hadn't seemed to recognize me, but where was the crime there?

She tapped her knee with the remote, staring blankly at the TV. After a couple of seconds, she announced, "I don't know *why* you're an asshole. I just know that you are."

She was beyond frustrating. I was getting shit thrown at me from every direction, but I hadn't done anything wrong.

"Okay. Well, I'm going to take my asshole-self out for a run," I replied, turning to the door. "Enjoy your magazine."

This had to be the first time *ever* an actor had been rejected *because* he was famous. Wasn't it meant to be the other way around?

But then, I'd reveled in the fact that she hadn't recognized me. That Lana had wanted me, Matt, not some Hollywood fantasy. I guess I couldn't have it both ways. I wanted a slice of reality when I'd come here to Worthington, and I'd gotten my wish.

ELEVEN

Lana

"Hey, Mrs. Wells," I said as I pushed the front door open. I was going to start locking my doors. Mrs. Wells should really do the same. We might be in Worthington, but there were plenty of strangers—and untrustworthy movie stars—during the tourist season. I put down the groceries on the counter. "Hey, Harold," I greeted the ginger tabby, who hissed and flung his tail in the air, giving me an uninterrupted view of his asshole as he marched out the door. How appropriate. That was exactly the kind of respect the world was showing me at the moment.

I finished unpacking the groceries and went into the living room to say hello to Mrs. Wells.

"I've been hearing all about your new neighbor," she said before my ass had even hit the chair. "A movie star, apparently."

I hadn't seen Matt since I'd blown up at him yesterday. Truth be told, I'd been avoiding him. I didn't really want to run into my one-night stand turned one-night nightmare. I didn't even want to think about him.

"I don't really follow these things," I replied, watching the muted television. Having Googled Matt, I felt stupid for not recognizing him.

"I hear he's handsome, too. You think maybe he's the one the spirits told me was going to be appearing in your life?"

I snorted. "Hardly." I didn't know what to make of him having a contracted girlfriend. It made no sense to me. Surely there were a thousand girls who would be happy to be his real girlfriend. Why deliberately choose someone he said had a boyfriend?

"You don't think he's handsome?" Mrs. Wells asked.

Of course I did. That went without saying. But then, really, how many ugly movie stars were there? "Looks aren't everything."

"True, dear, but that initial attraction is a good thing to have."

I rolled my eyes. She meant well, but I was in a shitty mood and had thought about Matt Easton enough to last me a lifetime.

"I've barely seen him. I guess he's working long hours." It was only a half-lie.

"Well, it's nice to be nice. He might be grateful for a warm Worthington welcome. Take him some of that lemon curd you make."

Was she joking? "I appreciate you trying to set me up and everything, Mrs. Wells, but I'm too busy to worry about making a man *lemon curd*." What, was this 1950?

"Oh, my dear, you need to put your priorities in order. One should never be too busy for love."

"You're right," I said to avoid an argument. I'd rather

head home and work on my collection. "Thank you, Mrs. Wells. Your groceries are put away. Give me a call if you need anything." I patted her on the hand and stood to leave.

"You're a good girl who deserves a good man."

Even if she was off where Matt Easton was concerned, it was nice to think that Mrs. Wells was rooting for me. "Thank you."

If Mrs. Wells had been right in her prediction—how this summer would bring turmoil along with a man—and it hadn't just been a coincidence, then at least it was over now. Getting caught in a sheet by a perfect stranger was as tumultuous as I could stand. I wasn't waiting for Mrs. Wells' storm to roll in. It had been and gone. And I'd survived.

My stomach grumbled. Lemon curd sounded like a fabulous distraction from thoughts of Matt Easton.

I shut the gate and headed back into town to pick up some supplies. I had plenty of sugar at home, but I'd need lemons and eggs.

As I came out of the grocery store, my canvas tote heavy with fruit, I looked across the street. Polly Larch and her sister Patricia were accosting my tall, handsome, Hollywood neighbor. He wore a baseball hat, but I could still see that his generous grin had spread to his eyes. Even though they surrounded him like twittering birds, he clearly didn't see them as a bother.

Mrs. Wells was right about one thing—he was very handsome.

I guess he'd told me he was an actor, even if he hadn't told me he was the hottest thing in Hollywood. I couldn't blame him for that. And maybe his arrangement with Audrey Tanner was normal in his world. Perhaps he hadn't cheated.

He looked over at me and our eyes met. I smiled, tightly. I shouldn't have lost my temper with him. Maybe I owed him an apology.

His grin grew wider and he gave me a two-fingered salute. My smile softened, and I looked away and started back to my cottage. If only he hadn't turned out to be a total asshole. I hadn't trusted anyone for so long, I'd been determined not to be blind to men's character flaws just because I found them attractive, just because I fell in love. I'd thought a night with Matt would be uncomplicated and maybe even the first step at rebuilding my faith in men. I'd thought that I would escape unscathed—it was meant to be simple. Didn't the universe realize I deserved to catch a break?

FIVE JARS of lemon curd later, I screwed on the lid to the last jar and set it down on the counter.

I scooped up four and put them in the refrigerator, then returned and picked up the fifth. I transferred it from one hand to the other. If he hadn't actually cheated, I *did* owe him an apology.

Would he think I was a complete lunatic if I turned up at his door with a jar of lemon curd? Probably. Maybe, I'd just leave it on his back doormat as a kind of peace offering, then turn around and disappear.

That sounded like a plan.

I took a deep breath and headed out of the back door.

Barefoot, I crept up onto his deck, not wanting to draw attention to myself. His car was in the driveway, but then again, it normally was, even when I knew he was out all day. As I got to the top of the stairs I heard music—Motown, Marvin Gaye—playing from the open dining room window. I grinned. He had good taste. I was just about to set the jar on the mat when his back door opened and I came face-to-face with his feet.

Damn it, even his feet—large, bronzed and poking out from his faded jeans—were sexy.

"Hi," he said.

I straightened and tilted my head to find him grinning at me. "I was going to leave this," I said, taking a step back and offering him the jar.

"Oh." He frowned, but accepted it. "Thanks."

"It's lemon curd," I explained.

"Oh. Great." He nodded.

I got the distinct impression he didn't know what the hell I was talking about. "You know, you can spread it on your toast in the morning."

As I said it, I realized how ridiculous that sounded. Looking at him, I doubted he'd ever tasted sugar. "You might not like it. I won't be offended if you don't—"

"It's perfect. You made it?" he asked.

I backed away, but he followed me out onto the deck. "Yeah. I had some left over and I wanted to apologize for losing my temper yesterday."

"So you brought me homemade lemon curd?" He shook his head and grinned. He seemed genuinely happy about it.

I shrugged. "I like to bake. Anyway, I'm sorry. I won't keep you."

"Hey, no. Don't go. I gotta taste this."

My toes curled over the wooden steps of the porch. "I think it's better if I leave."

"Please stay," he whispered from behind me.

I sighed. I should go back to my drawings, my cottage. I definitely shouldn't turn around. There were a million reasons why being in a ten-foot radius of the guy was a bad idea. "Do you have any sourdough bread?" I asked over my shoulder.

"Nope. Is that mandatory?"

I turned to face him. "No, any bread will do."

He held the door open and I ducked under his arm and into the kitchen. Face-to-face with the countertop we'd done God-knows what on the night before last. Flashes of his tongue, his muscles, and his musky smell invaded my brain.

I avoided his stare and rounded the counter, pulling the silverware drawer out to get a teaspoon. "Here. Just taste it on its own. Then if you don't like it, you haven't wasted anything."

He grinned as he took the spoon from my hand and cracked open the lid. His gaze flickered away from mine only for a second when he dipped the spoon into the yellow goop. I leaned back against the counter and watched as he brought the spoon up to his lickable lips.

"Wow," he said when he'd swallowed. "I mean, that's a whole lot of bad for me but it tastes too good. How come I've never had that before?"

"Maybe Los Angeles is too health conscious?" I wasn't Hollywood thin like the women Matt must be used to, though I'd never worried about my body or what I ate. Girls like Audrey Tanner must never eat.

"LA's full of crazy people eating cardboard and cotton balls or whatever the latest fad is. I ignore it. You can take the boy out of the Midwest but do not take the steak from the Midwestern boy's diet."

"Is that how you see yourself?" I asked. I released the countertop behind me and tucked my hair behind my ears. "As a Midwestern boy?"

A wrinkle formed between his eyes as he looked at me. "That's what I am."

"But you're a movie star."

He snorted and took another spoonful of curd. "Are you a shopkeeper? Or are you from Worthington, Maine?"

I transferred my weight from one foot to the other. "Both, I guess."

"Exactly. Just because I'm in movies doesn't mean that's all I am." He took a deep breath.

I knew what it was like to have people you didn't even know make judgments about you. I didn't know how anyone enjoyed being famous. I couldn't think of anything worse.

"I'm sorry I didn't tell you I was famous, but I was kinda enjoying the anonymity. It doesn't happen much anymore." He put the empty spoon back into his mouth and hummed as if he might have missed a speck of the curd. "I liked the fact that you didn't have me in that movie-star box. That you found me attractive without knowing who I was."

I folded my arms. "Oh, because no one ever found you attractive *before* you were famous."

He chuckled and screwed the cap back on the jar. "I'm not saying that I had a problem getting women to notice me. But these days . . ." He slid the curd across the counter. "These days I never know if a woman wants me so she can brag to her friends, tip off a tabloid, or because of some kind of . . . connection."

"Must be terrible," I said, shaking my head in mock sorrow.

He sighed. "Look, I'm not trying to make you feel sorry for me. I'm just saying that it was nice." He shrugged and his t-shirt pulled tight across his chest. "Refreshing, but I should have told you, I just—"

"No, I shouldn't have gone off like I did. You told me you were an actor. If I didn't have my head in the clouds, or went to the movies a little more often, I would have known who you were. I'm sorry for going crazy." I stared at my feet, embarrassed that I'd been so angry . . . and that I hadn't recognized him.

"I should be the one apologizing. Fucking Sinclair bursting in like that—I could have killed him."

"He's your publicist?" I leaned back on the countertop, my eyes flickering to the waist of his jeans. Was his body really as hard as I'd remembered?

He ran his hand through his hair. "Yeah. Came to check up on me, I think. And, as you witnessed, he has boundary issues."

Ruby had been right. "So he's mad at you stepping out on Audrey?"

His face lit up with a wicked grin. "Stepping out? Is that what I did the other night?" He moved closer, stopping right in front of me, leaving us only a whisper apart.

I should step back but it was almost as if I couldn't even if I'd wanted to. "Yeah, I think it's safe to say you stepped out on your girlfriend with me."

His fingers found mine, linking our hands so our palms were touching. "You know she's not my girlfriend, right? I can call her if you like, and she'll tell you herself."

I didn't shrug him off even though I knew I should. I needed to avoid the storm, not step right into it. "You'd call her right now?" Was he saying what he thought he had to in order to get a repeat performance from me?

"Sure, she wouldn't mind one bit. I've had dinner with her and her fiancé. He's a good guy too."

He dipped his face to mine. "You want me to?" He released my hand and took his cell from his pocket.

I hesitated, so he swiped the screen and began to tap. Then he put the phone to his ear and smiled at me. My knees fizzed under his gaze, and he let go of my other hand and pulled me tight against him. Instinctively, I pressed my palm to his upper arm to steady myself and as I touched him, memories of the night before last flooded through me. It had been so good. He'd seemed to know my body better than I did.

"Audrey, hey. I have a rather odd favor to ask you. I'm interested in a girl in Maine that I met. But she thinks we're dating—" He paused and smiled. "Exactly. We're very convincing. Especially as we're hardly ever seen together. Anyway. I guess that's Hollywood." He nodded. "Sure, I'll put her on."

My stomach flipped as he handed me the phone. "Hi," I said as I held the cell to my ear.

"Hey, Matt didn't give me your name, but I'm Audrey Tanner." I'd watched at least two of her movies, courtesy of Ruby, and it was either her or the best impressionist I'd ever heard. "Please don't tell anyone, but Matt and I haven't so much as kissed. I've been in love with my high school boyfriend since I was seventeen."

How on earth was I meant to react? "I appreciate you taking the time to—"

"And while we're sharing secrets, Matt has never asked me to talk to a girl he's interested in."

I pressed my lips together to stop myself from smiling.

"Right," I replied.

"He's a nice guy. Mainly. I think."

I let out a burst of laughter.

"Well, you know. For someone *that* good-looking," she said. "I imagine there are women around who think differently. He had a bad reputation back there for a while. But I don't think that's who he is. Not really."

I stared into Matt's blue eyes, then down to his full lips. He was *too* handsome. Like the man factory had made a mistake and put too much good-looking in the mixture. Some other guy had probably lost out as a result.

His palm flattened against my back and pulled me close. He began to grow and twitch against my belly. It would be so easy to give in to him right now.

"Thank you, Audrey. Congratulations on your engagement."

"Oh, you can't tell anyone." She sounded genuinely scared.

"Of course, I won't."

"If the press finds out, I'll be crucified in the tabloids for cheating on Matt. You know the women always come off looking like sluts."

"I promise I won't say a word."

"Girl to girl, I'm trusting you."

I nodded. "Thank you for talking to me."

"No problem, good luck with him."

I handed Matt his phone, then he and Audrey said their good-byes and he hung up.

I braced my hands on his arms. "You need to let me go."

"That's the last thing I should be doing." He glanced at my chest as I inhaled.

"I'm serious," I said.

"You know that I'm not lying about Audrey," he said, his grip loosening. "So I don't understand."

"I know, but that doesn't mean—you know." I gestured between our bodies. As much as the sex had been incredible, and he felt so good, I knew that Audrey was right, he was *too* good-looking. Not to mention famous and bound to attract attention wherever he went. That was a whole pot of crazy I didn't want to dive into.

"You don't want me to fuck you again?" His grin told me he was confident about his skills in the bedroom.

I rolled my eyes.

He bent and whispered into my ear. "Don't tell me that wasn't the night of your life." He dropped a kiss on my jaw. "You were perfect." He kissed me again. "*We* were fucking phenomenal."

I pushed at his chest and he released me, holding up his hands. I didn't move away. "The sex was . . ." Better than I'd ever thought possible? "Fine," I finished.

"Okay," he said, nodding as he grinned. "It was fine."

"But I'm not here for you to pick up and put down whenever your schedule allows. I'm busy. I have a life. And just because you want something, doesn't mean you get to have it." As much as the sex had been phenomenal, I didn't want to become a plaything for some guy passing through town.

He shifted his hips as if to give me a taste of what I'd been missing. "Okay. So what about the day after tomorrow? I was wondering if you wanted to drive up the coast with me."

I hadn't expected him to suggest a trip. I'd thought his mind was firmly between his legs. I knew mine was. "Where were you thinking?"

He pushed his fingers through his hair and I had to fight the urge to reach out and do the same thing.

"I just want to see some of Maine. Wherever you think best."

I wasn't sure if it was excitement or danger rumbling in my belly, but I wanted to show him my beautiful state. Just as I was about to accept and suggest we go to Bath, I realized there was no way that would be possible. "We can't just take off up the coast," I said.

He pulled me from the counter, turned me and walked me backward. "Why not? Are you working?"

"You'll be recognized."

He shrugged. "I doubt it. It's amazing what a hat and some old jeans can disguise. And if I am, I am."

"But, what about Audrey? Surely you can't risk someone spotting us."

"I promise not to kiss you, or hold your hand. Outside of New York and LA, it's rare to get photographed. And even if we do—"

"No. I want no part of that."

He frowned. "Part of what?" he asked.

"The fame thing. I don't want anyone taking my picture." Fear slithered down my spine at the thought of strangers gawking at me. That exposure and lack of privacy were what had sent me running from New York.

He cocked his head. "It's really not that bad," he said. "People are pretty friendly."

I shrugged. "You're not going to get branded a whore and a homewrecker if we get caught." There was no way I'd risk being seen. It would make life too messy.

He sighed, pausing in the middle of the kitchen. I could almost see the cogs in his brain crank into action. "What about if we just drive up the coast? We could take a picnic, but not stop anywhere with people."

He sounded excited—I hated to let him down.

"Come on," he begged. "I really want to get out and explore. You must know the places where there aren't any people."

"No restaurants," I said, prodding him in the chest.

"Promise." A grin twitched at the corners of his mouth.

"No PDA, either." I stabbed my finger twice against his hard pecs.

"I'll try to keep my hands to myself, but you really are impossible to resist."

I rolled my eyes. "Do you have an impulse control problem?"

"With you? Yes," he said. "Do we have a deal?"

"And promise to keep your hands to yourself?"

He grinned. "I promise."

"Okay," I said, reaching behind me, removing his arms and backing away from him slowly.

"Okay?" He followed me as I headed toward the back door.

"I'll see you the day after tomorrow." I turned to grab the brass doorknob.

"You're leaving?" he asked, sounding confused.

"I am."

"I'll let you go on one condition." He caught the door before it slammed shut.

"*Let* me?" I asked over my shoulder, as I headed to the edge of the deck.

"You heard me. Don't make me come over there."

I couldn't stop myself from smiling. "Okay, tell me."

"Wear a skirt," he said and my heart tripped. His confidence was a complete turn-on. "I saw you in one. I liked it."

Goose bumps scattered across my skin.

"Deal," I said.

"Perfect." He crossed his arms and watched as I turned and padded down the steps. As I got to my back door, I checked and he was still there, leaning against the cottage, his arms folded.

I couldn't help but think I'd just made a deal with a very handsome devil.

TWELVE

Matt

My thighs ached as I stepped out of the shower. I'd extended my run this morning. I needed to get rid of as much excess energy as possible because a day in the car with Lana without being able to touch her, kiss her or fuck her was going to keep my balls *blue*. Just as they'd been since I let her walk off my porch two days ago.

Blue, purple or fucking orange balls, I didn't care—I was looking forward to our trip today, even though I really should have cancelled. In fact, I shouldn't have suggested it at all. I'd had to *convince* her to come with me and that was a new experience. I wasn't used to working to get a woman to do what I wanted, but I liked the challenge. And she seemed worth the risk.

I dried off, then pulled on some shorts and a t-shirt. Nothing that would attract attention. Most of the women I'd fucked along the way had been desperate to go to the most photographed places in LA—needy for eyes on them and hopeful they'd be discovered just by being seen with me. But not Lana. She'd seemed horrified at the thought of someone seeing us together. Maybe she was just afraid she'd expose my relationship with Audrey, but something in the way Lana's whole body had tightened at the thought of discovery made me think it went deeper than that. I grabbed my wallet and sunglasses from my nightstand and headed out. I didn't want to be late.

My assistant had arranged for a nondescript car to be delivered first thing this morning complete with a packed picnic in the trunk. I hadn't driven the first one much, but just in case some photographer had clocked the license plate, I'd swapped it out. I wanted Lana to feel completely comfortable. And there was no point in taking unnecessary risks. I didn't want to needlessly jeopardize my career.

I took the steps to her porch in two strides and knocked on the door.

She swore.

"I heard that," I said with a chuckle.

"I just spilled—never mind. Come in!"

I opened the door and stepped inside. "Lana?" I asked when I didn't spot her.

She popped up from the other side of the counter. "Here. I just spilled my coffee." She held up a cloth as if to prove her point. "I'm not very coordinated in the morning."

Maybe not, but she was beautiful. Her cheeks were flushed and her chestnut hair fanned out over her shoulders. I scanned her body, stopping when I found what I was looking for. "Nice skirt." I tried to suppress my grin. She might make me work for it, but the reward was well worth it.

She lifted her shoulder as if it was no big deal. I knew better. I couldn't imagine Lana was the type of girl who did what men told her very often.

"You look beautiful."

She ignored my compliment. "Ready to go?"

"Your carriage awaits."

She beamed, the warmth of her unrestrained smile radiating out at me.

I held the door open and she passed by, leaving a trail of ocean breeze and roses. She was like an old-Hollywood movie star.

"Where's your car?" She paused at the top of the steps and looked back at me.

I nodded forward. "Right there. I thought I'd mix it up a little."

Her eyebrows drew together a little before she turned back and headed toward the SUV.

"You had a sports car."

"I thought this was a little less conspicuous. That okay?"

Her shoulders lowered as she approached the passenger side. "Yeah. It's more than okay." I unlocked the car and reached for her door. Our hands collided. "You don't need to do that."

"I told you, I'm a boy from the Midwest. That's what we do, so you'll have to put up with it." She dropped her hand and I took over. I wasn't sure if she liked me in charge or whether she relented out of politeness. Either way, it felt good.

She slid into the seat as if she weren't subject to the same rules of gravity as the rest of us. Fluid. Graceful.

I shut the door and rounded the trunk, spinning my keys on my forefinger. Yeah, today was going to be a good day.

"Holy crap, was I meant to pack the lunch?" she said, slapping her palms on her pleated skirt, the fabric riding up her thighs.

"I got it covered," I replied, trying to pull my attention from her legs to the rearview mirror so I could reverse out of the drive.

"You do?"

"In the trunk. I didn't make it, but it looks pretty good."

"That's so sweet of you."

"Hey, I can't exactly ask a girl on a date and then expect her to make the food." I pulled onto the street and glanced at her when she didn't respond.

"A date?" she asked, watching my face carefully.

"Yeah, a date." I hadn't really thought about it, but what else was it? I'd fucked her. I definitely wanted to fuck her again, and we were going to be spending the day exploring the coast *alone*. I was pretty sure this was a date.

"I thought I was just showing you my state," she mumbled.

I chuckled. "I don't want to sound like an asshole, but some girls might not be so downbeat at the thought of going on a date with me."

She folded her arms. "I'm not some girls."

"Well, that's for damn sure." I grinned as I turned onto Main Street.

"I just . . . I thought we were friends is all."

"We *are* friends. Doesn't mean we can't be more."

She took a deep breath. Would she deny it? She'd worn a skirt at my request, which didn't exactly scream "friend zone." How much of a fight was she going to put up?

"Where are we headed?" she asked, slipping her sunglasses over her eyes and slouching in her seat as we drove down Main Street.

"These windows are tinted. No one can see in."

"People are staring," she said.

"No, they're not, but even if they were, who cares? Why

are you so uncomfortable with a little attention? You're gorgeous. I'd have thought you'd be used to it."

"I don't like people knowing my business."

"So you decided to live in a small town?" I chuckled, turning out of Main Street and onto the main coastal high-way. "Aren't you better off in a big city?"

"Worthington is my home. I told you I went to college in New York." Her voice trailed off and when I glanced at her she was staring at her lap. "It didn't suit me."

I loved New York—the buzz, the ambition, the complete melting pot of people. It seemed so exciting compared to Gary, Indiana. Places like Worthington existed in the glossy pages of magazines and books, but I found it hard to believe people actually lived there. Not because it wasn't beautiful —it was too beautiful. Almost manufactured, it looked so perfect.

"What didn't you like?"

"In college, everyone is in everyone else's business." Her hands were folded across her chest and her answers were clipped. She was clearly uncomfortable talking about this and I wanted to know why.

"I think you get that wherever you go, though. People love to gossip. And the bad is outweighed by the good."

"Really?" She loosened her seatbelt and turned to face me. "Don't you hate people constantly taking pictures of you, regardless of what you're doing? Even if you're just coming out of the gym or going to a restaurant?"

"It gets old, but success as a Hollywood actor comes at a price."

"Isn't that too much of a sacrifice?"

"I can't really complain. It's like wanting to become a lawyer but not enjoying reading or becoming a baker but hating cakes. No job is perfect. And if I want to be successful in Hollywood, being recognized is just part of it. I just have to put up with it. It's my choice, and the upside is I paid off my dad's mortgage, bought each of my brothers a house. I mean, there's a lot to love about this acting gig." I grinned, and thankfully she smiled back.

"Must be a nice feeling, providing for your family like that." She rested the side of her head against the seat back.

I reached out, found her hand and laced our fingers together. "It is. And if I have someone taking pictures of me leaving the gym, well, I can handle that. It's not the photographs themselves that are a problem. The thing that bothers me most is how people in the industry think they know me because they've seen my picture. Or a movie I'm in. Or because I used to be a model. They make assumptions—people have opinions about me before they've even met me."

"I get that," she said. "People can judge. But that's true whoever you are."

"I guess." I sighed. "You've never wanted to be famous?" I asked. "Even as a kid?"

She shook her head. "Never. I've always loved jewelry and design. I thought at one point I'd want to do really high-end, exclusive pieces for the wealthy and fabulous."

"What changed your mind?" I asked.

She shrugged and turned back to face the windshield, pulling her hand from mine. "Dreams change. I wanted to be in Worthington, so the shop made sense."

I nodded. "I get it. When I left Indiana, I headed to Wall Street. I thought I was going to be some kind of finance whizz kid."

"Really?" she asked, turning back to look at me. "So you haven't always wanted to be an actor?"

"God, not at all. I wanted to wear slick suits and talk

about options and trading and be a king of Wall Street. I really thought I was going to be a stockbroker."

I glanced across at her and she was looking at me, her eyes wide enough to dive into.

I wanted to keep her attention, to share stuff with her in the hope she'd see a person I didn't show many people. I wanted her to see the man beneath the star. I wanted her to know the real me. "I was ambitious as a teenager, but also impatient. I couldn't wait to get out of Gary, and away from that world that belonged to my parents." I looked over at her again and she just nodded, encouraging me to tell her more. "They worked so fucking hard and still had nothing left at the end of every month. I knew I wanted more than that, but I also understood it wasn't going to fall from the Indiana sky."

"So, you didn't go to college?"

I shook my head. "Like I said, I was impatient. I wanted to get on with life, so I arrived in New York with like ninety cents in my pocket and got a job in the post room at an investment bank and used to listen in to telephone calls and the traders. I figured I'd learn as I went along." I'd wanted to be just like those guys on the trading floor. They smelled of money.

"So when did the acting thing happen?" She sounded genuinely interested, as if she hadn't heard this story before even though it was all over the internet. It surprised me. I had expected her to Google me—most women wouldn't have been able to help themselves—but now I wondered if Lana had stopped after she'd satisfied her curiosity about my relationship with Audrey.

"Modelling came first. I was approached in a nightclub and it was extra cash so I wasn't about to pass that up. After that, things happened really quickly. The money was good and people seemed to like booking me. I never looked back."

"So what didn't fall from the Indiana sky rained down in New York instead?"

I got that response a lot, especially in the beginning, and I understood that it sounded as though I'd had an easy ride but little came easily in life.

"What's that phrase? Something like 'the harder I work, the luckier I get.'" I drummed my thumbs on the steering wheel. "When I got signed, I spent hours with my agent, pumping her for information about the industry—what made a successful model. Why some just faded away, where was the money being made. You make it as a model when you land a big campaign—an aftershave ad or become the face of Calvin Klein. It's the equivalent of getting a franchise in acting. It's the pinnacle of success. So I figure, that's what I aim for—I wanted to be the best at what I did. I still do." That was why I was so focused on getting this fucking franchise, why I couldn't believe I'd almost fucked it up. I'd been so close to losing everything. "After I got my first paycheck, I bought every magazine I could get my hands on and I studied. I figured out which models were getting campaigns. Which were stuck doing low paid editorial crap but never landed anything big. I worked out why some models were labelled 'commercial' and others weren't." Those were the guys who made a living but weren't ever going to break out. I didn't want to be an also-ran. I could have stayed in Indiana for that. "I made sure I knew everything about every fashion photographer working at that time. I worked out three hours every day. I showed up on time, every time, and I took direction. I learned from the photographers what was good about my body and what I needed to keep hidden. And I booked many jobs so the right people saw my face. So yeah, it was some luck and a lot of hard work."

She nodded. "I guess I made an assumption. I'm sorry."

"Don't be. It's always better to be underestimated."

"I wanted to escape Worthington so badly as a teenager." She shook her head and smiled. "My best friend and I used to spend hours researching and planning."

"But you didn't like New York when you got there?" I asked. I wished I'd hired a driver so I could just keep looking at her instead of having to focus on the road.

She lifted her chin in the direction of the windshield. "There's just nothing that can quite top a view like that."

"Wow," I said as we turned to the right and the sea opened out in front of us.

"It's beautiful, isn't it? Never fails to take my breath away."

Her face lit with happiness and her skin glowed. "I know that feeling," I said. I'd worked with some of the most gorgeous women on the planet but none of them came close to being as breathtaking as the one sitting next to me.

"PULL IN RIGHT THERE," she said, pointing at the side of the road. We'd been driving a couple of hours and she'd relaxed after I'd talked about the upside of fame, as though she'd understood the fame wasn't something I chased. We'd talked and laughed about Worthington, LA and Gary. But she'd not mentioned why she'd left New York.

She was funny and clever and the more time I spent with her, the more I wanted time to slow down so the drive lasted forever.

I slowed and turned left up a sandy track. Thank God

I'd rented an SUV—my little sports car wouldn't have handled this terrain well. "Keep going?" I asked her.

"Just beyond the tree. I don't think you can go any farther." She leaned toward the windshield, trying to get a better view. After a few yards, we passed the chestnut tree and the track ended. We were surrounded by bushes planted in sand. I put the car in park and turned off the engine. How did she even know this spot was here?

"Let's go see the ocean," she said, grabbing the handle of the door. I followed her as she kicked off her sandals and ran between two trees, then disappeared.

"Lana?" I called. I reached the trees and looked down to find her waving up at me from the bottom of a small slope.

"I loved getting lost in these dunes when I was a kid," she said when I caught up with her.

"You have all the boys chasing you then?" Not much had changed.

"Of course," she said as I grabbed her hand and squeezed. "You agreed—no PDA." But she didn't pull away.

"We're not in public." I waved to a seagull flying over-head. "It's just us and the birds."

"What about drones?"

I chuckled. "I'm really not that interesting."

"I was kidding," she said, squeezing my hand.

We headed up the next dune. As we climbed higher, the sky expanded and the ocean came into view. "Wow." The breeze lifted Lana's hair and the strands splayed out behind her as if she were underwater. She looked like some kind of Grecian goddess standing at the top of the dune, looking out into the distance. Fuck, I could imagine starting a war for a girl like her.

She turned and smiled when she caught me staring.

Then she was off, running downhill and shouting, "Race you to the bottom!"

Struck still by her joy, I took far too long to catch up. She had time to turn and raise her hands in victory as I reached her, but I didn't stop, scooping her up and knocking us both back into the sand.

She squealed as I pulled her on top of me. "I haven't kissed you since Sinclair interrupted us," I said, brushing my thumb over the peach bloom of her cheek.

She bit her bottom lip and I rolled us over so she was beneath me. I liked it better this way. I got the feeling that if I let her slip out of my grasp for even a second, I'd never see her again. I dipped my head and her sweet breath hit my lips just before I pressed my mouth to hers. I couldn't help but groan. I'd been waiting for this since she'd left my bed. It was as if there'd been leftover cheesecake in the fridge and I'd been denying myself. But no more.

Her tongue met mine; her little sharp breaths telling me she enjoyed this almost as much as I did. She parted her legs and I ground my crotch against her pussy. I'd had a hard-on whenever I thought about this girl—just touching her was going to drive me to the brink sooner than I'd like.

"You're so fucking sweet," I choked out as I pulled away and dove toward her neck, sucking and licking. I wanted to devour her.

"I don't feel sweet when you kiss me like *that*."

I growled. "What do you feel?" I asked, dropping kisses from her neck down to her collarbone and over the top of her breasts. I wanted to strip her naked, place her on all fours and plow into her right there.

"Hot. Sexy. Like you own me."

"Fuck," I said, thrusting once, twice, then rolling off.

I pulled her toward me. "You're going to make me come if I'm not careful."

"Really?" she asked. "Is that a problem?" Her eyes narrowed as she waited for my answer.

I chuckled. "Not normally. But with you? Fuck, yes."

She grinned. "So, if I touch you . . ." She reached for my shorts and I caught her hand before she could make contact. The last thing I wanted to do was blow my load after a kiss. I had a reputation to live up to.

"Let's not find out." I linked my hands with hers.

"I think that would be a story I could sell to the tabloids."

I sighed. "Worse has been said about me by much less believable sources."

"God, I'm sorry. I was kidding." She pulled away, but I held her tight.

"Don't be. I made a lot of poor decisions a while back." I paused. If she didn't know what a fuckup I'd been, did I want to tell her? I did. I wanted her to see everything—the real me. Because I wanted the same in return. "I got out of control, too much partying, too much booze, too many . . ."

"Women." It wasn't a question or a judgement. Just a statement of understanding.

"Yes. A beautiful woman was always my drug of choice. Along with a lot of booze. Apparently, even as a kid, I preferred the company of women. But before I got to Hollywood, I'd always put work first."

"Did you end up in rehab?" she asked, her hand pressing into my chest as she pushed herself up to look at me.

I shook my head. "Nope. I wasn't addicted to alcohol. I think I got what I'd been aiming for and then wondered if that's still what I wanted. The partying was a way of distracting myself. I lost focus, forgot who I was and where I was from."

"And your focus is back?"

"I remembered I'm my dad's son. The parties, the women, the false friends all crumble under the scrutiny of my father's gaze."

Lana frowned. I guess I wasn't making much sense.

"He and my mother came to visit me one day, and I'd totally forgotten they were coming. I hadn't been home for days. When I wasn't at my house, he turned up on set and I was drunk." I sucked in a breath. "I saw myself reflected in his disappointment and I didn't like it. So, that was it."

"Just like that you turned over a new leaf?"

"More like I went back to my old leaf—driven, focused, hard working."

She laughed. "Oh, I got it. Hollywood almost seduced you but you escaped her clutches."

I chuckled. "A little bit." It was a good way to describe it. I'd been lucky. Many people weren't.

"You worried you might stumble again?"

I shook my head and pulled her toward me. "I'm really not. Others around me are. Hence Sinclair bursting in to my house unannounced. But I know I'd never go back there. It's not what I want for my life.

"What about you?" I was desperate to know her deepest secrets. I wanted to know everything. "Are men your drug of choice?"

She sighed. "Not really. I like to avoid drama, complications . . ."

"Life?"

"Just the downside of it."

"Is that possible?"

"I'll let you know. Or maybe you'll let me know." She

twisted her head and rested her chin on my chest. "Life's pretty peachy for you, no?"

I shrugged. Life was good. But lately, I'd been getting the sense that it wasn't just the franchise that I wanted. That there must be something that came after that. "I work hard, and as much as I enjoy acting, I know my time is limited. There's a lot of pressure attached to being the man of the moment—I can't put a foot wrong because it could all disappear tomorrow. I'm not ready for that yet."

"Because you love what you do?"

"Because I want to be successful. I see it as a means to an end. I want my family not to have to worry financially. My brothers don't earn a lot—none of us went to college. I want their kids—and mine if I ever have them—to have college funds and down payments for a first home. Life should be easier for the next generation, you know?"

I glanced down to find her gazing at me as if I were either crazy or fascinating. "Anyway, enough about me. You've got me revealing all my secrets. And we're getting far too serious."

"I like serious," she said without missing a beat. "It's real."

She was right. Our talks today were the most honest conversations I'd had in a long time. I thought about these things. A lot, while running and when deciding to do one project or another—when agreeing to pretend Audrey Tanner was my girlfriend. But I'd never told anyone what I'd shared with Lana.

"Shall we walk down to the ocean?" she asked, sitting up.

"If you promise to let me kiss you at the water's edge," I replied.

She patted my chest. "If there's no one around, I just might. You sure can kiss, Mr. Movie Star."

Mr. Movie Star. It rang in my ears. She didn't mean it to be deferential or to feed my ego. She was teasing me. And that was what I liked about her.

She stood, rearranging her skirt and lifting her hair to feel the breeze on her neck. Lana Kelly didn't treat me as if I was famous. She didn't *care* that I was famous. And she'd heard about my failures and seemed to like me anyway. I couldn't remember the last time I'd come across a woman like her.

Lana

"This lobster is delicious." I closed my eyes as I chewed, savoring the sweet seafood that had been included in our beach picnic.

"Well, we are in Maine. What did you expect?" Matt answered.

"And you just made a call and someone delivered the car with the food in the trunk all refrigerated and everything?" Matt had been clear that he couldn't take any credit for the magnificent spread—there was enough to feed *six*. It tasted like it was fresh from the sea this morning.

"Another upside to being famous. You want more champagne?"

"You trying to get me drunk?" I held out my glass.

"Will it make you easy?"

I tried to keep my hand steady as I laughed. "I've slept with you already, so I think it's well established I'm easy."

"I only wish that were true." He set down the bottle and crawled toward me. "You have a little something"—he licked the corner of my lip—"just there." He pressed his mouth against mine, and I dropped my champagne glass to wrap my arms around him. He pushed me back onto the sand and covered my body with his.

I wasn't sure he'd gone ten minutes without kissing me since he'd parked the car, and though I pretended he was such a bore, I loved it. I hadn't made out like this since high school.

We'd not seen a soul and it felt as if we were in our own private bubble so I hadn't fought off his kisses.

Matt was nearly a foot taller than me and so hard and muscular, I felt like a doll when he touched me. His hand slid up my thigh. "I want to make you feel so good."

He found the elastic of my underwear and slipped his hand beneath. I squirmed, trying to wriggle free.

"Hold still. I'm going to make you come."

I braced my hands on his shoulders. "Matt, no, not here. Anyone could—"

"We haven't seen a single person since we arrived. I need you to come." His fingers trailed up my folds and rounded my clit.

My body went weak at his touch. There was no saying no to him. I wanted to feel his fingers, wanted him to lift me higher and higher. Even though we'd only had one night together, I'd missed what he could do to my body.

"Oh yes, baby, I knew you'd be so wet for me." He abandoned my clit and I gasped at the change of sensation as he smoothed down my slick folds.

How could I be anything else but ready? The way he looked at me when he'd arrived, as if he were imagining me naked . . . I'd half expected him to push me against the wall and fuck me before we'd even gotten into the car. I'd been only slightly relieved that he hadn't. Was that how all those women who worshipped him from his movies felt?

His fingers circled my entrance, teasing out sensation from every limb, encouraging my pleasure to build and build.

"Matt," I whispered.

"I love seeing what I do to you move across your face. I love how your body tells me how much it wants me." He slipped two fingers inside me as far as they would go and rumbled, "You're so tight, Lana. So desperate." He thumbed my clit, circling and pumping his fingers in and out as he did.

"I can't," I gasped out. "I can't."

"Yeah, you can. Let it go. Let me give you what you need."

As if his words gave me courage to step off a cliff, I tumbled into free fall, arching my back and digging my fingernails into his shoulders.

My body sagged and Matt pulled me on top of him. "You look fucking astonishing when you come. I want to video it and have it play on a loop in my shower."

I tensed and pushed myself off him. "Hey," he said, trying unsuccessfully to pull me back. I sat, drawing my knees up to my chin. "Are you okay?" he asked, settling next to me and smoothing his hand over my back.

"No videos. No photographs. Not ever," I said, staring at my toes poking into the sand. The image that Bobby had plastered around campus flashed in front of me every time I blinked. "I don't do that."

"Okay, I'm sorry."

"I think we should leave." I started to stand but Matt pulled me back into his lap. "Let me go."

"Not until you tell me what's wrong."

I sat, stock-still, but desperate to run away. But I didn't.

Couldn't. I wanted to feel the heat of his body more than I wanted to escape.

"I had an ex who took my photo. It ended badly," I said eventually.

Matt brought his arms around my waist and pulled me closer. I took a deep breath, then exhaled, my body molding to his.

"I'm sorry," he whispered into my ear.

I hadn't given him any details, but it was almost like he was saying no matter what had happened, he was in my corner. I wanted Matt to know that I trusted him.

"When I broke up with him, he plastered pictures of me, naked, all around campus, sent them on email to the whole school. It was just . . . the worst thing that he could have done. It was such a violation." I took a deep breath, which evened out my pulse. "Ruby was amazing. She tore them down and sat with me while I cried." I paused, enjoying the heat of Matt's arms around me. "I never went back to class. I couldn't face it. Couldn't see all those people who'd seen such intimate pictures of me. It was . . . difficult."

I uncrossed my arms and placed them over his as he burrowed his face into my neck. "I'm so sorry. If I ever meet the weak little asshole, I swear I'll kill him." He pulled me closer.

"It was a long time ago." Five years was a lifetime, but every now and then, like now, it didn't feel that way.

"But not so long ago that it doesn't still bother you."

He was right. The memories of that afternoon were as fresh as ever today. As long as I boxed them up and shut them out it was fine, but even the smallest crack would have them back—bright and vivid.

"Is that why you don't like the city?"

"I love Worthington. Of course, like you I dreamed of leaving but, you know, you gotta be careful what you wish for."

"God, Lana, I want to make it better for you," he said, and I twisted in his lap to look up at him.

I smoothed my palm over the rough stubble on his jaw. "Holding me like this is good." I couldn't remember a time since my dad died when I felt so protected.

"Then we'll stay here all night."

I laughed. "It's not *that* good. I like my bed a lot."

"I can't wait to see what's so great about it."

I slapped him on the back of his hand. "Easy, Mr. Movie Star."

"Admit it. You're counting down the minutes until you can get me naked." He stood us up, holding me against him. "But not in public. You value your privacy. I get that now. I'm not going to put that at risk. Let's go home."

I smoothed my hand over his jaw. Wasn't he supposed to have the world at his feet? Have everything he'd ever wanted with the snap of his fingers? And yet here he was, comforting me, worrying about me. It seemed that Matt Easton was exactly what I needed in my life right in that moment.

THIRTEEN

Matt

I checked my watch as I opened the door of the makeup trailer. I'd barely made it on time. Lana's warm body had been almost too difficult to leave this morning.

"Hey, Matt," Jenny said, patting an empty chair. "You're mine today."

I grinned. "Perfect." The head artist was quick and friendly, which worked for me. I took a seat.

"How's it going up the coast? We haven't seen you in Portland at all," Jenny said.

"Yeah, Matt," Marie, the other makeup artist currently in the trailer, chimed in. "How come you're not staying with the rest of us? You should join in on our fun one night." She cocked her hip out and met my gaze in the mirror. "Maine has surprisingly good tequila."

"My head can testify to the good tequila," Jenny said. "And there's some really great seafood in some of these quaint restaurants in town."

"I'm trying to take it easy," I replied. I didn't want them

to think I thought I was too good to be staying in the same place as the rest of the cast and crew.

"You on some sort of detox or something?" Jenny tucked the paper bib into my collar.

"Kind of." I might have been sent to Maine, but it had given me a slice of normality that I found I enjoyed. It was a taste of home. It had been just what I'd needed. "It's peaceful, and I'm catching up on my sleep."

"Doesn't sound like the Matt Easton we know," Marie said, wiggling her eyebrows. "So is it true that Audrey has tamed you?"

I chuckled and closed my eyes as Jenny started wiping a sponge across my face. "Something like that." Audrey wasn't exactly front and center of my attention at the moment.

My phone buzzed, and I shifted so I could take it from my back pocket. "I'll be back in a few," I said to Jenny and headed outside.

"Hey, Catherine. I haven't heard from you in a while." Catherine and I had been friends since my modelling days in New York. She was an uncomplicated fuck who I trusted not to sell me out. She rarely called me though. I hoped nothing was wrong.

"Hey, handsome, I've been thinking about you."

Normally, I'd reply that I'd been thinking about her too, but I hadn't. And for some reason I didn't want her to get the idea that I had. "What's been keeping you busy?"

"I just finished a shoot for Gucci, so I'm having a celebratory sandwich."

I laughed. "Awesome, and congratulations, of course."

"Thanks. I have some time off coming up and wondered if you were still in Maine. You said you might give me a call."

When I'd found out I was going to be on the East Coast for a few weeks, I'd called Catherine. I'd caught up with her at least once a month since I started the thing with Audrey. And I'd been planning to make the most of the fact that she was signed up to an NDA while we were only a couple of hours from each other. But weeks had gone by and I'd not been in touch. I'd not even thought about her.

"Yeah, I'm on set right now, actually. I'm sorry I haven't called. Filming is really demanding."

"If you can't come to New York, maybe I could fly up for your next day off. I need to burn off this sandwich, and I'm pretty sure you could help me with that."

That was how it was between us. Casual. There were no expectations other than great sex. It was why our hookups had always worked so well. Normally, I'd jump at the chance to spend some time with her, but the thing was, I wasn't feeling very enthusiastic. "I don't have a day off any time soon—the schedule is totally killing me."

"Oh," she said, surprised. If she didn't believe me, she had reason not to. I had a day off in three days' time, and I was sure that if I told her that, she'd have booked flights before we hung up.

But I didn't want to see her.

The day after our trip to the dunes, Lana and I found ourselves on our respective porches, ended up enjoying the sunset, then going inside together. The next night was the same. And the night after that. In the week since the beach, I'd seen Lana every day. I'd slept in her bed each night. At the end of the day, I wanted to talk to her, hear stories about Worthington and jewelry, have her poke fun at me but know that she came like a train when I fucked her.

Lana and I weren't dating. It wasn't as if we were in a relationship. We were just temporary neighbors who fucked. I could easily stay in Portland with Catherine for the weekend. I just didn't want to. Not when I could be with Lana instead. I was into this girl and it had crept up on me.

"I'm sorry. Maybe when we've wrapped?" It was a hollow suggestion. Something told me that casual hookups were off the table for me while Lana was a part of my life. I couldn't imagine wanting someone more than I wanted Lana—to fuck, to talk to, to have fun or share ideas with. If I had a choice between someone else and Lana, Lana won every time.

"Sure, let me know," she said. "You know, you sound a little different. Like the Maine air is doing you good. Or maybe you met someone. Either way I'm happy for you."

I laughed. "You know me." But she didn't. Not really. But I had met someone who did. More than most people anyway. "I think I inherited George Clooney's mantle."

"If you say so," she said, though she didn't sound convinced.

Maybe I wasn't such a good actor after all . . . maybe Lana had gotten under my skin a little more than I'd realized.

FOURTEEN

Matt

As I got out of the car, I went straight toward the back door of Lana's cottage. Over the last few weeks, I'd spent less and less time at my place.

It was almost as if we were living together. Existing in a bubble built just for the two of us. With no one watching, there was no pressure, no expectations. We just enjoyed each day as it came.

I flipped open the screen door and called out as I opened the back door. The whir of a blow-dryer came from her bedroom and I went to track her down.

She was sitting at her dressing table in nothing but a robe, her brush in one hand, blow-dryer in the other.

I folded my arms and leaned against the doorframe, content to stand and enjoy the concentration on her face and the graceful way she moved.

Next week was my last week on set, and then I was headed back to Los Angeles. I'd thought about extending my trip—it would be great to spend some uninterrupted time with Lana before I left, but I'd received my schedule for my first week back in LA this morning. There was no way I could take any time off. The promo for my film with Audrey was going to have me busier than ever.

But I'd miss the easiness between Lana and me. The way I was able to just be me; the way Lana seemed to like who I was without the glitz and the glam of LA. I wasn't ready to give it all up. But Lana didn't belong in LA. I couldn't see how she'd fit into my world outside of Maine.

She caught my eye in the mirror and burst into a contagious smile. She turned and dropped her brush to the table. "How long have you been there?"

I shrugged and stepped forward. "Just admiring another beautiful Worthington view."

She rolled her eyes.

"Hey, I was giving you a compliment."

"Stop objectifying me and come kiss me," she said.

I didn't need to be told twice.

She tipped her head up as I stood over her. I brushed my thumbs across her cheekbones before I dipped my head to press my lips to hers. She tasted of summer and home and all the tension from my muscles drained away as our bodies found each other.

I pulled her up from where she was sitting.

"I just had a shower," she said. "It's been so sticky today."

"I'm going to get you sweaty again." I growled and bit down on her neck. "I feel like I haven't seen you for days." I always felt like that, as if I was constantly chasing more of her, as if I wasn't quite done. As if there was more to discover.

"You woke up in my bed, did wicked things to me

before you left for work just this morning," she said as she threaded her fingers through my hair.

She was right, it had only been hours since I'd had her, but that didn't mean I hadn't thought about her all day, hadn't wanted to be right here, buried in her.

I parted her dressing gown, revealing her milky white breasts, and closed my eyes for a beat. She was so fucking perfect. I pushed the robe over her shoulders and the whole thing fell to the ground, exposing her. That body had me running back to Worthington as quickly as I could.

I swept my hands over her waist. "Lie down," I said, lifting my chin toward the bed.

She backed away from me and sat on the bed. I raised my eyebrows, waiting for her to follow my command.

"Keep your feet on the floor."

Slowly, she lay back, reaching her arms above her head and arching her spine. Fucking perfect.

I stripped off my shirt and fell to my knees.

Stroking my hands up the back of her legs, I pulled her toward me and pushed her knees wide, zeroing in on her hot, wet pussy. I'd only been in the same room with her for a few minutes. Kissed her once, the contact bordering on chaste, but I could still see her wetness, still feel her heat.

She twisted under my inspection. "Matt," she moaned.

"So impatient," I chastised. "So desperate for my tongue."

I pressed my palms against the inside of her thighs, my thumbs scraping against her entrance. Her hips bucked off the bed and I grinned. I loved it when she got worked up this quickly.

I couldn't waste a moment to taste her, so I leaned forward and lay my tongue flat against her clit before circling and pressing again.

Her sounds turned from whimpers to moans as I delved deeper, coating my tongue in her wetness. Pulling my thumbs apart, I blew cool air against her hot entrance and she screamed. The noises she made—they weren't faked, or what she thought I wanted to hear—just honest reactions to the things I did to her. Fuck, every noise that left those lips was a complete turn-on.

I plunged one thumb into her as I continued to suck and press and lick. She thrust into my mouth, wanting more, needing more.

My erection pressed against my zipper so fucking hard I thought I might burst.

I pulled away, desperate to give my cock some freedom, stood to undress and glanced up at Lana, her hair spread across the bedspread.

"Turn around," I said. "I want your head here." I pointed at the corner of the bed nearest to me.

I kicked off my jeans as she turned.

"I want your mouth around my dick," I said. I wasn't done tasting her, but my cock needed some attention.

She reached over her head, grasped the back of my thighs and opened her mouth, ready to take me. I groaned and stepped forward.

In so many ways she was a wholesome girl from Maine, but the things Lana Kelly did to my dick should have her marked with a warning sign.

She took me in her mouth and sucked my crown. I swallowed hard, trying to regulate my breathing. Leaning forward, I braced my hands on either side of Lana's legs as she took me deeper. The smell of her pussy brought me back to the moment and I pressed her thighs apart, pausing to take in the beautiful swollen flesh before devouring her.

If this was heaven, I didn't ever want to come back to life.

The sensation of my cock hitting the back of her throat as I flicked my tongue over her clit and the moan that vibrated down my shaft was almost too much. She pressed her hands against the back of my thighs, trying to get me deeper into her, and I was only too happy to help. She gagged and I tried to pull away but she only sucked me in harder. This fucking woman. There was no one like her.

Her moans around my cock grew louder as I continued to lick and suck, press and push. Every reverberation around my dick brought me closer to the edge and urged me on to soak up her wetness. There was no way I was coming alone.

All too soon she stiffened and thrust against my mouth.

I stilled, pressing my flattened tongue against her as I finally allowed myself to spill into her mouth.

I panted against her pussy, my legs weakening, my body too sated to move. Holding her beneath me like that, taking me so willingly as I fucked her mouth, the trust it took—it felt as though something had burst through and taken us to a different, more intimate level.

She wanted me. Came *for me*. Not the movie star. Just me. Matt. The guy who'd grown up in Indiana, the kid who'd travelled the world but never really left the Midwest. It was the biggest turn-on I could ever have imagined.

I wasn't ready to give it up.

Lana

It had been an intense welcome home. I'd caught him watching me from the doorway and he had his mouth on me in seconds. As Matt pulled the sheet up around us and I huddled into his side, I wanted him to confirm what had just passed between us had been more than sex. Trust had formed the basis of my orgasm—intimacy. I wasn't sure I'd ever experienced that with a man.

Over the last few weeks, we'd spent every minute he was in Worthington together, but between his hours on set and my work at the shop, it never felt as if I got enough time with him. But now things had grown from something physical into something . . . more.

I just wasn't sure what that *more* was.

Whatever it was hadn't usurped the sex. There wasn't much point in wearing clothes with Matt around. He liked me naked and the feeling was mutual.

He swept his hand up my body, his fingers and then his mouth finding my nipple. I groaned at the sharp pain that burst into pleasure as he squeezed and then bit. Somehow he seemed to know exactly how hard I liked his teeth, how deep I wanted his bite. I swiveled my hips and he stilled me, his fingers pushing into me immediately.

"What's got you so worked up?" I asked, only barely able to push the words out.

"I need to get my fill of you. I've missed you today."

I sucked in a breath as he removed his fingers.

"Turn over and look back at me," he demanded.

I slid onto my front, pushed up on my elbows and threw a glance over my shoulder.

"You're so fucking beautiful."

He smoothed his hands over my ass. I knew what came next and braced myself as his palm cracked against my skin. I groaned—a sound pulled from the middle of my belly. It hurt so good.

"Perfect," he said, sweeping his hand over where he'd just smacked me. "And I bet you're even wetter than you were." His fingers tripped over my sex. "Oh yes. Very nice. Very nice indeed."

The bed dipped on either side of me as he straddled me and worked open a condom.

Nights like this were perfect. He came in, desperate to fuck. There was some cursory foreplay, but what he wanted was to ram himself into me until he came. Tonight had been slightly different. But it was all good. I wanted everything.

I slid my hands toward the headboard as he raised my hips and pressed my chest to the bed. I loved that he took exactly what he wanted from my body and that was exactly what I needed.

He possessed me, and I let him.

He nudged at my entrance and I took a big breath.

He let out a groan as he pushed deeper.

It always felt so primal like this.

"You like that, don't you?" he asked. "You like me telling you where to lie. How to offer yourself to me. I decide how we fuck and you love it."

I moaned into the mattress.

Yes. I couldn't get enough. I'd never had so much sex in my life, never spent the day feeling the aftereffects of fingers, teeth and cock, my only regret that I couldn't have more than the memory.

I'd always enjoyed sex but I'd never yearned for it. Never physically craved a man as I did Matt. And it was exactly because there was no pressure on me. He took what he wanted and knew what I needed.

He slammed deeper and deeper and I tried to keep my orgasm at bay. I wanted to be stronger than I was, for him to have to fight for my orgasm, but as soon as he touched me, I was always seconds away from my climax. I screwed up my fists and tried to block out the drag of his dick, his hot breath on my neck as he told me how many times he was going to make me come.

My climax rumbled like distant thunder. "You wanna come again, Lana?"

I nodded.

"You always want to come as soon as you get my dick."

I'd hate him for being so arrogant if it wasn't entirely true.

I spread my fingers wide and let my orgasm ripple across my body as Matt continued to thrust into me. He liked to fuck me through my climax. In the rare event that I didn't have another one soon after, he'd double down until he had me coming for a second or third time.

Tonight, the third one was beginning to build even though the second was still a series of aftershocks. He pulled us to our sides and wrapped his arms around me, never losing his rhythm. He reached for my nipple, pinching and rolling it between his finger and thumb, injecting a fresh shot of pleasure directly between my legs.

His other hand went to my lower belly and brought me closer, thrusting deeper. I called out, desperate for some respite. But I needed it harder and deeper.

"Feel this, Lana? I knew the first moment I saw you, soaked to your skin, screaming at me, that this was what you needed. My cock, driving deeper into you, my fingers pinching your nipples. You screamed out how bad you needed to be fucked this hard."

The rest of his words blurred into my climax as it ripped through me and I could tell by his sharp thrusts that he was coming with me. "*Lana*," was the only sound I heard through the pounding of the blood in my ears.

"You smell like the ocean," he whispered on an exhale as our bodies continued to pulse and quiver.

I reached back to cup his jaw. "You smell of determination. Something got into you tonight." We'd had sex every day since our trip up the coast, but something had shifted in the way he'd touched me tonight.

I turned to face him and he grinned, and I shook my head. "I can see that joke forming in your brain. You know what I mean. You got something on your mind?"

"I got my schedule for my first week back in LA."

My stomach flipped. Next week was his last on set and then he was going back to California. He'd never pretended that he might stay, but I would miss him. I'd gotten used to having him in my bed every night.

"You have a schedule sent to you? You don't just, I don't know, wake up and get on with your day?"

He rearranged us on the bed so we were facing each other and pulled up a sheet. "No, because the press tour for the movie Audrey and I did starts almost immediately. I also have a couple of interviews and meetings with directors and stuff. There's a lot more to the job than just filming."

I nodded and placed my hands between my face and the pillow.

"Will you come out and visit me?" he asked, taking a strand of my hair and pushing it behind my ear.

"In LA?" We'd never talked about what happened after he left Worthington. Things had started off so casually between us, and it was always so clear that we only had limited time together. I didn't have any answers, but I wasn't sorry that he'd brought it up. I wanted to see inside his brain.

"Yeah, in LA." His fingers smoothed over my waist.

Where did he see this going? There'd been plenty of times over the last few weeks that I'd wanted to stretch out time so he'd be in Worthington longer, but it had never occurred to me that once he'd left we could see each other again. Not until tonight.

"I'm not a city girl—you know that. I have the shop here. My life is here. What would I even do in LA? You can't risk being discovered with another woman, and I don't want any attention—"

"I'm not sure if you're really concerned about any of these things, or if you just don't want to see me."

"I'm really concerned about all those things." Mostly, I was worried about being seen with him. I didn't want that sort of attention for either one of us. "You know I don't want people taking my picture, or knowing my business."

He pulled me toward him, so we were touching. "You've never thought how you'll miss how I can make you feel?"

"You're trying to distract me." I smacked him on the chest.

He chuckled, pulling my hand to his mouth and kissing it. "Just reminding you what you'll be missing. And I can sneak you in. No one will ever know you're staying with me. We can stay in bed the whole time."

I trailed my fingers from his collarbone over his chest. Was that possible? To go unseen to the house of a Hollywood heartthrob? "Surely there are plenty of women very happy to spend all day in bed with you in LA?"

He drew in a breath. "Look, I'm just kidding about staying in bed all day." He paused. "I think. I like hanging out with you, but I'm leaving soon. And I don't want to stop hanging out. I'm just suggesting we have some more time together. No pressure."

"And you think we could do it without the press finding out?" I focused on his eyes, trying to determine if there was reticence behind them.

None.

He brought my leg across his hip, snaking his hand up the back of my thigh. "Yeah. I have high fences."

"We won't be able to go out, though. Not for lunch or anything." Surely he wouldn't want to be cooped up at home for a weekend.

"I can get any restaurant in town to do takeout for us." He seemed certain that this was what he wanted, and I wouldn't turn down an extra few days with a man who knew my body so well. And had also gotten to know my mind pretty well too. A man who I enjoyed sharing my day with, who could make me laugh, who not only didn't mind my yoga pants but found them sexy. I liked Matt. And I wasn't so sure I wanted him to disappear from my life all of a sudden.

I bit back my grin. "Only if you promise me *a lot* of sex."

"Now that's the easiest promise I've made in the last month." He pressed his lips against mine. I tightened my leg, pulling him toward me.

Would it be as easy as he made it sound, sneaking into his house and not being seen? A famous guy was the last person I'd want to date if that was even what he was suggesting, which I wasn't sure about. But I wanted to let him go even less.

FIFTEEN

Matt

Sitting out on Lana's deck while she worked was one of my
new favorite things to do. She was curled up next to me on a
long bench, sketching jewelry designs while I made notes
on a book I was reading. The sound of the ocean was incredibly soothing, and I'd grown so used to it that I'd decided to
look at real estate in Malibu when I got back to LA. The
only problem was Lana wouldn't be there sharing the view
with me. I'd never been interested in just hanging out with a
woman, which wasn't to say I wouldn't take naked-Lana
over dressed-Lana any day of the week, but just being with
her was better than I'd ever thought possible.

"It's going to rain again," she said without looking up.

"How can you tell?"

"You can't feel that shift in the air? Must be those ions
or something." She glanced across at me and grinned.
Christ, she was beautiful.

We hadn't mentioned her coming to visit me in LA

again since we'd talked about it a few days ago, but I could tell she was thinking it was a possibility.

As if on cue, the sky rumbled. She raised her eyebrows. "Told you so."

"You right about everything?"

"I wish. I'd love to be able to tell the future." She looked away and blushed, but I couldn't figure out why.

"What are you thinking about?" I swiped her hair off her shoulders and cupped the back of her neck.

"Nothing. How's the book?" She lifted her chin toward my current read, *The Brothers*, about kids growing up in the Midwest who discover a body.

"It's not a kids' book though?" she asked.

I shook my head. "No more than *Stranger Things* is a show for kids."

"I love that show," she said. "It's unadulterated entertainment but you can see respect for the audience."

I grinned. "Exactly. So much stuff now is dumbed down. But you can tell the things that are made for ratings compared to other things that are clearly made by people who want to be real fans of the end product. This," I said, jiggling the book, "would make an awesome movie."

"You keep saying that," Lana said, concentrating on her drawing again.

"Because it's true." It was the second book I'd read since coming to Maine that I could see on the screen. If not a movie, then maybe as a Netflix series. "You'd have to get a director who wasn't afraid to be a little dark and you couldn't aim it at kids. As soon as you do that, you lose what this book is about. Kids are sophisticated." I pulled her legs onto my lap. "This book could be about me and my brothers, growing up and on our bikes in Gary, getting up to God knows what. But we weren't naïve. We knew exactly what was going on. We knew the auto mechanic at the corner of Virginia Street and Fifteenth sold drugs and stolen phones. We knew my dad's best friend fooled around on his wife. Adults underestimate kids. And the scriptwriter would have to understand how worldly the characters are in this text despite their age."

Her smile grew wider.

"What?" I asked.

She shook her head. "I like to hear you talking like this. With passion. It suits you."

"It's this book. It would make *such* a great movie."

"Has the author sold the rights?" She tilted her head and continued to sketch.

"I doubt it. It's a book about four kids who stumble across a murder. Not the sort of thing that gets snapped up by studios and production houses."

"Maybe you should think about seeing if the rights are available."

I placed a bookmark between the pages and lay it down next to me on the bench, tugging her feet toward me. "You think?"

She nodded. "Yeah. You could be the one to get it made. It's often the oddball choices, the movies that take a risk, that do really well."

I chuckled. "Hardly. I'm a pretty face. I don't get books turned into movies." Brian was forever telling me how lucky I was that I'd made it when so many models tried to break into acting all the time.

"Don't a lot of actors produce?" She glanced up at the roof of the porch as if impatient for the rain.

"When they've been in the business a long time. Earned their stripes."

"You don't think you're there yet?"

I'd never really thought about going behind the scenes. "Well, I'm all about the franchise at the moment. Everything's aiming for that."

"Because that will make you a lot of money?" she asked. I'd talked a little about my future career plans and Lana understood my goals.

"I guess that's part of it. I like to be able to give my family what they've never had, so none of them have to worry. But for me it's more than that. It's about being the best. About getting to the top."

She nodded. "And after you have that?"

My plan was always to make as much money as I could while I was hot, then make a graceful exit. "I'm not sure I'll ever be producer material. I was a model, remember?"

"I'm looking at you. I don't need to remember. That doesn't mean you can't be a producer." She pulled out the blanket from underneath the bench and began to unfold it. "But you like this book. Can't you option it or something? Is that the right word?"

"Yeah, it's the right word." How could I explain that it wasn't as easy as she was making it seem? "The author is unlikely to sell their rights to me. I don't have a production company or studio backing or anything."

"Doesn't mean you can't get all those things. Surely you have contacts?"

I lifted my arms as she placed the blanket over both our legs. Despite the fresh breeze, I wasn't cold, but I liked that she was trying to make me comfortable. "Yeah, maybe." I could mention it to my agent, I supposed. The book was phenomenal, but I knew the lack of adult male leading roles meant it wasn't likely to ever get to the big screen. But if Lana believed in me, then maybe it was worth a try. "You think it's possible?"

"I never hear what you're shooting for when this franchise thing is in the bag. Won't turning a book you love into a movie be something to aim for?"

When I went for my first audition as an actor, I'd come out of the meeting knowing that if I got the part, I'd do every job it took to be a success. I was determined not to squander the opportunity.

"I think passion for success has gotten you a long way. Have you ever thought that you could have passion in a different way, for the actual work? Maybe you need something more."

My heart began to beat through my chest. *Something more.* Looking back, it was probably what I'd been wanting for a long time. I'd pushed the feeling down by partying and then by focusing on getting back what I almost lost. But being here in Maine, with Lana, the feeling had grown. But it wasn't so scary anymore. "Maybe I'll call Brian and talk it over with him."

Taps on the roof gave away that it was raining before it was possible to see for sure. "You see? Rain."

"So what about you?" I asked, nodding at her drawing pad.

"What about me?"

"What are your big dreams or future plans? What's your *more*?"

She looked out over the ocean. "I have everything I ever wanted here. My shop. A beautiful cottage. A million-dollar view."

"The view is spectacular. But what about these?" I asked, pulling her notebook over to see what she'd been working on. "You don't want to market these to high-end retailers? Sell them in New York and London and Paris? They're incredible."

"They're just sketches, and I like Maine. I don't have to be selling jewelry all over the world to be happy."

She fished a necklace out of her blouse and held out the pink stone that hung around her neck. "My less expensive designs are just as cute, don't you think?"

"You know I think you're super talented. I'd just like to see you make one of these things." I ran my fingers over the folio of work she kept. "Rather than just draw them."

She sighed. "I will. One day."

"How about I promise to call Brian if you make me something? I want to see one of these incredible designs come to life."

"It's not that easy. It's a huge investment. I'd have to buy the gold and these pieces here"—she drew her finger along the left side of the jeweled collar—"are sapphires. It's not like I can stop off at Jerry's Foodstore and fill up my shopping cart."

"Whereas Jerry's got a two-for-one sale on turning a book into a movie."

She pursed her lips and narrowed her eyes. She hated to lose, and usually I was happy to concede outside the bedroom. But I wanted her to think about this.

"Okay. I'll make you something if you promise to call your agent."

She was so damn cute that it took everything I had not to grab her, pull her onto my lap and kiss her into next week. But then, I was always fighting that feeling.

"One of your designs. In your studio. Not more lemon curd."

"Something wrong with my lemon curd?"

I'd spent the day trailing smears of sticky yellow across her nipples, over her pussy and in her belly button. There was absolutely nothing wrong with her lemon curd. "I think we both know how much I enjoyed it, but I want you to make me jewelry."

"And you'll make some calls about the book?"

I nodded.

"You got yourself a deal."

"Good," I replied.

"Making deals with you gets me hot," she said. "Wanna get naked?"

"Always," I said, discarded my book, stood and pulled her to her feet.

SIXTEEN

Lana

"What are you thinking about?" Matt asked from the bathroom door, his chest speckled with water droplets.

He'd come back early from the wrap party last night. When his car pulled up at just before eleven I'd assumed it was someone else. I'd been a little too pleased to see him, which worried me. Tomorrow he'd be gone. He was just supposed to be a summer lover. But every day I spent with him, I yearned for a week more. And it was getting worse not better. This house would feel empty without him. *I'd* feel empty without him.

I was trying to untangle the damp knots in my hair and not think about how after tomorrow, there'd be no one around to ask me questions like that. "Everything. Nothing. Why? What are you thinking about?"

"I'm thinking that—" He paused and looked at his watch. "I've known you for nearly six weeks."

"It's been that long since I saved your life? Death in the

bandstand? I really should have let you get struck by lightning. It would have made a good headline."

He grinned and strode toward the bed. "Six weeks since you verbally abused and harassed me."

I tilted my head back to look up at him. "I think you got off easy."

"I wouldn't change a thing." He stroked his thumb over my cheekbone.

"I wonder if your fans know how sappy you can be. I heard you were a player, a ladies' man. A heartthrob." I shook my head. "What happened?"

He chuckled. "I have no idea. You have a magic body and soul. And Jesus, you give the best blow job in the whole of the US of A."

"Okay, maybe you're not so sappy." I rolled my eyes.

He dipped and placed a kiss on my lips. How was I going to get used to him not being here?

"I have something to show you," I said.

"Seeing you in my shirt, knowing you're not wearing anything underneath is enough," he said.

"I think you'll like this almost as much." I pulled out my dressing table drawer and brought out the cuff I'd been working on over the last week that I'd carefully wrapped in acid-free paper. I'd barely been in the shop at all, wanting to make this before Matt left. "I figured I could maybe put a commission tab on my website and use this as an example." I placed the piece on my dressing table and unwrapped it.

"Wow, Lana. This is beautiful."

I rolled my lips again and watched him take in the gold bracelet that matched the more intricate collar in the Bastet collection. It was smaller, but also less expensive to make.

"You don't think you could just sell it? It's the sort of thing I'd expect to see at the Oscars."

"In Worthington, Maine? I'm not sure Hollywood types come around here very often." I poked him in his rock-hard stomach just above his towel. "There's always the odd exception, I suppose."

"Regardless, *I'm* proud of you. You're so talented, Lana," he said, rubbing himself down and climbing into his briefs.

"Thanks." I looked away. Truth be told, I was pretty proud of myself. Five years had passed and I'd sometimes thought I'd never make any jewelry again. I'd seen it as something I'd left behind in New York. It represented my old life and old dreams. "And did you keep your end of our bargain? Did you speak to Brian about the book?"

He rubbed his towel over his head, making his damp hair point every which way. "I've put a couple of calls in to him. Left him a message."

"You make him a ton of money, but he doesn't call you back?"

"He normally doesn't return my calls if he thinks I'm going to make the wrong decision about a script or something. Some kind of passive-aggressive power play." He scraped his fingers through his hair.

"You don't think he liked your idea?"

Matt shrugged. "Probably not. I told you—I'm just a pretty face to him. Nothing but a pussy draw." He pulled on a t-shirt, his abs dipping and clenching.

I grimaced at his words. "But it's not Brian's decision, right? You could talk to the studios yourself?"

"Yeah, I might do that when I'm back home."

For some reason, his description of going home sliced through me like a knife. "Sounds like a good plan. You'll need something to keep you busy."

"Until you come out and visit," he said. "You are still coming, aren't you?"

"Sure," I said. We hadn't made any definite plans and I wasn't convinced it would actually happen. Matt Easton would forget all about me as soon as he got back to LA.

His phone buzzed and I turned back to my dressing table to find my mascara.

"Hi, Sinclair," he said.

I lay the back of my hand on my cheek, trying to cool my face. Every time Sinclair called, I couldn't help but remember how he'd seen me naked in bed with Matt. Apparently Hollywood boundaries were different from the rest of the world's.

"Yeah, Lana has her laptop. Lana, can I check something out on here?"

"Help yourself," I replied, twisting open my mascara.

He winked, then turned back to his conversation. "Are you serious? What does it say?"

"Shit," he said under his breath as he began to tap at the keyboard. "They have pictures?"

I glanced across at the screen, but he'd turned it away from me so I couldn't see whatever it was that he was getting riled up about.

"MT fucking Z. Unbelievable. They must have had someone on a boat." He looked up out my bedroom window. "There's no way they could have got that shot otherwise."

My blood ran cold as Matt's voice merged into the screaming in my head. Pictures? Taken here?

I gripped the edge of the table in front of me as my head began to spin. "Matt?"

I hadn't even finished saying his name when I felt him

beside me. "It's okay. You can just about make out it's me, but they can't tell it's you."

"Show me," I blurted out.

"I'm telling you, it's not that bad."

"Show me," I demanded. "I need to see for myself."

He grabbed the laptop and set it in front of me on the dressing table, bottles and makeup flying everywhere. "It looks like they were taken last week. But they were so shitty, they had to wait for a slow news day."

I peered closely at the grainy pictures of us on Matt's deck. How many were there? I grabbed the mouse and clicked through. One. Two. Three. Four. Four pictures. I went back to the first one of us having lunch on his deck. That must have been on his last day off. Most of our time we spent at my place, but I remembered last week we'd taken our food to his cottage because I'd run out of ice. "It was Tuesday."

"Yeah, but look, baby, they can't see you."

In the first two shots, it was only just possible to make out Matt's identity. If it hadn't been for his height and strong jaw, it would have been easy to mistake him for someone else. In the first one, I was hidden behind the clematis trellis. In the second one, I stood behind him. I wasn't in the rest of them.

"They just know I was with someone. That's all."

Thank God. I wasn't going to be dragged through the tabloids. Still, this posed a problem for Matt. "Is Sinclair mad?"

"Sinclair's always mad," he said, tossing his phone to the bed. "But I'm on my deck, eating lunch. There's not much he can say. Don't sweat it."

"But your franchise. I thought you wanted to portray an image of dependable and trustworthy . . ."

He closed his eyes and shrugged. "It's not like we're kissing or anything."

"I'm so sorry." I put my arms around his waist, and let my head rest against his stomach.

He pushed his hands through my hair. "It's my fault, not yours."

"No," I said, tilting my head to look at him. "This is the guy who hired a boat in order to invade your privacy's fault."

He smiled, but it was dull and without life. I couldn't decide whether it was the invasion of privacy or the thought that he might have created problems for his career that worried him. Guilt churned in my stomach. Matt and I had snowballed into something that I'd never intended. Suddenly, I was putting his future at risk. All for a relationship that was never going to go anywhere. Matt might be used to his fame and attention, but I knew I never would be. There was no time when I was going to be okay with people taking my picture and publishing it across America. And that's what it would mean to be with him. These grainy photos were a warning of what would happen if things continued between us, if things grew deeper.

Tomorrow, Matt would leave and I'd wave him off and remember a beautiful summer. But that's all we could ever be. The way he held me close, kissed my head? It made me think he understood that, too.

There was no way a Hollywood superstar and a girl from Worthington, Maine, were meant to be together.

SEVENTEEN

Lana

Keep busy. That was my mantra. Right now, that meant polishing the front windows of the shop.

I pulled out the linen cloths and grabbed the vinegar from under the cash register. I had to get used to Matt being back in LA. It wasn't like he was traveling for work or on vacation—we lived on opposite sides of the country. Which wasn't even the biggest obstacle in our relationship. His fame, my not wanting to be out in public with him, him having every woman under sixty-five having a desire to jump him—none of it sang out *happily ever after*. I should have been stronger and ended whatever there was between us, but he was so hard to resist. Especially when I didn't want to. Instead I let myself hope that his draw would wane over the next few days.

We'd spoken twice since he'd left yesterday. Once when he landed and another just before I went to bed last night. Apparently, Matt was almost as good at phone sex as he was at the real thing. Almost. I blushed as I came face-to-face with Mr. Butcher.

"Good morning, Lana." He poked his head around the open door. "It's going to be a beautiful day. Better get those windows done quickly. You can't do them in the sun."

"Oh, now that's an old wives' tale," I replied.

"It's true," he insisted. "The heat from the sun warms the window and dries it too fast, which makes streaks."

"Well I gotta work faster then."

"I heard your neighbor moved out. Are you very disappointed?" he asked, lingering by the door.

I tried to keep my face still and my smile constant. "We have another renter in on Wednesday, so it's all good as far as I'm concerned." I was pretty sure that if anyone in Worthington had caught wind of a romance between Matt and me, I'd have heard about it, but something in the way he asked made me think maybe he suspected.

Mr. Butcher smiled but dropped the subject. "I'm glad to see your property business is booming. What about the jewelry? How's that going?"

I stopped what I was doing. "Actually, if you have a few minutes, I'd love to get your opinion on a piece I've been working on." I'd been so happy with how the gold cuff had turned out that I was desperate to show it off.

"Of course. I'd be honored. You know what a talent I think you have."

"And you know I adore your taste and value your eye, Mr. Butcher."

"It's in my blood, darling. What can I say?"

From Paris to Poodles, good tailoring to a sunny Maine day, everything Mr. Butcher felt passionate about was *in his blood*.

"If you'll excuse me while I just go and wash my

hands?" I held up my palms, then turned and headed in back. "Take a seat and I'll be right out."

I threw the cloth by the side of the basin and washed my hands before drying them carefully. I hadn't shown anyone other than Matt the cuff, and I was pretty sure I could have sawed off the end of a baked bean can and Matt would have told me how talented I was.

Mr. Butcher, on the other hand, wouldn't hold back with his criticism.

I pulled the wooden box from the filing cabinet where I'd been keeping it and headed back out. Mr. Butcher was standing in front of the glass display case that doubled as a counter.

"So, what have you got?" he asked.

I really hoped he'd like it. It was the first piece I'd made since leaving New York, and I hated to think I'd lost any of the skills I'd learned.

I pulled out a black-velvet mat and placed it on the glass, then opened the box containing the cuff.

He gasped. "My dear, it's magnificent. Did you make this yourself?"

I beamed at him. "Yeah, it's my first piece since college. Gold-plated platinum."

"Good grief, Lana. With this sort of talent, you should be in Saks, Barneys and Harrods."

I shifted from one foot to the other. "I wasn't planning on selling it in the shop." Excitement and uneasiness churned in my stomach.

"Well of course not. Do you have other pieces?" He held the cuff up to the light. "It truly is remarkable. Very luxurious—it doesn't have that homemade feel to it."

"I think that's down to the materials." So many jewelry

designers skimped on quality because of costs, but I'd wanted to do this right. "You really like it?"

"I really do." He placed the bracelet back on the velvet and turned to me. "I'm quite serious when I say that you are very talented. I could make a few calls, or—"

"Thank you. For now, I'm just going to add a section on my website and say I take commissions. I don't want to get ahead of myself." It was enough to know that I could make beautiful pieces, and that people I trusted liked them. I'd left my dream of adorning the rich and famous in New York. I had a different life now.

He clasped his hands together. "But, darling, you need to share these with the world, not hide them away."

I wasn't hiding, was I? I'd achieved so much in the five years since college. My dreams had just changed.

Mr. Butcher was wrong. "I'm not hiding anything. I just know what I'm capable of handling right now."

Matt probably agreed with Mr. Butcher. He didn't understand my desire to stay in Maine.

As much as I enjoyed spending time with Matt, I wasn't sure I saw him in my future. Maybe because I knew deep down that however much he protected me, if we were going to survive as a couple, the whole world would know who I was—I would never be okay with that kind of exposure and scrutiny.

"Knowing your limits is good, Lana." Mr. Butcher tilted his head, and the look in his eye made me wonder if he knew about what had happened to me in New York. "But pushing them here and there is even more important. It's as true in business as it is in love. When you believe in something, sometimes you have to jump and trust the net will appear."

Why did I get the feeling that Mr. Butcher was trying to

deliver a sermon? "It's scary, jumping without knowing something will catch you. I prefer my feet on the ground."

"Yes, it is. It requires faith in yourself and the people around you." He sighed and turned toward the window and the view of the ocean. "I spoke to a journalist just yesterday who I found wandering down on the beach."

I turned back to the counter and my stomach flipped as I started to put away the cuff. "You did?" Surely a journalist wasn't looking for Matt? "From the *Portland Press Herald*?"

"No, it wasn't anyone from Portland. Someone from out of town, looking for the gossip on Matt Easton."

I froze, then fumbled with the box in my hand. "Really? What were they asking?"

"Just that he'd heard Matt was staying here. He said he was following up on some photographs."

I couldn't look at Mr. Butcher, but I was desperate to know what had been said. Did Mr. Butcher guess it was me in the photos?

"I told him that if we'd had someone as handsome as Matt Easton in town, then I'd be the first to crow about it." I turned to Mr. Butcher to make sure I hadn't misheard him. "Outrageous. To think he could turn up in Worthington and we'd just spill our secrets to some stranger."

A smile twitched at the corners of my mouth.

"We look after our own. You know that."

I exhaled, relieved. Even if Mr. Butcher did know something about Matt and me, he hadn't said anything. "Well, Matt's gone now. Hopefully the journalists are, too."

"I hope Matt will be back. He was very handsome."

"Who knows? Anything is possible," I said.

"That's the attitude. You need to be open to possibilities, that's all I'm saying."

"I thought we were talking about jewelry?"

"We're talking about your happiness, Lana. Worthington will always be here, but that doesn't mean the rest of the world isn't worth exploring. Just be open to everything this wonderful life has to offer you."

I sighed. He was right. I needed to be brave, deal with things as they came up rather than avoiding things in case they hurt. But it was easier said than done.

"I was thinking that I might get some professional photographs taken of this piece for the website, so I can show what I can do," I said as I packed up the bracelet. "Then, maybe you could send one to one of your contacts, if you don't mind."

Mr. Butcher's eyes danced. "It would be a complete pleasure."

"They might hate it, of course."

"Or it might not be the right time," he said, shrugging his shoulders. "It's a risk. But it doesn't hurt to try. To dip your toe in the water."

"Thank you, Mr. Butcher."

Instead of terrified, I felt excited about the prospect of someone with real power in the fashion industry seeing one of my designs. Sending a photograph to some stranger on email didn't require me to leave Maine. And if it led to opportunities that were too overwhelming, I could always say no. I really had nothing to lose and everything to gain.

EIGHTEEN

Matt

I stared up at the ceiling of my bedroom, my hands behind my head. I'd never enjoyed sharing my bed, preferring to starfish on my mattress to my heart's content. But this was the tenth day of waking up in Los Angeles on my own in bed, reaching over, hoping to find Lana's warm body, only to pull away disappointed.

Three days, and she'd be here. I couldn't help but grin as I pictured her in my bed, naked beside me. I snaked my hand down to grip my morning erection. I wouldn't have to waste these when Lana got here.

My dick twitched in my fist and I closed my eyes, imagining Lana's hand rather than my own. My eyes flew open as my cell buzzed. Hopefully that was her, ready to talk dirty to me.

I grabbed the phone. Brian. Just my fucking luck.

I released my cock and sat up against my headboard. "Hey."

"Thank God you're back in the right time zone. I have Sinclair on the line as well."

"Hi, Sinclair. What can I help you with?"

"You're always all business, Matt."

"You know me. What's up?"

"It's about Audrey. We've been doing some media management since those photos in Maine, and we need to bring your breakup forward."

"I don't see why. The studio will want to wait until publicity for the film is finished."

"Look, the press is on your tail after that photograph with the brunette," Sinclair said.

"Why? Those pictures weren't incriminating. And for future reference, her name is Lana." Jesus, the way people were referred to in Hollywood as their most prominent body part was fucking ridiculous. "And she's my girlfriend." As I said the words, my throat constricted. Was she my girl-friend? I'd been happy to be casual about what we were to each other when I'd left Maine, but having been separated from her, I wanted to put a label on it. Did she feel the same?

"Whatever. I'm telling you—the press is looking for a cheating story. They're going to start clocking the time you and Audrey spend together, or go looking for reasons why you're apart. She could even be caught out with her fiancé. This could all end up a big mess."

If Sinclair was right, the whole situation was a ticking time bomb. "Do Audrey's people agree with this?"

"If you're on board, that's my next call."

I sucked in a breath. "Let me speak to Audrey first. She called me about the breakup, so I should be the one to make the first move." Hopefully she'd see this could avoid a scandal for her as well. "But how will we play it with the studio? Won't they be mad?" What I didn't want to do was piss off the producers, who were all banking on the chemistry between Audrey and me to generate ticket sales. Hollywood was a small town. The whole point of dating Audrey in the first place was to show that I was responsible and reliable. I didn't want this backfiring.

"I think we can spin this so people become interested in the breakup, wonder if you'll get back together. Particularly if you're close on the red carpet. People are going to speculate about what's going on and who broke it off with whom," Sinclair said.

I could imagine the studio being okay with that. The tabloids speculated all the time whether co-stars' chemistry spilled off set and into real life. And a breakup would lead to a lot of questions and commentary. "You think you can convince them?" I asked.

It was difficult to know how Lana would react, but surely it was better for the guy you were sleeping with not to be in a relationship with someone else, even if it was fake. Lana and I had never had a conversation about what we were to each other, but I knew I wanted her in my life. The sex was fantastic between us, we made each other laugh and we'd spoken twice a day every day since I flew back to LA. For the first time in my life, I didn't consider myself single, and I was a mile past okay with that.

"Come on, it's me you're dealing with. I can sell sand to Arabs," Sinclair said.

"Let me talk to Audrey and I'll let you know. I don't want you leaking anything to the press in the meantime." I also needed to speak to Lana. Audrey and I splitting up was a good opportunity to discuss what we were.

"So what does this mean for me going forward?" I asked.

"If you're thinking you can go back to fucking everything with a pulse, then you're sorely mistaken," Brian chimed in. "If you want to—"

"I take my career more seriously than you do, Brian. You might have to convince some of your clients what's good for them, but I'm not one of them. I've learned my lesson."

"I was hoping you'd say that," Sinclair said. "Because I've found the perfect girl for you."

"You're suggesting another contracted relationship?" Obviously, that had been the plan, but in the last few weeks, I'd been thinking that maybe Lana might be my real girlfriend.

"Kristin Cooper. She's beautiful, just finished an arthouse picture that Sundance loved, and has signed on to the latest Joel Schumacher. She's going to explode over the next twelve months. It will be great publicity for you." I expected him to elaborate, but his silence suggested he thought that he'd presented a slam-dunk solution.

"But I'm seeing Lana. I don't see why I can't just be with her. It's not like I'm going to be out partying."

Brian groaned. "No civilians. You just said that you were prepared to do whatever it takes to get the franchise—this is what it takes. The publicity with Kristin will really help keep you hot."

I moved to the edge of the bed and pushed my hands through my hair. "The whole point of being seen in a relationship was to prove that the press had it wrong and that I wasn't a kid in a candy store—that I was reliable, stable. That I had some self-control. The publicity was an extra benefit, but not the purpose of this."

"But a huge benefit nonetheless. And anyway, Kristin will help cement this new version of you," Sinclair said.

Brian and Sinclair had always wanted what I wanted—a franchise, for me to be the most successful movie star in Hollywood. We might not always agree but they knew what they were talking about and I trusted them. But this time, for the first time, I wasn't convinced we all wanted the same thing.

"Surely it doesn't matter who I'm in a relationship with as long as it's monogamous. Why can't it be Lana?"

"Because Kristin is beautiful and—"

"So is Lana," I replied, interrupting Sinclair. She had that old Hollywood glamor thing going on. Sexy and feminine . . . but could swear like a sailor.

"A relationship with Kristin keeps you front of mind. You'll be the only thing this town is interested in. And she's got as much to gain and lose as you have," Brian said.

I slumped back onto the bed. I had no doubt in my mind that objectively he was right. But I wasn't feeling it. "Is she single?"

"That's my boy," Sinclair said. "Yes, she's single, and I know for a fact that she thinks you're hot, so it could turn into a real thing, you never—"

"I'm with *Lana*," I said through gritted teeth. "If Kristin was seeing someone, too, then it might be easier." At least then Lana wouldn't have to wonder whether any lines had been crossed. Things would be less messy. "It won't work if she's single."

"We can make it work," Brian said.

"If you keep seeing Lana in private, without publically dating someone, people are either going to think you're gay or fucking everything that moves unless you're a public couple," Sinclair said.

"I don't care if people think I'm gay."

"You don't need me to tell you that you're not going to

get a franchise if there are more than three rumors that you might be gay." As usual, I hated what Sinclair was saying, but he wasn't wrong. "The only alternative is to date Lana seriously and publicly. But I don't like that option. It doesn't give you the publicity push. And it could get very messy. We need someone who understands the game."

Fuck.

I was pretty sure that Lana wasn't suddenly going to be okay with going public. Hell, *I* wasn't even sure if I was ready for that. Privately dating someone was something I'd only just got accustomed to—would it survive media scrutiny?

I sighed.

"I can set up a dinner for you and Kristin, see how it goes," Sinclair said.

"No. Don't do anything. Yet."

"Listen, Matt, you don't know how this Lana thing is going to go. I know you like her now, but she's a long way away and she's not used to the pressure of Hollywood." Sinclair had a point. "You think she's ready for all the attention and publicity? Give it twelve months with Kristin, then if you're still crazy for Lana we can transition you into that relationship. By then the franchise is in the bag."

"I don't know." Audrey and I had managed, but she'd been with the same guy since high school. More importantly, I hated the idea of pretending someone other than Lana was my girl.

"It's the smart move, Matt. And like you say, you're serious about your career," Sinclair said.

"Don't try to manipulate me, Sinclair. You know I hate that. I'll make my decision and let you know."

"Why don't you just have a drink with Kristin? I think you'll get along with her really well."

"No. I'm not going to do that. Not yet." If I gave Sinclair an inch, he'd take a mile. I just couldn't see how dating one person but wanting to be with another was a good idea.

But I wasn't sure I could convince Lana to date me publicly, anyway. I knew she didn't crave fame or publicity, which was one of the things I liked about her. She understood the beauty of being in Maine and stepping out of city life. Her motives were clear to see—she wanted peace and happiness. How could I deny her such worthy aspirations? I didn't want to be the one to take it all away.

Brian continued on about Kristin, but I was only half listening. "I said I'd call Audrey, but I don't want to talk about it anymore." The other end of the phone fell silent. "What I do want to speak to you about is *The Brothers*. Did you approach the author's agent?"

Brian cleared his throat. It was how he built up to bad news. Shit. "I'm just not sure this is the way to go for you at the moment, Matt. You need to stay focused."

Whose career was it, though? "Does that mean you haven't approached the author's agent? What about Fox? Did you talk to them about a production deal?"

"You don't have any experience producing. And you came from modelling. It's not an easy transition. You need to look focused. It's not good to be overcommitted."

"Every actor out there has a production deal." I swept my hand through my hair.

"I know, and I understand that this might be frustrating to you."

I hated when he adopted the tone of a parent of a two-year-old having a tantrum.

"But you need to take this business one step at a time. What you don't want to happen is to get a production deal too early and then have it fail."

I took a deep breath. He had a point. "Surely we can still option the book?"

"You think a decent agent would recommend an actor without a production deal taking an option on this? It's not like you're going to take it to a studio and say you'll star if they make it. That I could get behind. But I read the fucking thing. There are no adult male leads in the book."

Christ, Brian could be a douche. I was very close to telling him to fuck off. When someone told me I couldn't do something, it lit a fire under me. If Brian wasn't going to play ball then I'd have to change up my game. I hadn't made it this far by playing things safe. "Okay. Well, keep your ear to the ground. If you hear of anyone else looking to option it, let me know."

"Sure will," Brian said. I genuinely believed he thought he was acting in my best interests, but it didn't seem like we were aligned on what those were anymore. Yes, I wanted the franchise, but I could option the book and try for a production deal at the same time. I could do both, couldn't I?

And as long as I wasn't getting into trouble, I didn't see why I needed any woman in my life other than Lana.

I'd never felt so out of sync with my team as I did right now.

NINETEEN

Lana

I pulled my suitcase off the carousel, imagining the chaos on the other side of baggage claim if Matt had decided to turn up at the airport, despite the fact that we had agreed I'd take a car to his place. He'd be surrounded by screaming women, thrusting their phones and God knew what in his face. He'd never felt like a movie star to me. He was just Matt—the guy who sheltered in the bandstand in a thunderstorm, the man who could make me come again and again and again.

I set my suitcase on its wheels and headed for the exit. Nerves fluttered about in my stomach. What happened if things were different between us in LA? Our time together in Maine had been easy, but in Los Angeles, Matt was surrounded by the most beautiful women on the planet every day. Would he see me and wonder what he'd done by inviting me to come out?

After baggage claim, I paused before I took the final few steps to the sliding doors out to the real world. Matt had said he was going to send his driver to collect me, so I'd look for someone holding a card with my name on it.

I took a breath and walked toward the exit. Jolting to the side, I grabbed for my suitcase handle, but went flying onto my ass.

What the hell?

No one stopped to help and as I glanced up a huge, burly security guy strode past. "Hey," I called out as I struggled to get to my feet. The sliding doors opened and a hundred flashbulbs went off. What was happening? I brushed down my pants and strained to see what was going on. As I caught up with the security guy who'd knocked me over, a tiny woman in frighteningly high wedges slowed for the photographers. Great. I'd been pushed aside by some celebrity's security. I couldn't help thinking it was some kind of warning, that being with Matt would land me on my ass.

I spotted my name written on a white board and I headed toward it.

"Miss Kelly," the man with the sign said. "Let me take your bag. I have the car right outside."

My stomach began a full-on churn. There was no turning back now. "Thank you."

The car was a Range Rover, less conspicuous than I'd expected and parked right by the entrance. The driver opened the door and I climbed inside.

I squealed when I realized I wasn't alone.

"I thought I'd surprise you," Matt said, grinning at me, and enveloped me in a hug.

"Oh, thank God." I wrapped my arms around him and buried my face in his neck, grateful I wasn't being kidnapped, and so happy to see him at the same time.

"Are you okay?" he asked, pulling me away from him and inspecting me as if I'd lost it.

"Fine. Just glad to see you." I beamed at him.

"I couldn't be happier to see you," he said, holding my face and swiping his thumbs over my cheekbones. I melted into his touch. He had magic hands—all my concerns and nerves seem to fade away when we were together.

"How come you're here? I thought I was going to meet you at home."

His grin filled his face, and I couldn't help enjoying the fact that I was part of the cause of his smile. "I couldn't wait," he said. He turned his head and reached for something on the armrest. A buzz sounded and a screen came up, separating us from the driver just as we began to set off. "I wanted to see you as soon as you touched down. If I hadn't known you'd kick my ass, I would have been waiting for you inside."

God, it felt good for someone—Matt—to want me so much. I couldn't remember ever feeling so adored. "Well, I'm glad you waited. This way, I don't have to claw a thousand women's hands away to get to you."

He chuckled. Then his eyelids dropped as he pressed his lips to mine.

Heat coursed through my body. I'd forgotten how when he touched me the whole world fell away, leaving only the two of us.

I pushed my hands through his hair and he moaned. Oh, how I'd missed that sound. I loved how I could make him do that.

"You smell of the ocean," he said, breathing me in.

I turned, trying to get my body closer to his. He lifted me and placed me on his lap. As I put my hand out to steady myself, my palm grazed his erection and I gasped as my pussy pulsed. I'd missed his body, his kisses, his cock. How had I ever considered not taking this trip? No one had done the things to my body he had, as though he had some special, secret code that gave him access to a different level of my pleasure. I couldn't give that up easily.

I pushed my hand down his thickness, but he grabbed my wrist to stop me.

"I won't have you in the car like some disposable model, actress or whatever," he said as he pulled back. He gripped my waist and placed me in the seat next to him, then sat back. "We gotta save it until we get back."

"Okay," I said, unsure of what had just happened. "You worried I was going too fast?"

His head snapped around. He reached out his hand and I took it. "I'm concerned I won't be able to hold back if I kiss you. These two weeks have dragged like you wouldn't believe, and I don't want to cheapen what we have by fucking you in the car."

I squeezed his hand.

"But don't be lulled into a false sense of security. As soon as we close the door to my house I'm going to fuck you in every room, on every surface. I won't stop until we're raw and wrung out. You hear me?" He raised his eyebrows as if he really wanted me to answer him.

I smoothed my thumb across his wrist. "I like the sound of that."

"Twenty minutes and then you're mine," he growled, my nipples pebbling at the promise.

The thought of being his was intoxicating. Every woman in the world wanted him and he'd picked me. A girl from Worthington, Maine, who yelled at him for being stupid the first time she'd ever met him. How had that happened?

I shook my head. I couldn't overthink these things; I just had to enjoy it while it lasted. There was no way we had a future together. Our worlds were too different; we lived so far apart. We couldn't last. But I was determined to savor being with him while I had him.

For now.

Matt

How I'd held myself back from yanking down those cute pants and slamming her onto my cock as soon as the car door shut, I had no idea. But somehow, I'd managed it.

Twenty minutes passed like fifteen hours—my dick threatening to explode with pent-up lust with each mile—but finally we pulled up at the gates of my Beverly Hills Spanish-style bungalow.

"Oh, this is pretty," Lana said, dipping her head so she could see out the window. "And it's so secluded."

My place was on a gated street behind a high, stucco wall and a solid-wood gate. There was no way paparazzi could get a look inside. I wouldn't risk her privacy or mine. "I like to keep the important things private," I said.

"You have a gardener?" she asked, scanning my front yard. I barely noticed the flowers and shrubbery. I just wanted it to look nice. Beyond that I didn't give a shit.

"What do you think?" I asked, pulling her closer.

"I think you have people."

"You're right. My fingers are best saved for important work—like getting you naked."

She rolled her eyes and I fought the urge to spank her. Maybe I would when I got her inside.

The car pulled up and I climbed out. "Wait there," I said. David got out and as he reached for Lana's door, I asked, "Can you bring her bag in?" He nodded and left me to open her door.

She winced at the sun as I opened the door but still managed a cute half smile.

"Welcome to LA," I said.

"Thank you for inviting me."

David followed with Lana's suitcase, but when we got to the front door, my urge to be alone with her overtook me. "I'll take the bag inside if you just leave it there. You'll be back at two?"

"Yes, sir," he said, and he turned back to the car.

"He's coming back tomorrow?"

"Or tonight, depending on how you look at it. I have a little trip planned. Just the two of us and not in public. But you might want to take a nap because it's kind of a middle of the night excursion."

She put her arms around my neck. "I don't feel like napping."

"Then I'll have to see what I can do to tire you out," I replied. "We have twelve hours before he comes back but I'm not sure that's enough for me to do all the things I have planned."

She pulled her bottom lip between her teeth as I pinned her against the door with my hips.

"You are so delicious." I pushed my mouth against hers, desperate to taste her, dying for her to understand how much I wanted her.

I had to get her inside. Without breaking our kiss, I dug out my keys and tried to open the door behind her.

"Matt," she whispered against my cheek before pulling away. I lifted her and she wrapped her legs around my waist, kissing my neck. I got the door open, dragged her suitcase into the entrance hall and carried her inside.

"I have a house rule," I said.

"Yeah?" she asked, leaning back as I slammed the door behind us and strode toward the bedroom.

"No clothes."

She grinned.

"And you're breaking that rule."

"But you just told me." She fumbled with the bottom of her shirt, then pulled it over her head, exposing the delicate white lace of her bra. Her breasts pushed out of the cups in a way that got me harder than a baseball bat and itching to bite down on the soft flesh.

I shook my head. "Don't play innocent with me. You don't follow the rules, you gotta pay the price."

She squirmed in my arms, trying to get free. "What price?"

"You're mine until you leave LA. That means I get to do exactly what I want while you're here."

Her breathing became choppy as she stared into my eyes. She liked me in charge. Of her body and mind—at least when we were in bed—and that suited me. I hated it when women tried to take over in the bedroom. It had gotten worse the more famous I got; the nameless women I'd fucked treated sex with me as an audition, constantly trying to impress me. Lana, on the other hand, just reacted to what I did to her, seemed to do whatever seemed right in the moment. It was never forced between us, just phenomenal.

I let her fall onto my bed, scanning her body, drinking in the sight of her finally, finally in my home.

She glanced around and her smile faltered. "What is it?" I asked.

She shrugged. "I bet this bed has seen a lot of action."

Of course, she would think that. My history preceded me. "I've never been with another woman in this bed."

Buying this place had been a turning point for me. I'd bought it when I'd stopped the wild parties and meaningless sex.

She pursed her lips, clearly thinking I was bullshitting her. I leaned forward and opened the fly on her pants. "I mean it. This is my home. The first place I've ever owned. The only woman who's entered this room is my housekeeper."

"Really?"

"I've never lied to you," I replied.

She softened and reached to release the catch on her bra. "I don't want to be breaking the rules, now do I?"

Her breasts fell free, her swollen pink nipples begging me for attention. She might just be the perfect woman. I slid her pants off to reveal matching white lace underwear. "Christ, I'd forgotten how tempting your pussy is. How tempting *all* of you is."

I got undressed as quickly as I could, my gaze never leaving her body. I should have taken her panties off before I started to undress myself. The view would have gone from incredible to spectacular.

As if she were reading my mind, she slipped her thumbs into either side of her underwear and dragged them down. I fisted my cock as I eyed her glistening pussy now she was finally naked. Slowly, she opened her legs under my inspection. "That's right. You know what I like," I said, taking a step forward. I grabbed her ankle and pulled her toward me.

Her hair spread out around her like arrows pointing toward her beautiful face. "How did I get so lucky?" I asked. A small smile curled up her lips.

I wanted to be anything but soft with her now. I wanted to fuck. Hard. Fast. Relentless. I grabbed a condom from my nightstand and rolled it on as quickly as my shaking hands would allow. I couldn't wait to feel her around me. "We'll do slow later. Right now, I need to be inside you, baby."

She nodded. "I want that, too."

I groaned as I guided the tip of my cock to her clit and then pushed down her slippery folds to her entrance. I leaned over her, clamping my hand on her shoulder. "You ready?"

She reached over her head, her breasts lifting. "Please, Matt," she cried.

I slammed into her in one fell swoop, my hips hitting her thighs. "Oh God, yes," she said, fainter now. The booming in my ears had taken over, and I had to try to think of something other than the way she was pulsing around me, the way I could feel her surrounding my cock, how she was looking at me. I needed to see her come, remind her what I did to her body. I had to show her how good this was, that it was worth it.

I pulled out and she whimpered. "Oh, baby, I won't deprive you." I just wanted to feel her heat, her skin next to mine. I moved us up the bed and hovered above her, looking into her eyes. I wanted to memorize every second with this woman. She widened her legs, her palms pressing against her inside thighs, spreading them as far as they would go.

I pushed in, watching her as she took my cock, deep, right up to the root. The expression on her face was desire mixed with relief, as if my dick was a life source. As if she depended on it, worshipped it, needed it.

I shuddered.

"You missed me, baby?" I asked her. "You missed my cock, driving into you like that." I slammed into her again. "Your fingers aren't the same, are they? They can't fill you up like I do."

"Yes," she whimpered. "I want . . ." She was too far gone to form full sentences.

I pressed my hand on her belly, stroking my thumb over her clit. Her body began to twitch and jerk. I clasped her shoulder, trying to keep her in place. "Just take it, baby. Take my dick."

"Oh God, oh God, oh God," she chanted, her voice breathy and desperate.

She grabbed my wrist. "I don't think I can . . . It's too much." She looked at me, almost pleading with me to stop, to keep going, to give her release, to make it last. I knew how she felt. She wanted everything at once.

That's how I felt every moment I spent with her. She was almost too much for me. Too good.

But I knew what she wanted was for me to take what I wanted from her. I picked up my rhythm, pounding into her again and again, not stopping as her grip around my wrists tightened, her fingernails digging into my skin. But I didn't stop. I just kept fucking and fucking, my skin getting hotter and hotter until seconds, minutes, hours later, she screamed out my name and her orgasm coursed through her body.

I paused, panting as I enjoyed the way her whole body shook and her muscles milked my dick all the time as she looked straight at me.

Jesus Christ, I wanted this to last forever. I wanted us to do this again and again. I wanted time to stand still.

I began to move but she cupped my neck and pulled me toward her. I kissed her, fast and sloppy. I was impatient. I wasn't nearly done. My dick was throbbing, and I wanted her to know how much I'd missed her. I wanted her to feel how much.

I pulled out and flipped her over to her stomach and

lifted up her hips. She groaned as I positioned her just as I wanted—her ass in the air, her face in the mattress.

I slid my hand over her ass, focusing my attention on her hot, wet pussy as I teased her entrance with my crown.

I wanted her to need it, beg for it. It wasn't enough that she was just ready for me.

"Matt," she cried as she twisted her hips.

I stayed silent, pulling back when she shifted to try to get more of my dick.

"Matt. Please. I want it. Please."

That was better. And I couldn't say no to her. Not ever.

I gripped her hips and slammed into her as she groaned. I gasped in relief. "Yes," she screamed as if it was all she'd been waiting for her whole life.

It was so deep like this. We fit perfectly. I couldn't stop. I wanted to give her whatever she wanted. I needed to take from her more.

I pressed my palm on her lower back, desperate to keep her in position, not wanting to waste a single thrust.

Her hair skirted her skin as she leaned up on her elbows and turned her head to look at me.

It was like a bullet to the chest. She was so beautiful, her eyes heavy with desire, her mouth slightly parted, the need in her expression. How had I got so fucking lucky?

I wanted to come on her. Over her. In her. I wanted her whole body covered in me. She quivered the way she always did before she came the second time and it was too much. Seeing her undone sent blood rushing to my dick.

Her desire for me—not the actor, model, star, but just me—tipped me over the edge. Her eyes widened and she lingered on the cusp of orgasm, begging for release. I was happy to give it to her. Three final, sharp thrusts and she arched her back and called out my name. She couldn't get any more perfect.

I fell onto the bed and rolled to my back, pulling her into my arms.

She twisted her legs, linking them through mine as she always did. Who would've thought I'd have a postcoital routine that existed of something more than a piss and a good-bye.

Our breathing hadn't even returned to normal before I started imagining Lana gripping the edge of my dining room table while I pounded into her from behind. "You're wicked," I said, kissing the top of her head.

"I am?" she asked.

"You make me insatiable."

"I'm pretty confident you had that covered before I arrived," she said.

My sexual past wouldn't stop hovering around us like a bad smell. Did it bother her? Worry her?

I shifted so she was on her back, then propped my head up with my hand and stared down at her perfect naked body. I slid my palm between her breasts and over her belly. "You get that this is different for me, right?" She caught my hand before it could go lower. "You're different. For me. That's why you're here, in LA, in my home, in my bed. I can't pretend there haven't been women before you, and I can't change that—don't want to. But you're the only one that I want to be with. I hope you feel the same."

She traced my eyebrows with her finger as if buying herself time to think. "Kiss me," she said simply. It wasn't any kind of declaration, but she never had to ask twice.

And anyway, it was enough.

For now.

Lana

Between orgasms, I had managed a little sleep thanks to the difference in time zones. So although I was tired, it could have been worse. I still wasn't sure I wanted to go out in the middle of the night, but Matt seemed excited. I'd rather have stayed naked and in bed with him.

"Are you ready?" he called through the bathroom door. We'd agreed to have separate showers or we'd never manage to get out of the house.

"Just coming."

He snickered and I couldn't help but roll my eyes and grin as I pulled on a pink blouse and a pair of skinny jeans.

Being here in LA with him hadn't been as awkward as I'd imagined it might be. We'd spent a lot of time together in Maine, but I'd been worried he may be someone different at home. Sometimes people changed depending on their environment.

Part of me had thought this trip would be a release. I'd be able to leave and say to myself that Matt wasn't the man I'd thought he was and that we'd go our separate ways. But so far, Matt was the same, which was both wonderful and terrifying.

I scrambled through my bag for my mascara. Even though Matt had said I didn't need makeup tonight, I was pretty sure there wasn't a woman in Los Angeles who went completely barefaced. Mascara, blush and maybe a bit of lip balm would be the absolute minimum while I was here.

"Car's here," he yelled.

I almost ran into him as I came out of the bedroom. Excitedly, he grabbed my hand and practically pulled me out of the house.

Matt held my car door open as David slid into the front seat. "You're okay with the route?" Matt asked.

"Absolutely, sir," he replied and then Matt flicked the switch that brought the screen up between us.

"You've never been to LA, right?" Matt asked, taking my hand and clasping it in his lap.

"Nope. Ruby and I were going to go after graduation but then . . ." But then my ex had ruined our plans. I hadn't even attended the ceremony.

"If I ever meet him, he's going to get knocked into next week."

I kissed his shoulder. "You're sweet, but I wouldn't want him to have the satisfaction of knowing it still bothers me." Bobby had wanted to control me, to punish me, and releasing those photos had given that to him. In my own way, I was finally trying to take some of that power back, here, with Matt. I was getting on with my life.

"Have you seen him since it happened? To confront him?"

"No, never laid eyes on him again." The damage had been done and confronting him would just have given him the attention from me that he wanted. "There was no point. I just walked away."

He pulled me closer to him. "Always a lady."

"Not when I'm in yoga pants and socks."

"Especially then. That's your sexiest look."

I elbowed him in the ribs. "You've got all the right words today."

He kissed me on the lips, then moved away and tapped on the tinted window. "This is Rodeo Drive. You've heard of that, right?"

"With all the stores? Can I roll down the window?" I asked. "I like the breeze and I want to see better."

He grinned and reached for the button.

"No one will see you, right?"

"Not at all. We'll be moving too fast."

The warm air slipped into the air-conditioned car, making me shiver. "It's so hot, even so late." The street was quiet and still, and reminded me of a film set, all new and perfect.

"We can come shopping tomorrow if you like." he said.

"Like you can just walk into stores without people noticing you." I laughed. "And anyway, I'm not much of a shopper." He'd promised me we wouldn't go out in public. Hopefully he wasn't regretting that decision.

"And now we're turning on to Sunset Boulevard," he said as we turned right. "Like the movie."

"And the musical."

"That," he said, pointing to the left. "Is the Beverly Hills Hotel."

The familiar white cursive font on the side of the green building poked out from between the palm trees. "We're not going there though, are we?"

He shook his head. "It's a real celebrity haunt. There'll be photogs there. I thought you might just like a drive around town—your own private Hollywood tour. You can't visit the city and never step outside my gated community."

"I'd be okay with just being with you." As soon as I said it, I realized how cheesy it sounded. But it was true. I'd come to LA to see him, not the sights. "But this is really thoughtful of you. Thank you."

Each side of the road was flanked with green—trees and shrubs and grass. "It's cleaner than I expected. And greener."

He chuckled. "Yeah, this end is nice. It changes as we go along. You'll see."

We sat holding hands, looking out the window, the scent of a Los Angeles night filling the car as the trees buzzed by. Without warning, the greenery disappeared, and flags on both sides of the street welcomed us to West Hollywood.

"And this is the beginning of the Strip."

Billboards took the place of the landscaping. Car horns honked in the distance and our trip didn't seem so private anymore. "Should we close the window?"

Matt shrugged. "It'll be fine. I have my hat if things get busy." He leaned forward and pulled out a navy-blue Yankees hat from the pocket in front of him.

"The Yankees? You know you're in LA, right?"

"I used to go when I was in New York. Can't turn me now."

"You know it's not an invisibility cloak though, right?" I asked. A piece of clothing wasn't going to transform him from Matt Easton to some tourist from the Midwest.

"Let me worry about being recognized. I promise, it won't happen."

I needed to trust him. This was his town, his fame. And it was as important to him as it was to me that we weren't seen together. "You ever been on one of these billboards?" I asked, pointing up to a huge sign that had Jennifer Aniston on it.

"Yeah, once or twice. It's a weird feeling, driving past one. But good. It means the movie's getting publicity if you're thirty feet high."

I shuddered, though a movie billboard was probably different than having your naked body plastered around campus. Matt had signed up for it, agreed to it, even aimed for it. But I wouldn't ever crave people's eyes on me like that.

"That's the Viper Room, a club that you might have heard of," he said, leaning toward me and pointing to the right.

It sounded familiar, but I couldn't remember why. "We're not going there though?"

"No." He chuckled.

"What's so funny?"

"Nothing really. I used to go a lot. But you're right. It's not really your scene. And I mean that in a good way."

I didn't say anything, but this part of LA was less glamorous than I'd imagined it to be. I wasn't sure what I'd expected, and maybe things would look different in the light of day, but it looked run down in places.

"That's the Comedy Store," he said and I slid over a little, some of my hair catching the breeze and escaping out the window.

"Hey, look at that," I said, glancing back at Matt to make sure he'd seen what I'd seen. "A train. Is that a restaurant?"

"Serves great hot dogs."

"It's super cute."

"We can get takeout from there if you like."

Of course, we couldn't actually just go to dinner. It was almost as if we were in a bubble, cut off from the rest of the world. It was a romantic thought, but it was also a little odd. I'd never noticed how limited Matt was while we were in Maine, probably because I was in my world and my day wasn't impacted by Matt's stardom. But going to a restaurant should be the most natural thing in the world. It bothered me that we couldn't be normal, or spontaneous. "Maybe," I replied.

"Oh, and that's Chateau Marmont—an old Hollywood icon."

"That place?" I asked, staring at the white building on the left, hidden by the trees.

"Yeah. I like that place. Maybe we'll go one day. You know, when this Audrey thing is over."

I smiled but didn't say anything. Even when the Audrey thing was over, I didn't want to be together in public. I thought he understood that.

We kept going and the restaurants gave way to banks and offices. I wasn't sure if we were going somewhere or were just driving around.

"And this," Matt said, "is Hollywood. You know how you can tell?" he asked as we pulled over.

"How?"

"The sidewalk."

I poked my head out of the car to see stars all over the sidewalk. I grinned and turned back to him. "That is so cool."

"That's Grauman's Chinese Theater," he said, lifting his chin.

"Oh, yes. Of course," I said, recognizing the striking building from watching the Academy Awards. "Have you been to the Oscars?" I asked.

"Never been nominated or invited. I've been to the after parties, but never the ceremony."

I wanted to ask whether or not he wanted an Oscar, but surely every actor did.

"We're going to drive along up here for a couple of blocks." He pressed a button and told David to go to the next place. Matt had obviously put some thought into this trip and it was kind of adorable.

After a few minutes, the car slowed to a stop again. "I thought you might want to visit your namesake, Lana Turner, and then I have a map and we can go and see anyone you like." Matt's eyes were lit up. "You brought your phone, right? For a picture? David will take one for you."

"I can selfie," I said. "You okay to stay here?"

He nodded and I could feel him watching me as I slid out of my seat. Even at this time of night, there were people around. He'd definitely attract attention if he followed me.

I found Lana Turner's star quickly. I couldn't help but be a little sad my dad wasn't here for this. He was the Lana Turner fan. But I knew wherever he was he'd be smiling down, happy if I was happy. Which I was.

I was full to the brim.

So much so I couldn't quite believe any of it was real.

Matt

"You've heard of the Hollywood Bowl, right?" I didn't want Lana to think I saw her as some hick who knew nothing about the world, but I remembered coming to Los Angeles and everyone pointing out all these places as though I should know what they were or understand their significance when I hadn't had a clue. I really wanted to show her LA tonight. I just wished we didn't have to hide.

"A concert venue, right?"

"Yeah. It's outdoor, and I really like it. And here we are."

"Stay," I said as I opened the door, got out and rounded the trunk to her side. As I opened her door, she said, "We're getting out? Like, *you're* getting out? What if someone sees?"

"It's closed tonight," I said, helping her down from the Range Rover.

"Closed?" She frowned.

I held my hand out and guided her to the entrance. "To the public, but I thought it might be fun to explore."

"We're breaking in?" She sounded genuinely concerned.

"No, they've let us come after hours. I know a guy who knows a guy."

"Oh, to be a famous movie star," she said and giggled, poking me in the ribs.

"Hey, I said it had its perks."

I'd arranged for us to enter at the back of the venue so that when we came out, she'd feel the size of the place. As we turned into the bowl, she gasped. "It's huge."

As I'd planned, the stage was lit in blue, as if someone was about to come out and perform. "Let's make our way down to the front," I said, tugging her hand.

As we got closer, we slowed, taking in the lights and the stage. She twirled. "I can't believe we have this entire place to ourselves." She slid her hands up my chest and around my neck. "Thank you for planning something so special. If only your screaming fans knew how adorable you really are."

I spanned her waist with my hands and dropped a kiss on her lips. "I look after the people who are important in my life, that's all. Come on. I have something arranged." I turned and led the way to our left.

"Glass of champagne?" I asked as we came to a table covered with a white cloth. On it was an ice bucket and two glasses, along with two hot dogs from Carney's. I loved that she'd spotted the restaurant on our way here.

"Champagne and hot dogs?" Her eyes were bright with excitement. "This is too much." She held out her hands as if welcoming the food and alcohol.

Seriously, she might just be the perfect woman. Or *my* perfect woman anyway.

I poured two glasses of champagne and handed one to her. "To hiding in plain sight," she said.

"With the most beautiful girl I've ever known."

She tilted her head. "You have all the words, my friend. All. The. Words."

What she didn't realize was that I wasn't trying to tell her what she wanted to hear, I was just saying what I felt. There was no one on the planet I'd rather be with right there and right then.

I sat and pulled her onto my lap.

"It's true, champagne does go with everything," she said, setting her glass back on the table in front of her. "Even hot dogs."

"Are you enjoying LA?" I asked. I hoped it wouldn't be long before she came out again.

"Yeah. It's different than I thought it would be. It feels less like a city than New York."

I chuckled.

"You know what I mean—it's more about the outdoors than Manhattan."

"I'd like to think this won't be your only trip."

Her gaze darted from my mouth to my eyes and she just smiled.

"I was talking to Sinclair about the pictures taken in Maine."

She glanced back at the stage and leaned into my chest.

"Audrey and I are going to announce our breakup on Tuesday after you fly home."

"Really? Before the publicity tour for your movie?" She linked her fingers through mine.

"Yeah, the studio thinks it might create good buzz if

they spin it right. It's just there will be additional scrutiny on Audrey and me after the photos."

"I'm sorry if I ruined that for you."

"You didn't do anything. And maybe it's for the best. Audrey won't have to wait as long to get married. And, you know, things are going well between you and me so . . ."

She stopped stroking my wrist. "But Audrey isn't the only reason why you and I aren't public."

"No." I took a deep breath. "But maybe now we have options."

She put her hand on my chest and turned to face me, her eyes narrowing. "Options?"

"Well, I won't be with Audrey. And Sinclair is talking about another contracted girlfriend." She raised her eyebrows. "I said that we were together so I didn't need another girlfriend."

"What did he say?"

"Well, he wants me to be in a relationship. Thinks it shows me as being mature and reliable." Sinclair might want me going out with a star, but if Lana was amenable, I'd rather it was her.

"So you're going to get another girlfriend?"

"Well, I was hoping you were going to tell me that I'm already taken," I said, pulling her closer. "I want you to be my girlfriend."

Her frown deepened. "I don't understand."

"Look, I don't want another fake girlfriend when I have you." I paused, wanting her to agree, but her face was frozen. "The thing with Audrey was easy," I explained. "I was single and she had a serious boyfriend. But now that the shoe's on the other foot, I can't imagine why she signed up. Not when she was with someone else."

"What are you saying? You don't want a contracted girlfriend?"

"I'm saying, let's go public. I don't want to have to hide." Her eyes widened in shock. "Not right away. There needs to be some time after my breakup with Audrey."

She tried to wriggle away but I held her tight. "Would it be so bad for people to know I'm your boyfriend?"

"Let go of me. I need to—"

I released her and she scooted off my lap and onto the chair next to mine. "You know I don't want that sort of attention."

"But you've seen how my fame can be a good thing—think of the positives."

"It's not something I'd ever choose. You know that. I feel like you're changing the rules on me here."

"How did you think this was going to play out? We can't stay a secret forever. Not if we're serious. And I'm here to tell you I'm serious. I really like you. I haven't dated a woman since high school—I've never had the urge. But I want to spend all my time with you, whether I'm in the house or going to a premiere." It felt good to tell her.

"A premiere?" She looked at me as if I'd suggested we boil ourselves in acid.

I shifted my body toward her and brushed her hair behind her shoulders. "You'd look beautiful on the red carpet."

She pressed her palm flat on her chest. "I can't breathe."

I made sweeping circles on her back. "I'm not saying that we need to issue a statement. I'm just suggesting that when the Audrey thing has died down, in a couple of months, then we could just not make such an effort *not* to be seen together."

"In a couple of months?" Her question sounded hopeful.

Maybe she was open to this. "Yeah, nothing has to change right away."

She took a deep breath. "A couple of months is almost as long as we've known each other."

"Exactly. I just want you to think about it. Sinclair's asking me to meet this new girl for a contract and I just—"

"Maybe you should." She dragged her fingers through her hair. "Anything could happen between us in a couple of months. You're going to be travelling to promote this movie. I'm going to be busy in Maine . . ."

"Hey," I said, ducking down, trying to catch her eye. Her stare was planted firmly on the ground. "Just because I'm going to be abroad doesn't change anything. I can arrange for you to come out to wherever I am on the junket, and if I have some down time, I'll come back to Worthington for a few days."

"I don't think that's a good idea."

"You don't want me to come to Maine?"

She sighed. "I do, but not while your profile is going to be higher than ever. You'll have just announced your split with Audrey and the press is going to be looking for the reason why. I don't want to be the answer."

"Fair enough. And Sinclair would probably have a—"

"I don't give a shit about Sinclair. I'm telling you, for now I don't want you to come to Worthington."

I wanted her to tell me that all she cared about was me and she'd do whatever it took to be with me. But she was saying the opposite. "Okay, I promise not to come to Maine." I tried to sound level and unconcerned but the rejection stung.

"Okay," she mumbled under her breath.

We sat silently as the minutes ticked by. Had I read this situation wrong? We'd practically lived together in Worthington and she'd agreed to come out to LA. Did she expect things between us to fall apart?

Would it really surprise me if she did? My past was hardly one of committed monogamy. But I *wanted* to be committed to her. Somehow, I'd gone from wanting to fuck everything that moved to wanting one woman and one woman only—Lana.

I just wanted her to feel the same way.

"I'm sorry if I overreacted. I have a lot to lose, and I can't give that up just because it's convenient for your career." Her voice wobbled as if she was close to tears. This was not how this night was meant to go.

"You think I'm using you?" That was the furthest thing from the truth.

"I'm not saying that. I just think that we wouldn't be having this conversation if it weren't for your career and Sinclair and the franchise."

Well, I couldn't argue with that. If Sinclair hadn't been on my case about getting another girlfriend on contract, I never would've brought up going public with Lana. I knew how she felt about it.

I wanted her to be happy. More, I wanted to be the one who made her happy. "I'm pushing too hard," I said. "And you're right, going public with you in a few weeks would be convenient for my career. But it's more than that, Lana. I like you, like being with you. Part of me wants to show you off, tell everyone you're taken. Have people see how fucking lucky I am."

She grabbed my hand and squeezed. "I know and it's so nice. It was just not what I was expecting. At all. I'm not sure where it leaves us if one of us wants one thing and another wants something different."

I took a steadying breath. I needed to be strong and calm. To tell her everything was going to be okay, that I could guide her through this. One way or the other, we'd resolve this. "Listen. Above everything, I want you to be happy." A tugging in my gut said that wasn't the whole truth. I wanted this franchise, which meant I had to have a girlfriend. Only after the ink was dry on the contract could I do what I wanted. If Lana wanted our relationship to remain under wraps, then maybe I should take the lunch that Sinclair was trying to set up.

"I want you to be happy, too. I'm just not sure what that means," she said, glancing up at me.

I took her face in my hands. "We're going to take things step-by-step. I'm going to stop pushing and we're just going to enjoy our time together." I dropped a kiss on her lips. "Agreed?"

"Okay," she said. "And I'll definitely think about it."

I smiled, trying to mask my concern. Los Angeles didn't have thunderstorms very often, but a rumble in the distance told me unless I could change her mind at some point, we weren't going to last very long.

TWENTY

Lana

The metallic taste of blood hit my tongue, and I pulled my thumb out of my mouth to see the skin by the side of my nail bleeding. Shit. I stopped pacing and tried to concentrate on the ocean as the voice on the other end of the phone kept talking about *talent* and *meetings* and *New York*.

"So can you make a meeting next Thursday?" Beatrice Gravel, the senior buyer at Barneys, asked. It was the second time and I couldn't put off my answer any longer. This was exactly what I'd been aiming for when I'd sent my drawings and photographs of the cuff I'd made to a contact of Mr. Butcher's two weeks ago.

"That would be in Manhattan?" Of course it would. Where else would it be? I hadn't been back since college. But the possibility of having a jewelry line in Barneys? Was I *really* going to pass that up because of my ex?

"Yes. We can have lunch, talk about next steps and show you some of the other designer jewelry we have in the store. We think your designs would be a beautiful fit."

If Ruby was here, she'd rip the phone from my hand, accept on my behalf and then tell me it was going to be okay. So would Matt, for that matter. I took a deep breath. I could always pull out later if I totally freaked out. But as I stood on my deck, overlooking the ocean, sheltered from the storm that I could feel was just a few minutes away, I felt brave. Powerful. Like I was standing on the edge of my destiny. "That sounds great."

"Wonderful. If you have any more designs, bring them with you. We love the Bastet collection and we definitely want to start with that, but we absolutely want to see anything else you're working on."

I pressed my forefinger against my bleeding thumb. "I'll see what I can find."

"Great. Well, I can't wait to meet you in person after all these phone calls."

"Yeah, it will be . . ." I searched for the right words. Why was I so awkward when people were being complimentary? "Nice to meet you, too."

I cringed, but we said our good-byes and I hung up, wondering what I'd gotten myself into.

I jumped, my phone buzzing in my palm. I grinned as I saw who was calling and then swiped the screen. "Hey, Mr. Movie Star. How's Italy?"

"Hey, beautiful," Matt replied. "I just got to the airport."

I couldn't hear the normal hustle and bustle of airport noise in the background, but then he was probably in some kind of VIP lounge.

"Sweden next?"

"Yeah, I think so. Although, at this point, I really have no idea."

He sounded exhausted, which made sense. He was

getting close to the end of his publicity tour and every time we spoke he came across a little less enthusiastic about his job.

I laughed. His schedule was ridiculous. I'd flown to London a couple of weeks ago and we'd spent a few days together holed up in the Dorchester hotel, but he hadn't had much time off.

"How did your call with Barneys go?" he asked.

I bit back my lip, pleased he'd remembered.

"I'm going to meet them in New York on Thursday for a meeting."

"That's great," he yelled, and I had to hold the cell away from my ear.

"I figure I can always cancel."

"Hey, don't do that. This is a fantastic opportunity."

"I know, I just . . ." I leaned over the railing toward the ocean. I knew it was time to put to rest all my old ghosts. But that didn't mean I was looking forward to it. "I won't cancel. I just need to prepare myself."

"You're stronger than you think you are," he said. "Don't underestimate yourself. And hey, I'll see what I can do to fly back."

"Your tour doesn't finish until that Friday, and anyway I'll be okay."

"You can stick around for the weekend and I could meet you there? I'll check my schedule and talk to Brian and let you know."

"It would be good to see you." During my trip to LA, things had solidified between us and we had transitioned from a summer affair to a relationship where we spoke every day and tried to see each other as often as we could. But he wanted more—for us to go public. I understood and I knew I wanted to be with him. I just didn't know how it would work. I hoped he'd give me the time I needed to figure it out.

"I want to be there," he said.

"Seeing you would be a good incentive to visit the city again," I said.

"More so than a jewelry line at Barneys?"

I laughed. "Maybe the same." The business opportunity seemed too good to be true. Just a few years ago it would have been more than my wildest dreams. I'd thought I'd been forced to leave the dream behind, but it had been reignited in me.

"Okay, I'll talk to Brian about it and see if I can make it happen. I miss you. I don't want to go more than two weeks without seeing you."

"Is that a rule now?" I asked.

"Not a rule, just—if this is going to work, then we need to minimize our time apart."

There hadn't been a day since he'd left Maine that we hadn't spoken to each other, but neither of us had mentioned the idea of going public again. He'd promised not to push me and he'd been true to his word. In fact, he'd said that while he was in Europe he was going to meet with Kristin Cooper, an actress Sinclair thought might make a good *girlfriend*.

His split with Audrey was over a month old. I guess he had to make a decision. Was he waiting for me to bring it up? I could talk to him about it again in New York. See how his meeting had gone.

"Okay. Were there a lot of Audrey questions today?"

"Yeah, at least one in each interview. But it must be so dull listening to us. We have our script down on this one. 'We're still such great friends, distance and work schedules, blah, blah, blah.'"

"Distance and schedules, huh?"

"Yeah, it's like a resigning politician saying he wants to spend more time with his family."

Distance and work schedules. They were so plausible that it made sense that they were well-worn excuses. "If you can't make it to New York, I can always fly from there to LA." I didn't want distance to be the thing that proved to be our undoing.

"You don't need to do that. I'll make New York work."

I sighed. "You will?"

"I will, I promise. I can't expect you to always fit around my schedule. Your work is important, too." He had all the right words, all the time.

"Are you sure you're not a figment of my imagination?" I asked, taking a seat on the bench.

"Maybe I am. But just go with it," he said, and I laughed. "So what are you doing tonight?"

"I'm just going to sit out here on the porch and wait for the storm to roll in." It would be a good way to relax.

"I wish I were there. We could watch it side by side, then get naked and fuck all night." He growled into the phone.

Even though we'd spent more nights apart than together since he left Maine, I still missed his body every morning when I woke up. "You'll have to save it until New York."

"I'm not sure I can wait that long," he said.

"Keep telling yourself how I'm worth it. You'll start to believe it's true."

The man a million women wanted only wanted me.

TWENTY-ONE

Lana

"You don't think it's weird to be drinking in a place this dark?" I asked. The lighting was so dim in the uber-cool cocktail bar buried deep in the East Village that I could barely see Ruby, even though she was close enough I could reach out and touch her.

"Not everything is ocean air and clapboard siding, Lana. You've been in Maine too long. New Yorkers like the dark." There was some dim, amber lighting at the bar and a tea light on each table, but nothing else. It looked like the owners were trying to save on their energy bill.

"You remember you grew up in Worthington, right?" I asked her. I'd known Ruby for a long time, so even in the dark I could sense her eye roll and shrug. At least the music wasn't too loud and we could actually talk.

"I can't believe you're *here*. How does it feel?"

I'd gone straight from the airport to the hotel last night and hadn't stepped foot outside until the meeting with

Barneys this afternoon. "Better than I thought. It helps not being near the campus, obviously."

"There's no way anyone would remember anything, you know. It was ages ago in college time."

"I know." Someone remembering wasn't the problem. It was how tarnished the city had become for me. When I'd arrived for college, New York had been a symbol of my future, of my dreams and aspirations, but it had morphed into a representation of bad decisions and poor judgement. As much as I hated my ex for posting those photos, I should never have let him take them. I'd never make that mistake again.

"Tell me about the meeting." Ruby took a sip of her cocktail.

I blew out a puff of air. "I just don't know what to say. They want to stock the Bastet collection. I told them how expensive it will be, and that it will all be made to order, but apparently they don't care." The meeting had gone far better than I had expected. They had opened with a very generous offer, which I'd have been happy to accept, but after talking to them about the quality of the materials and time it took, they'd increased their offer and made it *impossible* for me to say no.

"Will you still be able to keep the shop?" she asked.

I released the black straw I'd been toying with and swallowed. "Yeah. Although, I'll have to get additional help and spend more time actually making stuff if there are orders."

"Of course there will be orders."

"I don't know. The pieces are *really* expensive."

"But they're beautiful. People pay a lot more for a lot less."

I wasn't sure if it would matter if I didn't sell any at all. Just the experience of being stocked at one of the most exclusive stores in Manhattan was recognition of what I'd been working toward.

"Let's toast to you being in Barneys," Ruby said, raising her glass. "I can't believe it." She laughed. "That's not true. I can totally believe it. You deserve it."

We clinked glasses and I drained the rest of my drink.

"You think you'll end up moving back here? I'd so love to have you back in the city like we'd always planned. We could get a place together."

I shook my head and reached for the cocktail menu in front of me. I used my cell phone light to read it. "I doubt it. There's no need for me to move." If I thought too far into the future, then I'd have to think about Matt, and what was going to happen between us. And all that was in a box marked *complicated* that I wasn't about to open.

"But if you're going to be in Barneys you'll visit more often, right? I can't believe you wouldn't stay with me, even if you are being put up in some fancy hotel."

"I'm sorry. It was closer to the store and I was getting in so late."

"When do you fly back?"

"Sunday night." Her eyes lit up and I cringed with guilt. I knew I wouldn't get to hang out with her. "Matt is flying in tomorrow. We're going to spend the weekend."

Her face went blank, but I knew a thousand questions were gathering in her head. "So, it's serious between you two?"

I angled the flashlight on my camera onto the menu. "I like him."

"You ever worry that a relationship with him would be all one way? All about him and his dreams and aspirations?"

It'd never felt that way. Matt never acted like a star with me. "I don't think so. That's not really who he is. He was so excited about my meeting today. And he's flying in to New York especially to see me."

She smiled. "I'm glad. I really am. I heard he broke up with Audrey."

"You know that was a fake relationship, right?"

She leaned forward. "Yes. But does that mean you two are going to be together officially?"

A sharp tug in my stomach drew my attention from the menu. "He wants us to be. But I don't want my picture flashed across the tabloids." There was no way I could handle the scrutiny.

"But it's not like you're just sleeping together—you've been dating a while now. And you're not going to be naked. Isn't he worth it?"

"It isn't a question of him not being worth it." My feelings for Matt grew every time we spoke and exploded every time we were together. I was getting dangerously close to loving him. And I didn't want to lose myself and make another bad decision. "I just don't want the scrutiny."

"So don't be the couple who calls the paparazzi every time you go out for coffee. You don't even have to be the couple that does the red-carpet thing together."

"Maybe it's best if he does another contract with another girl," I said, settling on my next cocktail and placing the menu down. "He's having talks with an actress at the moment." Matt hadn't mentioned how his meeting with his potential new official girlfriend had gone. And I hadn't asked. It would take the pressure off me if he was publicly with someone else.

"Wait, you want him to pretend to date someone while he's really dating you?"

"He had this sort of arrangement with Audrey, and it worked."

"But that was before you came along. Do you really want to see pictures of him gazing at another woman on the red carpet when it should be you?"

I folded my black cocktail napkin in half. Of course I didn't want that. But I understood that Matt couldn't be publicly single for too long. "It's no big deal. And it means I can keep my privacy."

"You don't think he'll start to believe you don't care enough to commit to him?"

I'd never considered the possibility that he'd view my desire for privacy as a reflection of my feelings for him. "He knows how I feel." Right? I'd flown out to LA and London. That showed him that I cared, surely?

"So, what? He just dates someone else fake until what? You two break up? It's not like he's going to suddenly stop being famous."

I winced. "Who said anything about breaking up?" I'd never felt this way about anyone before Matt. I certainly didn't want things to end between us.

"Well, if you can't be seen in public together, surely the stopwatch is running down on your relationship. I'm not judging." She shrugged and took a sip of her drink. "If you want to keep things casual between the two of you, then good for you. Do that. But if you want something more, you might have to give something up."

"I didn't say things were *casual*." Was I kidding myself? Were we just treading water before things ended between us?

"But you're not prepared to go out in public with him?"

"Are you saying you'd be okay with having your face in every hair salon in America?"

"Absolutely."

"Are you serious? You don't care about people knowing your business? About giving up all of your privacy?"

"I grew up in Worthington, Maine, just like you did. How much privacy do you really have? Everyone knows everyone else's business."

"Yeah, but at least you know theirs, too. The people in Worthington care about each other. They're just not flicking through the pages of *US Weekly* looking for salacious details of the last celebrity breakup."

"But who cares what strangers think? As long as you know who you are and you know who Matt is, why do you give a shit about anyone else?"

I stirred the ice cubes left in my drink with my black cocktail straw. Ruby made it sound so straightforward. Like there was a button I could press with white writing on it that said, "I don't care what people think." But there was no button, and I didn't know how to just stop caring.

"I'm just trying to say you need to decide how much you like Matt. If he's worth making some sacrifices for."

I could compromise on a lot of things. I could travel to LA or wherever he was in the world. I could spend less time in the shop. But inviting the press into my life, giving up the anonymity I'd worked so hard to establish was such a *huge* sacrifice. Was that what was required?

"I get that what happened in college really fucked you over, I really do. But are you going to let your asshole ex stop you from doing what you want, with who you want, your whole life? Doesn't that give him way more power than he deserves? Why not live your life and ignore the things that don't matter?"

It felt as if Ruby was handing me one good reason after another for going public with Matt. And my arguments for keeping our relationship a secret were collapsing under the strain.

"I don't want you to lose something amazing because you're too scared to try again," she said.

"Losing? Why do you keep talking about *losing* Matt?"

"I'm just saying that wanting to stay hidden makes things complicated. It adds a layer of pressure. On both of you and the relationship. And it seems temporary. To me and, I imagine, to him also."

I'd just been living moment to moment with Matt. I tried not to think beyond the next time we'd see each other. But the thought that our weekend in New York could be the last time we had together, that his patience might be wearing thin, made my palms sweaty.

"It's not temporary. Not for me. And I don't want to lose him." I tipped back my empty glass, swallowing the last few drops of bitterness that came from the mint stalk. I needed to talk to Matt. I couldn't lose him. The realization that it might be a real possibility came crashing down around me.

Only one question really mattered. Was losing Matt worse than losing my privacy? And the answer was yes. Much worse.

I wanted him more than I wanted to hide. And I needed to tell him.

TWENTY-TWO

Matt

"The wallpaper looks like it's spun gold," Lana said, glancing around the hotel room. "And the number of chairs, even in the bedroom? We could invite most of Worthington over and they'd all have a place to sit."

I chuckled. "Yeah, let's not do that."

"If you're used to the Presidential Suite at the Mandarin Oriental, what were you thinking booking my little cottage in Maine?" she asked. "You could fit both cottages in this place."

I was learning that wherever Lana was, I felt at home. Even if it was Friday at just past six and we were naked, in a hotel bed, overlooking Central Park. I pulled her closer. "Hey, I love your place. This suite is ludicrous. They upgraded me. I would never book something this huge. I don't need two bedrooms."

"But now that we're here, we have to take a bath in that tub. That view is just—"

"There's no better view than looking at you."

"Who writes these lines for you?" she asked, lifting her head from where it rested on my chest.

"It's all my original work. And I mean it. If you're in the bath, I don't give a crap about the view. Your boobs are awesome."

She giggled. "That's the best compliment I've ever heard."

"Like you said, I have all the words."

She dipped down and kissed my torso. My dick twitched.

My phone buzzed on the nightstand and I groaned.

"Sinclair," I said.

"Take it. Otherwise he'll keep calling."

I slid my finger across the screen. "Hi, Sinclair."

"We're stuck in traffic. We'll be twenty minutes," he said.

"You'll be where in twenty minutes?"

"Kristin and I will be with you. We agreed to this last week."

I'd told Sinclair that I wouldn't sign the contract with Kristin Cooper until Lana had met her. "But we said tomorrow night." I'd not had a chance to get Lana up to speed. Talking about your next girlfriend wasn't the kind of conversation you had over the phone with your current girlfriend.

"No, we said Friday night. Christ, are you not in the hotel?"

I glanced at Lana. "Yeah, we're here."

"Good, we'll see you in twenty minutes." He hung up.

Lana frowned. "He's coming here?"

"I said we'd see him tomorrow. He swears we agreed tonight. But he's bringing Kristin. I wanted you to meet her before we sign contracts."

"Sign contracts?" Lana's whole body stiffened. "I didn't realize that deal was done."

"You knew I was talking to her." I'd deliberately not mentioned it a lot because I didn't want Lana to think I was pressuring her into going public. But I definitely had told her that things were progressing.

"And she's coming here tonight to sign?"

"And to meet you. In twenty minutes."

She shook her head and bounced out of bed. "I'm getting first shower," she said as she ran into the bathroom.

It wasn't anything I was looking forward to. I didn't want to live this lie. But at least we'd get this over with. Hopefully Lana would be comfortable with her and everyone would be happy.

Lana

Staring into the mirror on the dressing table, I applied a thin layer of blush. Kristin Cooper was beautiful. Blonde. Not much more than a hundred pounds. She probably had her hair professionally blown out and her makeup done by a glam squad. And here I was, my trusty L'Oréal cream blush smeared on the back of my hand, hoping to make myself look healthy, rather than like I was trying out for a circus. The thought of coming face-to-face with Matt's next girlfriend, even if she was fake, filled me with complete and utter dread.

My conversation with Ruby had brought everything into focus. I didn't know what the future held for Matt and me, but I knew that I couldn't lose him. I'd been waiting for a moment to tell him, in between kisses, that I wanted to be with him and that I'd put up with the scrutiny, the lack of privacy, and that I just wanted us to have a proper shot at being together. If that meant we didn't hide, then so be it.

Sinclair's call might have come at the exact wrong time. But perhaps it was fate. Wasn't it better this way? Didn't I get the best of both worlds—Matt *and* my privacy?

In the bar with Ruby, as soon as I'd decided that I'd go public with him, a weight had lifted off my shoulders. I'd been happy with my decision and I couldn't wait to tell Matt.

I hadn't understood that negotiations with Kristin had gotten this far. It made sense that Matt wouldn't tell me all the details—it was awkward and uncomfortable for us both. But if I'd known we were due to be meeting Kristin tonight, then I would have told him. Perhaps I still should. But there was still that voice at the back of my head, telling me that this was what I'd wanted.

But was it?

What I wanted was Matt.

Hell, if it hadn't been for him, I wouldn't be in New York at all. I wouldn't have had the courage to start making jewelry again, and I wouldn't have had the confidence to follow up on an introduction Mr. Butcher made for me to one of his contacts in the fashion industry.

I dressed quickly—we weren't going somewhere fancy— and checked my lip gloss and fluffed my hair before going to find Matt and Kristin.

I walked in to the living area from the bedroom just as Matt passed Kristin a drink. She was even more gorgeous in real life. She wore skinny jeans and a cami. Her makeup was flawless and her glossy blonde hair looked like she'd just stepped out of a Pantene commercial. My gaze flitted between them as I took them both in. They looked perfect together—two beautiful, talented actors. The public would lap them up.

I patted my stomach, trying to stave off the nausea that stirred in my belly, and went across to join them.

"Kristin," Matt said, rising when he spotted me, "this is my girlfriend, Lana." He held his arm out to me as I neared them and slid his hand around my waist. "And Lana, you know Sinclair."

I nodded at Sinclair, images of me naked in a sheet still flashed through my head. "Hi," I said, reaching out to shake Kristin's hand.

She ignored my hand and pulled me into a hug. "It's so good to meet you. You're so pretty," she said. "Matt's a very lucky guy."

I smiled. "Thank you. You're even more beautiful in real life."

She chuckled and patted my arm. "I have a team of people that work on me. I do *not* wake up like this."

I laughed. She was nice. Maybe she and Matt should sign contracts today, and then I'd have more time to get used to the idea of a public relationship.

"Shall we sit and go through the paperwork?" Sinclair said, clearly keen to close this deal.

"Sure, do you have an itinerary?" Kristin asked as we all took our seats around the dining room table. Kristin sat next to Sinclair and Matt and I opposite them.

"Yeah, there's a lot going on over the next six months because of Thanksgiving, Christmas and then Sundance followed by the awards season," Sinclair said.

"My publicist should have sent you over a copy of all my fixed dates," Kristin said. "I swear, if this job was just acting, it would be a hell of a lot easier."

Matt chuckled.

Kristin was more down-to-earth than I'd expected. Less starry. She didn't treat me like I was a second-class citizen just because I wasn't famous. She seemed humble and normal.

Sinclair could have picked someone worse. Up until last night, I would have been happy for Matt to sign a contract with Kristin. But now?

"Yes, I got your list, Kristin, thank you," Sinclair said. "It works that you're both in LA and neither of you have travelling commitments. But I think a trip over the holidays would be a good idea. Maybe Cabo. Or even Europe."

Kristin and Matt were nodding but I couldn't help but wonder why the hell a vacation was necessary. And would I be going to Cabo with Matt and Kristin or would they be going alone?

"Any functions or trips other than home to see your family, please ensure you keep your team informed," Sinclair said. "We just need to know what to say to the press if you're not together and we get asked."

Sinclair slid a piece of paper across the polished wood table to Matt and gave another to Kristin. "Everything should be set out there."

"I have the charity gala lunch at the Beverly Hills Hotel that should be on the list for next month," Kristin said.

"Yeah, I had that down anyway. I did it last year," Matt said.

"Will that be our first public appearance?" Kristin asked, looking up at Sinclair.

"Yes. We have a lunch planned for next week at the Ivy. We expect press interest to start then and then the gala will be your first official public appearance."

Matt had spoken to me about the gala. It was being held to raise money for the children's hospital. It should be me going with him to that event. Not Kristin, however sweet she was.

As they talked, I found I was watching rather than listening, trying to figure out if this really was what I wanted. Could I encourage my boyfriend to put his arms around another woman, even if we all knew it was pretend?

I'd been hiding since New York, denying myself my hopes and dreams, but I'd sacrificed enough.

That I might lose Matt because I wanted to hide might actually be worse than seeing my naked picture all over campus. At least back then I'd been able to go back to Worthington and lick my wounds. But if Matt and I split? Maine was where I'd met him. How would I be able to heal if we broke up if he was everywhere I looked, everywhere I slept? He was in my heart.

The conversation with Ruby and now watching him in the same room as Kristin, seeing a glimpse of him with someone else, solidified my decision. If anyone was ever going to be worth fighting for, worth risking everything for, it was Matt Easton.

He was worth a picture in a magazine.

Worth enduring the internet's scorn.

Worth risking getting hurt for.

Worth loving.

"I'm going to start working with your team on the following six months' itinerary," Sinclair said. "We just wanted to get the big things noted down before we signed." He pulled out a small bundle of papers from his bag. "And so if everything's in order with the schedule, then we can sign and we're done."

Kristin reached out for the papers, but before she could pull them toward her, I slammed my palm down on top of the bundle, stopping her. "I'm sorry, but no," I said.

This couldn't be our lives for the next twelve months. Despite thinking it might be for the best, I couldn't let this happen.

Matt squeezed my hand. "It's okay. I've seen the contract and so has my lawyer."

My gaze flickered from Kristin to Sinclair and landed on Matt. "I should have told you before now, but I don't want you to do this."

Matt sighed. "I thought this was what you wanted."

I shook my head. "No. I want you. I want you no matter the circumstances or consequences. I'm sorry, Kristin." I glanced at her and she was staring back, wide-eyed and smiling. "I didn't realize this was so far advanced." I turned back to Matt. "I want to be with you. And the tabloids can go to hell."

"What are you saying?" Matt asked.

"I'm saying, it's time."

"Time?"

"For lunch at the Ivy."

I stared at him and he didn't say anything for the longest time. "You want to go public?" There wasn't much enthusiasm in his voice.

I lifted my shoulders. "I just thought that maybe we could try. You don't seem so sure." Had he changed his mind? Kristin was definitely the easier option in many ways.

"I would love that. You know that." He shifted in his chair, his whole body turned toward me. "But, it's going to be difficult to *try* this. I mean, once we're spotted together, there's no putting the genie back into the lamp. You get that, right?"

I nodded. "Yeah, I get it. But I want to do this. And if

you're by my side, I think it can work. I want to be with you."

Matt's smile lit up his face, but before he could speak, Sinclair cleared his throat. "This isn't something to make a snap decision about. Maybe take some time—"

"This is all I've thought about for weeks," I said. "And after last night, I realized this is what I want." I nodded.

"Last night?" Matt asked, turning to me and holding my face in his hands. "What happened last night and why have you waited until now to say anything?"

"I wanted to tell you in person. And you kinda sprung this meeting on me. I didn't realize—"

"I'm really sorry about this, Kristin," Matt said, pulling me toward him. "And whatever I can do to make it up to you, let me know. But if Lana's happy going public—"

She put her palms up facing us. "Of course. I wouldn't dream of standing in the way of such a cute couple. No hard feelings." She stood and picked up her purse. "I was on my way to a dinner engagement anyway."

"I think we should discuss this," Sinclair said. "I'm not sure you've thought of all the consequences."

"Come on," Kristin said, pulling at Sinclair's arm. "This is done. You saw that look in his eye when she told him she was ready to go public. There's no faking that. This is what he wants."

Kristin pulled Sinclair out the door, leaving us alone.

"You're sure?" Matt asked, cupping my face again.

I nodded. "I want to be with you."

"I want to be with you too."

"I figure we can get through it together. I'm strong enough to do this with you if you're by my side."

"There's no place I'd rather be."

He slid his tongue along the seam of my lips and then

pushed into my mouth. My body sank in response. Then without warning, he pulled back. "What changed your mind? You're not just jealous of Kristin, are you? Because, I'd never—"

I pressed my fingers against his lips. "No." I paused. "Well, yes, I'm jealous of Kristin, but not because I think you'll cheat." I paused again. "But I don't want the world to think you're hers when really, you're mine."

I glanced down and fiddled with the button on his shirt. "And I talked to Ruby last night and she made me see that if you and I are going to have a shot at being serious, then I can't hide. That you're worth *not* hiding for."

"So you made up your mind about this when you spoke to Ruby last night? I wish you would have called."

I trailed my fingers over his lips. "Yeah. I wanted to tell you in person. And I realized the world doesn't care about me. It's you they're interested in." I smoothed over his eyebrows.

"And the only person I'm interested in is you," he said.

I wasn't sure how I got so lucky.

TWENTY-THREE

Lana

I dabbed the excess lip gloss from my mouth, then tried to get another look at my ass in Matt's miniscule bedroom mirror. For someone so good-looking, I would have expected him to have more mirrors in his house.

"Your ass looks fantastic," Matt said, coming up behind me. "In fact, I'm happy to stay in tonight and focus exclusively on that, if you'd prefer."

I laughed. "You're losing your charm, Mr. Easton." I swatted away the hands grabbing at my bottom. I wouldn't have been so nervous about going public had Matt and I walked through the lobby of the Mandarin Oriental hotel in New York together, then strode hand in hand through Central Park as soon as I'd told him I was ready. I'd been so certain then. But life wasn't that simple. Apparently, we had to wait until Audrey had been spotted out with her fiancé, and she confirmed she'd moved on. So we waited a couple of weeks between our meeting and the first shots of us together.

The problem was, the more time I had to think about it, the more I worried.

"Are you ready?" he asked as he tucked his wallet into his jeans.

"As ready as I'll ever be." I hooked the strap of my handbag over my head and let it rest against my hip. We were heading out to dinner at Chateau Marmont because Matt loved it and Sinclair had agreed it was a good place to be seen together for the first time. Apparently, he'd tipped off a friendly photographer.

"Oh, shit, hang on, I have something to give you," Matt said, then disappeared out of the bedroom door, coming back just a few seconds later and offering me what looked like a bank card.

"What's that?"

"It's a credit card."

"Thanks. I went to school. Why are you giving it to me? Your wallet is in your pocket. Why don't you put it in there?"

"Because this one is yours. It's linked to my account, but I want you to have it in case you need anything."

I took the card. Sure enough, it had my name on it. "Buy what? Groceries?"

"I don't know. Clothes. Shoes. Makeup. Whatever. I know you have your own money, but I don't want you to worry about having what you need to avoid tabloid criticism."

"I can afford to buy things. I don't expect you to pay for everything just because I'm your girlfriend."

"I know, and when my assistant asked whether she should arrange a monthly bank transfer as well, I said no."

I spluttered. He couldn't be serious. "She asked if you

wanted to set up a regular payment? She gets that I'm not a hooker, right?"

He chuckled. "Calm down, crazy head. It's just how things are done in LA. You know how weird it is here."

"It's normal to give your girlfriend a credit card and a monthly salary?"

"No idea about the salary. But I do know how hard this is for you. I want to do what I can to make it easier. It's really the least I can do—being my girlfriend shouldn't mean you're having to spend more money than you normally do. If dressing in Stella McCartney every day will help, then that's what I want you to do."

"Well, guess what, Mr. Movie Star, you don't have to pay me to be your girlfriend." I handed him his credit card. "You can go down on me regularly—that's payment enough."

He laughed. "What, so I'm paying you in sex?"

I waved my hand in the air. "Whatever you want to call it."

"Look, keep the card. You never know—there might be an emergency. You don't have to use it." He handed it back to me. "It would make me feel better if I thought I was doing something to help."

I couldn't very well say no to that. I took the card and turned it over and over in my hand. He was being sweet and protective. "Okay. But I'm not going to use it."

"You're my favorite person in the world right now," he said, then leaned over and kissed me on the head. "You're not anything like these LA girls."

"I'll let you know in a couple of hours how I feel about you." I grinned up at him.

"Ready?" He held out his hand and, instinctively, I took it. "You nervous?" he asked as he led me out to the car.

"A little," I replied.

In just a few minutes we were passing the Beverly Hills Hotel. It seemed ages ago that we'd last taken this route. So much had changed between us on that trip, and all for the better. We were a couple now. I trusted him and I knew he wanted to make me happy. I hoped I was going to weather the storm that the tabloids would inevitably create. But like Mrs. Wells had said, a storm brought good things as well. Matt was worth it.

"Sinclair took you through everything, right?"

I chuckled. "He did. He was very thorough." I'd spent the last three days with Sinclair and his assistant, who'd trained me in how to deal with paparazzi and warned me of the worst-case scenario when it came to social media trolling and tabloid lies. I was pretty sure Sinclair had half hoped I'd run screaming back to Maine. On more than one occasion, I'd been tempted. His best advice? Smile.

"I have my game face on. Look." I pulled my practiced grin to my mouth. Not so wide as to show teeth but wide enough to not look miserable.

He chuckled. "Thank God it's impossible for you to look anything but beautiful."

"Sinclair told me I had resting bitch face."

"That man is full of shit."

I released a wide, genuine smile. Matt always brought out the best in me. "You don't believe that, and anyway, I think he's right. I just have to grin and bear it."

"I'm not sure my beating heart will be able to withstand the constant smiling." He clutched at his chest and I play slapped him.

"He also told me I should toss out half my wardrobe. That it was the best the mall had to offer—and I'm pretty sure he meant that as an insult—but it wasn't good enough for the girlfriend of *the* Matt Easton."

Matt shook his head. "Seriously, ignore him. He's a snob."

"Banana Republic is my drug of choice," I said. "I'm not ashamed."

"Have you considered that perhaps what Sinclair was trying to say was that you just wear fewer clothes? Maybe you should spend most of your time naked." He nuzzled into my neck and set off sparks across my body.

"You're ridiculous," I replied, pushing him away.

He pulled me toward him and went to kiss me, but I put up my hand to stop him. "You can't ruin my lip gloss just as we're about to get photographed for the first time."

He groaned. "Can we go back to sneaking around? At least then I could kiss you whenever I wanted."

"I wouldn't want you to feel deprived," I said. "I'll make it up to you." I wanted to kiss him, but I didn't want to look like a clown the first time I appeared in a tabloid. Sinclair's assistant had arranged for someone to come to the house to do my hair and makeup, and I'd even given in when someone else had arrived with three different outfits for me to try on. I'd gone with a white, Stella McCartney pantsuit after the look Matt had on his face when I'd tried it on. He'd insisted I keep it, even if I didn't wear it tonight.

Although I felt a little less *me* than usual, I didn't feel as if I was going to embarrass myself in yoga pants and a pony-tail, which was my normal outfit of choice.

"Lucky for you, we just arrived," Matt said as we turned off the road. "Otherwise, I'd have insisted you make good on your promise, right here, right now."

"Oh, honey, there's not room enough in the car for what I plan to do to you."

He pulled me closer and dropped his mouth to my ear. "Promises, promises, Miss Kelly," he growled.

Matt's driver opened our door and Matt got out before me, then turned to help me out of the car.

"Matt!" various people called as soon as they saw who it was. A whoosh of lights greeted me as I stepped out of the car. I'd expected the gentle introduction of just a single photographer, but three paparazzi rushed toward us. As instructed, I took Matt's hand and looked straight ahead while keeping a slight smile on my face. Apparently, it was an expression meant to indicate contentment without acknowledging or enjoying the attention.

The driver had pulled up as close as he could to the entrance, so there wasn't much opportunity for the photographers to get pictures. Hopefully, they'd get enough and leave us alone the rest of the night.

"Who's your new girl, Matt?" one of them yelled. Another asked about Audrey. Sinclair had warned me that they'd try to provoke a reaction so they could get a more salacious shot, but my Sinclair-approved smile stayed safely in place.

Matt gripped my hand as we slowly but steadily made our way uphill to the entrance of Chateau Marmont. Neither of us said a word to each other. It was as if we were holding our breath until we got inside. If this was what it was like every time Matt went out, it was no wonder he liked Worthington so much. It was so peaceful. So quiet.

We slipped through the entrance and Matt's hand immediately went around my waist. "You did great," he said, pulling me close.

Being here, in public with him, after having my picture taken felt like I'd reached Everest base camp. It was a huge relief and a big accomplishment, but the mountain itself still towered in front of me. But for now, I was with Matt and we were both happy and that was all that mattered.

TWENTY-FOUR

Lana

Two weeks later, as I reached the sliding doors after baggage claim at LAX, I paused and pulled out my sunglasses, bracing myself for the glare of the LA sun. Hopefully Matt would be waiting for me in the car.

The photographs of us together at dinner had been published online and in the tabloids. There'd been a mixture of coverage, but no one had identified me. It hadn't been half as bad as I thought it would be.

I picked up my weekend bag and continued to the exit.

As the sliding doors parted, I scanned the waiting faces, looking for Matt's driver.

"Lana Kelly," someone shouted and I snapped my head around expecting David, although it wasn't like him to shout.

I was met with a bright flash and I froze. What was going on? The voice got nearer. "Lana, is it true you starred in a porno?"

My heart began to thunder. Someone was accusing me

of being a porn star? I couldn't tell whether it was a professional photographer or some random member of the public.

A flash of light burst in front of me again and I tried to remember what Sinclair had said—keep walking, hold a semi smile on my face. But I didn't feel like smiling. I wanted to know what was going on and I didn't know where I should be going. I turned right out of instinct and tried to keep moving forward.

Where was David?

I wanted to get out of this place. My hands were sweating and my head was spinning. Was this what I had to put up with? Accusations of being a porn star?

"Did you break up Audrey and Matt?" It was the same voice as before but in front of me now. It must be a photog, surely a member of the public wouldn't just accost me like this. My gaze hit the floor but I kept on walking.

Although Sinclair had warned me that paparazzi would try to provoke a reaction, I just wasn't prepared for this ambush. Luckily I had my sunglasses on, or he would have seen the shock all over my face.

I had to get out of there. I couldn't go back inside—security wouldn't let me.

Before I could form a plan, someone was at my side, taking my arm. "Miss Kelly, this way."

David. Thank God.

He grabbed my case with his free hand and we picked up the pace.

"You look like you've put on some weight since that naked picture was taken," the stranger in front of us said.

As soon as he'd said naked picture, I knew exactly what he meant. Someone must have seen the photo Bobby had taken with me.

My knees weakened and if David hadn't been by my

side, I was sure I would have collapsed. Tears began to sting my eyes and panic rose in my throat.

How had he gotten hold of that photograph? It was five years ago, and even Bobby hadn't been so cruel as to put it on social media.

David led me out to the waiting car. I fumbled with the door handle, desperate to get into the car, praying Matt would be there to put his arms around me.

David opened the back door and I scrambled inside only to find myself alone. I locked the doors and slid away from the windows. At least I'd escaped the photographer, but where was Matt?

I took out my phone and began to dial just as David got into his seat.

"You okay, Miss Kelly?" he asked.

I tried to smile and nod but I just wanted to talk to Matt. I called, but it went straight to voicemail. I pulled the screen from my ear to check if I had service. Four bars. I dialed again. Voicemail.

"David, do you know where Matt is?"

"At home, I believe."

I wanted to ask him why the hell he hadn't picked me up. Had he known the photographer would be lying in wait at the airport? I tried his number for a third time. Voicemail again.

I changed tactics and Googled myself.

I swiped down through the headlines.

Was Matt Cheating on Audrey?

Matt Easton's New Girlfriend's Porno Past!

Matt Easton's Naked Love!

My stomach churned. I clicked on the first porn-related headline. As the page loaded, the familiar photograph of me, lying on the bed, facing my then boyfriend, came into view.

I couldn't breathe.

My worst nightmare had become reality. The media had gotten a hold of the picture Bobby had littered around campus. Except now my humiliation wasn't confined to a few thousand college students and teachers. This had spread across the internet. Anytime someone searched for Matt Easton, this would come up.

And where was Matt? I needed him by my side. I slumped back in my seat and stared at my phone, willing him to call. The screen remained blank and my palm hot and sweaty.

The ride to Matt's seemed to be over in just a couple of minutes and, as the wooden gates opened, I craned my neck, hoping to see him in the driveway, waiting for me. But he wasn't there. Was he even home?

I climbed out of the car and loitered as David took my bag from the trunk. I followed him as he unlocked the door to the house and placed my bag inside.

"Thanks so much, David." I smiled, trying to pretend that Matt not being here to greet me was normal. Where was he? Was it possible that he hadn't seen my picture on the internet?

David shut the door behind him and voices drifted in from the patio. It wasn't as if I hadn't been here before, but I still felt a little uncomfortable as I made my way through the living area and out onto the patio where Sinclair and Matt were seated around a large wooden table. Matt snapped his head around as the door clunked behind me.

"Lana!" Instead of the broad grin that normally lit up his face when he saw me, he drew his eyes together. I realized he knew. I'd been able to hold off the tears until then but realizing he'd known made it more real somehow. He strode toward me, leaving Sinclair at the table.

"Lana, thank God you're here." He cupped my face and I sagged against his hard, warm body. "I have some difficult news to share."

He drew in a deep breath.

"There was a photographer at the airport," I said. My voice was quiet. Why was Sinclair here? I wanted it to be just Matt and me. I didn't want my pain to be public.

"Fuck," Matt replied and pulled me against him. "I didn't come to pick you up because I thought I might lead them to you. I'm so sorry. What did he say?"

"I saw the stuff on the internet. They have the picture of me."

He nodded and pulled me closer. "Oh God, Lana. I wanted to be the one to tell you."

Eventually, his grip on me loosened. "Sinclair's here to help us deal with this," he said and took my hand. We headed toward the table.

"It will all blow over in a couple of days." Sinclair shrugged. "The less attention we give it the better. I keep telling Matt the same thing."

"That's easy for you to say, Sinclair," Matt said, and I squeezed his hand, appreciating the support.

"My advice is still the same as it was two weeks ago. Ignore it," Sinclair replied.

I looked up at Sinclair. "What do you mean two weeks ago? At Chateau Marmont? Surely this is different? I didn't expect the press to get hold of these old pictures."

Sinclair seemed to disregard me and stared at Matt. I glanced across at Matt and he was glaring at Sinclair. There was something they weren't telling me. I couldn't shake the feeling that things were about to get a lot worse.

Matt pushed his free hand through his hair. "We hoped it wouldn't come to this." My heart began to beat against my ribcage. I clearly wasn't getting the whole story.

"You both need to tell me what's going on."

Matt sat back in his chair. "Can I get you a drink?"

I twisted in my seat so I was facing him. "No thank you. I just want to know what you mean by you hoped it wouldn't come to this. Did you suspect that Bobby would leak the picture?"

Sinclair began to speak. "About two weeks ago, right after you went to Chateau Marmont, Bobby approached me with an offer. Your photograph, in exchange for a lot of money. He threatened to sell it to a tabloid if we didn't agree."

I tried to swallow but my throat was too tight. I couldn't believe what I was hearing. More betrayal by Bobby but this time on a far grander scale. How had I not realized he was such a worthless human being?

"Sinclair, why didn't you tell me?" I asked. I turned to Matt. "Did you know about this?" It would be one thing if Bobby had contacted Sinclair and he'd handled it without saying anything to Matt, but another thing entirely if Matt had known and hadn't said anything. But surely he wouldn't do that to me.

He nodded. "Sinclair told me and I asked him to handle it. I'd hoped it would go away and you'd never have to find out about it."

"You both knew and didn't warn me?" I twisted my hand out of Matt's. I couldn't believe what I was hearing. How had Matt known about this and kept it from me? We were meant to be a team. I pushed my chair back from the table and put my head in my hands. My life was being managed by two people without me knowing anything about it. And the whole world had seen me naked.

Matt smoothed his hand across my back but I shrugged it off. I didn't want him touching me. We'd spoken every day. How many times had he called me right after he'd been talking about me with Sinclair?

"Sinclair is really experienced at handling these kind of situations. It's what I pay him for. It's just that Bobby got impatient and went with an offer from that internet gossip site. Your ex is a real scumbag, Lana."

"I know that. But I thought you were different."

"Hey, I know you're upset. We've been trying to make this situation better." He tried to pull me onto his lap as he'd done a hundred times but I pushed against him with my fisted hands.

"No," I snapped and he released me.

"We can handle this," Matt said, stroking my hair. "Like Sinclair said, this is an old college photo. No one will remember in a week. And this is as bad as it will get. There's nothing more to find. You're over the worst of it now."

"Over the worst of it? You don't think I'll live the rest of my life knowing there are stories on the internet calling me a porn star? I didn't sign up for this shit. There's no upside for me. You have a career and a bright future. What do I get for having my personal life exposed to the world?"

Bobby's betrayal paled into insignificance compared to Matt keeping such important things from me. He didn't understand why I was so upset. *At him.* "How could you have kept this from me? Why didn't you tell me this was happening?" I scraped my fingers through my hair and looked at him.

"I wanted to protect you. We thought it would come to

nothing. We thought we'd pay Bobby off and that would be the end of it."

I slumped back in my chair. I'd never have thought Matt would be so secretive.

"Were you ever going to say anything?" This was my life, my reputation, my worst fears coming to life and everyone had known about it and hadn't warned me. "The photograph was of *me*."

"I didn't want to concern you with it. You were worried enough about going to Chateau Marmont. Then that went so well, even better than I'd hoped. I didn't want this to trouble you if it turned out to be nothing." His brow was furrowed as if he was totally confused as to why I might be upset with him.

"So you lied?" I asked.

"I didn't lie," he snapped.

"You didn't tell me the truth, either." I didn't understand why he thought that it was okay to keep information about me secret. He was supposed to be the good guy. The guy I could trust.

"This is Sinclair's job. He's the best. What good would it do for you to have known? There's nothing that you could have done."

"That's not the point. The fact is it was my picture, my problem. At the very least I could have prepared myself for being accosted at LAX by a paparazzo."

Matt winced.

"Lana, I promise you, in a week's time, this will be old news. You don't need to get yourself so worked up," Sinclair said. "There are a hundred stories like this every day. No one will remember tomorrow."

I shook my head. "There's only one story that involves me. One that my boyfriend and his publicist *lied* to me about." I stood and the chair scraped against the stone patio. "And I just don't understand why. Is it because my thoughts and feelings just don't matter? Or is it because you've been so focused on the fallout for you and your career that I've just been abandoned by the roadside like I'm worthless?"

"What?" Matt asked. "That's not it at all. I've been trying to protect you, keep you away from all this Hollywood bullshit. It's an easy fix as far as my career is concerned."

"Oh, well I'm glad I'm not too much of a burden." I laughed bitterly.

As Matt stood, his chair fell backward. "Lana, come on. We were just trying to make this better."

"But that's not your job."

He swiped his hand through his hair. "It's exactly my job. You said it yourself. That we're in this together, that you could only do this with me by your side."

I nodded. "That's right. By my side, not out in front. Not by filtering what I can see, especially not when it's *about* me."

"It could have been so much worse. This is nothing," Sinclair said.

"It's nothing to you, because you're thinking about Matt's image. About *his* career."

Sinclair shrugged. "That's what I'm paid to do."

I turned to Matt. "You might be happy to have other people run your life for you, but that's not who I am."

"Hey, people don't run my life. Sinclair is here to help."

"They don't? Then why haven't you optioned that book you loved so much? Is this your career or Brian's or Sinclair's or whoever else is on the payroll, making decisions about your future?"

I turned and headed back into the house. I had no idea

where I was going to go. I was locked in some kind of LA prison. Would David still be in the driveway? But I knew I wanted to be away from Matt, from Sinclair, from all the cover-ups and scandal. I wanted to go home.

"Hey," Matt said, catching up with me and grabbing my arm.

I twisted away from him. "Let me go." I kept walking across the marble floors toward the front door.

"So, that's it? You're just going to leave?"

"What is there to say? You don't even understand why I'm upset."

"Of course I do. Having those photos leak is your worst nightmare coming true."

I paused. A few weeks ago, if anyone had asked me what was the worst thing that could happen to me, Bobby selling my picture to a tabloid would have taken the gold medal. But now that it had happened, I realized there was something far more damaging. "No. Having my boyfriend lie to me, having the person I risked everything for treat me as a problem to solve, rather than his equal, is far worse."

The echo of Matt swearing was all I heard as I opened the door and strode into the drive. Thankfully, David was still there, washing the car. "Can you take me to LAX?" I asked.

David glanced behind me to where Matt lingered in the doorway. "Sure, Miss Kelly." He dropped his hose and unlocked the car.

"Don't go," Matt shouted as he came up behind me. "Stay. I want to work this out."

I took a deep breath. But what about what I wanted? For this not to have happened. For us to have dealt with it together. "I want to leave. It's not always about what you want," I said, putting my purse on the back seat.

"Don't run, Lana. We can face this side by side if you just stay. You can't run away and hide from problems your whole life."

"I'm not running. I'm going home."

He sighed behind me. "Are you sure? Are you certain you've not just been waiting for an opportunity to leave me? This relationship? Isn't this just convenient?"

I spun around to see if he was serious. "You think I'd wait until the internet had called me a porn star if I planned to run?" How could he say something like that just to deflect attention from what he'd done? "I've faced my worst fears, risked *everything* for you. And you don't think enough of me to tell me the truth."

"I was trying to protect you. And I'm sorry. But don't leave. Not now." His hands snaked around my waist. "If you don't want to be in LA, then I'll come to Maine."

Part of me wanted to say yes. I wanted to rewind and relive those moments locked in our Worthington bubble where we were just two people enjoying a thunderstorm.

"Lana, I want to make this better."

There was no way he could. If only he could have been the man I thought he was, the man I'd agreed to give up my anonymity for. But he'd turned out to be someone entirely different and no one I could trust.

"I need to leave. Don't come to Maine." Matt's presence would bring more attention, not less. And I wanted to disappear.

I wasn't running. I just wanted to go home.

To wave at Polly Larch as she walked her cat.

To hear the sound of the ocean as I sat on my porch.

TWENTY-FIVE

Matt

The LA heat was stifling, but the way the air conditioning cut to the bone was worse. I sat out by the pool on the swing that I'd bought for Lana. I'd wanted to have a piece of Maine in Los Angeles for her when she arrived, but now I wondered if I'd ever get to show it to her. Maybe I'd ship it to Worthington. All I'd been able to think about in the week since she'd left was everything I'd lost. What my job had cost me. She was gone and she wasn't responding to my calls or messages.

My phone buzzed in my pocket, so I pulled it out and tossed it next to the script for *The Final Battle*, which had arrived a few days ago. Brian's name flashed across the screen. No doubt he was checking up on me, making sure I loved what I was reading.

Far from it. It was pretty much the worst script I'd ever read. I was about half of the way through and although the part I'd been talking to him about was the lead, there were only a few pages of dialog, most of which was cheesy. Nothing about this film screamed box-office smash.

"Hey, Brian," I answered.

"How's my favorite client today?"

He wasn't usually so chipper. "I'm your favorite? Why's that?"

"I just got off the phone with Anthony Scott's people. I have an offer for you."

My heart sank. "Oh, great." Even to my ears, my voice sounded flat.

"Great? It's a fuck-load more than *great*. You have arrived. Have you read the script?"

Lana's words continued to echo around my brain. Had I been allowing Brian and Sinclair to run my life? Make decisions for me? I'd been clear since I'd come to LA that what I wanted was to reach the top, and the pinnacle of Hollywood success was landing a franchise. Brian and Sinclair had been on board, so that was what we'd all been pushing for. It was why I'd agreed to date Audrey. It was the reason I'd said yes to the last three films and hellacious schedule. Every decision I'd made had been leading to this moment. It had been what I'd wanted. Brian and Sinclair were just doing their jobs.

Except that I'd never asked myself if it was worth it. I'd never stopped to wonder if this was what I *still* wanted. And now, with success within my grasp, all I could think about was Lana.

"Not finished with it yet," I said, sliding my hand over the pages. "But I was thinking—I'm still interested in making *The Brothers* into a movie."

He groaned. "You're not still talking about that book about the kids?"

I took a deep breath. "Yeah." Reading this Anthony

Scott script wasn't getting me excited, but the thought of bringing that book to the big screen gave me goose bumps.

"Are you fucking crazy? You need to kiss Anthony Scott's fucking ring and be grateful he's even heard of you. We can start talking production deals when your abs go doughy."

I sighed but didn't reply.

"This is an Anthony Scott movie and they're willing to pay you eight figures. And it's likely going to turn into a franchise. Frankly, you should do the movie for fucking free, it's such good exposure."

Eight figures was a lot of money. But it was more than that. An Anthony Scott feature and a possible franchise was a lifetime pass to A-lister status. Signing on to this would transition me from rising star to Hollywood royalty. It was exactly what I'd been aiming for all these years.

Fact was, if I never worked again, I would be more than okay financially. I'd paid off my parents' mortgage and set up college funds for my nieces and nephews. My family had never asked me for anything, and Lana had showed me that doing what *I* thought was best for people wasn't always what *they* wanted. Every time I spoke to my dad, he told me the only thing he wanted was for me to come home and visit more often. I'd been doing things for people I loved without understanding what they really wanted from me and that wasn't my money. It was my time and attention.

Lana hadn't wanted me to solve her problem. She just wanted me on *her* team.

I'd been so controlling of my career and my image in the last eighteen months, that I'd simply tried to do the same for Lana. Except what she'd needed from me wasn't control—it was honesty and support. I'd taken over and kept her in the dark about something that was hers to deal with. I'd been trying to do the right thing but it was stupid and selfish. I got that now. But it was too late. I'd been too focused on the end result and hadn't cared about how I ended up there. It was the same with my career.

I hated this script, so why was I even thinking about doing it? It was all a means to an end. And I wasn't sure that was enough anymore. In fact, I wasn't even sure that getting a franchise fit my definition of success anymore. Things had changed. I wanted to be happy. I wanted to make *The Brothers* into a film. I wanted Lana.

The thought of working with Anthony Scott should have me popping champagne corks left and right. But being on the set of a movie I knew was a pile of crap wasn't what I wanted to do with my career. Not anymore.

"Yeah, well I'm not going to do it for free. In fact, I'm not going to do it at all. It's not the direction I want to go." Instead of the panic I'd expected to swallow me whole, my shoulders felt a hell of a lot lighter.

Brian swore. "If you think this is the way you're going to make it to the top, you're sadly mistaken—"

"I've made my decision. I hope you can respect that, but I understand if you feel you can't represent me any longer." It felt good to have said no. I wanted something more than fame, money or success. I wanted to enjoy what I did and be proud of who I was. I needed to be less fixated on getting to the top and more focused on who I was and what that meant. "I hope that's not what you decide to do, but if we continue to work together, we need to sit down and figure out where to go from here."

The silence from the other end of the phone was deafening.

"You're a fantastic agent, Brian. But it's my career, and my life."

Brian sighed. "That script for *The Final Battle* is a pile of fucking shit, anyway."

It was the last thing I'd expected him to say. I chuckled. "Well, we can agree on the quality of the script, at least."

"I'll tell him you have a scheduling conflict. Honestly, it will do okay at the box office but it won't be one of his best. If it tanks, it's not going to turn into a franchise like they think it will."

"If it does, I don't care. I really want to produce *The Brothers*."

I could almost hear Brian's brain whir over the phone. "I'll see what I can do. It might work better on TV, though. I could talk to Netflix, see if they'd be interested."

It was exactly what I'd been hoping he'd say when I first talked to him about it. "Sounds great."

"I'll make it happen. I'll come by later this week and we can work out a new plan for you. Christ, I've seen drinking, drugs and women change the direction of an actor's career, but rarely does one of my clients fall in love and see the light."

"Thanks. I appreciate you supporting me." He thought I'd seen the light? Why had he never said anything before? Had he been too busy fighting to get me what I wanted? What I *thought* I'd wanted? Brian had only ever done what I'd asked him to—make me successful, secure me a franchise —but my priorities had shifted. He'd just been trying to deliver everything I wanted only for me to discover I needed something else entirely.

All I wanted to do was pick up the phone and tell Lana about my conversation with Brian. I grinned. She'd be happy for me. Even proud of me. If only I could show her how much she'd taught me. If it hadn't been for her, I don't think I would have ever dreamed I could produce something. She'd made me believe in a different future for myself —want something different, something *more*. She'd changed the direction of my life forever, whether or not she would share it with me.

"How is Lana? I heard from Sinclair that you two had a huge fight."

I sighed. "She's in Maine. And she's not really talking to me. I'm trying to give her space."

Life without Lana was empty. But the thought of her pain was worse and I hated myself because I'd caused it. I had just been trying to protect her from inevitable trauma, but when I saw what that had done to her, I knew I should have spoken to her. I shouldn't have kept it from her. I'd made a dreadful situation even more appalling and she'd run. Maybe she always would have. Perhaps she was just looking for an excuse. But I shouldn't have been the one to give it to her.

I was doing my best to give her what she'd asked for when all I wanted to do was jump on a plane to Maine and hold her, comfort her, tell her how sorry I was. I wanted to fight for her. For what we had. But that's not what she'd asked for. I'd learned my lesson and I was listening to her. Waiting for her. But I wasn't giving up. Not ever.

Still, I had to do something.

At least I could clean up the mess I'd made.

As much as was in my power, I needed to make things right.

TWENTY-SIX

Lana

I shouldn't have done it, but three tabloids in the grocery store had Matt on their front cover, and I just couldn't resist buying them. I missed him. Horribly. More than I thought was possible. I'd thought Bobby's betrayal had hurt me in college, but this was far worse. Matt had deliberately deceived me, and I couldn't recover from that. No one should make decisions about my life but me.

Maybe it was never destined to work out. He couldn't make himself less famous. He was always going to be Matt Easton, and I was always going to be the girl from Maine who didn't want to live with the attention.

I stuffed the magazines into my Kelly Jewelry tote. I'd have to wait until I'd dropped Mrs. Wells' groceries off before I could scurry back home to read them. I didn't understand why he was doing so much press when his film with Audrey had been open a month already. Wasn't publicity supposed to have finished? I needed to stop caring.

Just as I got to Mrs. Wells' gate, Polly Larch waved from

across the street and headed toward me. I hadn't been out in town very much since my pictures had been made public. I'd just wanted to hide away while people's memories grew fuzzy. Despite her crazy lady appearance, Polly's memory was as sharp as a tack, and I pulled my shoulders back, ready for her inquisition.

"I've not seen you in the longest time, Lana. I just wanted to tell you that tomorrow night I'm going to be throwing Molly a party to celebrate one year together. It's a last-minute thing, but I hope you'll come."

"Wow, you've had her a year already?" The fact the cat was still alive surprised me more than the fact she was having a party for her *cat*. This was Worthington, after all. I stifled a giggle and wished I could message Matt to tell him. He'd get a kick out of the story.

"A whole year. Can you believe it? Say what you like, but that leash works. Will you come?"

"Sure, but Ruby's back tonight. Can I bring her?"

"Of course." She waved as she turned on her heel, her long, full skirt lifting slightly in the wind. "The more the merrier."

I smiled and shook my head as I watched Polly bounce down the street. She couldn't have been happier if she'd just been told she'd won the lottery. She hadn't even mentioned the pictures. Maybe she hadn't seen them, or maybe she just didn't care. Either way I was relieved.

By some miracle, the photos of me had not made it into print, and I hoped it stayed like that.

It could have been a lot worse. To my surprise, Bobby selling my photograph to the tabloids took up less of my concern. Perhaps on some level, I'd expected it from him. What cut deep was Matt's betrayal. And the loss I felt because of that.

I unlatched Mrs. Wells' gate and pushed my sunglasses up to the top of my head as I took the stairs. As usual, I let myself in. "Mrs. Wells, it's me, Lana."

The TV echoed from the living area and her gray curls stuck up over the back of her easy chair. Without turning away from the screen, she waved. "Hello, dear."

Ruby would be here in a couple of hours, so I didn't have long to chat. I'd started work on another piece for Barneys, and I wanted to see if I could finish it before she arrived. I put all the groceries away in their familiar homes and headed over to spend a few minutes with Mrs. Wells.

As I approached, she moved her quilt from the chair next to her, and I took a seat. Twice I'd delivered groceries to Mrs. Wells since I'd come back from LA, and she hadn't once mentioned Matt, the photographs or anything else about her prediction of storms and a man coming into my life. It was almost as if Worthington, Maine, was in a bubble, cut off from any of the less-pleasant aspects of life. It was why I'd come home after New York, and it had been just as healing this time.

"I hear Ruby's home this weekend," Mrs. Wells said, pointing her remote control at the TV and pausing the action in *General Hospital*. "She's a good girl."

"She is. We've been friends a long time." I sat back in the chair. I couldn't remember a time when I hadn't known Mrs. Wells. She'd always been a part of life here in Worthington. I wasn't sure she'd aged a day in the last twenty years.

"Old friends are important," she said. "But new ones are, too. What happened to that handsome boy who rented the cottage from you this summer? The movie star?"

I stiffened. "I don't know. I guess he's back in LA."

She turned to face me. "You know he's the one for you."

I stared past her at the TV. "Mrs. Wells. Please." I wasn't sure I could cope if she told me Matt was my destiny.

"I don't want to interfere, but with your father gone, I think you might need someone with a little gray hair to give you a bit of advice."

I hadn't expected her to mention my dad. It had been four years, and I still missed him every day. But these last few weeks had been worse than usual. I'd just wanted him to tell me everything was going to be okay. He'd always been right when he'd said it before, and I needed that certainty right now.

I sighed but that didn't stop Mrs. Wells. And anyway, a part of me wanted to hear what she had to say.

"Your father loved you so much. You know he and your mom didn't think they could have kids."

I nodded. My dad had told me I'd been an unexpected surprise. We hadn't talked much about my mother. I'd been five when she died, but it was times like this that I wished I knew everything about her.

"Whenever I saw him in town, all he ever spoke about was you. Even when he got as sick as he did, he found his voice well enough to tell me what you'd been up to at college and how talented you were."

I took a deep breath, trying to keep my tears at bay. He'd gotten so frail by the time I got back from college, but I'd always been grateful for the twelve months I'd had with him back here. As much as I hated what had happened to me in New York, it had given me that much, at least.

"He was always quick to tell us how much like your mother you were."

"Really?" I couldn't remember my dad ever telling me that I reminded him of my mom.

"She was a talented painter when she was younger."

How had I not known that?

"I know he didn't talk to you about her much—I think he was worried you'd idolize her, want to live up to a woman whose faults you'd never know. He knew that no one's perfect."

I barely remembered my mother, just the curve of her smile and the way her hair smelled like roses. She was like some kind of fantasy goddess I knew had existed at some point, but simply accepted wasn't part of my life. My dad had been my world and I was happy enough with that.

"He always said that you were the gift she gave to him, and that he could never be angry or sad because the happiness you brought him outshone anything dark in his world."

I took a shuddering breath, trying to keep the dam inside me from breaking.

"Have you noticed that about life?" Mrs. Wells asked as she patted my hand. "The good always manages to outshine the bad. There's so much suffering in our world, but the sunrise, the birth of a baby, even the smallest human kindness always makes sure that the darkness is kept in check. But it will always be there. We can't get rid of it entirely."

I let her words sink in. My father must have been so devastated to lose his wife, but I'd never seen him with anything but a smile on his face. How had he done that?

"You think my dad would be proud of me?"

"How could he be anything but? You're a beautiful girl with an incredible, kind, generous heart." She squeezed my hand and I tried to hold back my tears. "But you can't avoid the darkness. There's always a dose in life. You deserve to be happy, but that doesn't mean you can run from the storm. Sometimes it's good to get a little rained on."

I couldn't ignore what she was trying to tell me. Was I expecting a relationship to be perfect? Had I run away to try to avoid the pain? There was no doubt Matt should have told me that Bobby had tried to sell him the photograph. Was it just a mistake or a reflection of how he saw me? The press intrusion, the way everything revolved around Matt and his career, even the interest in me and my life . . . was it worth putting up with all of it to be with Matt?

I wasn't sure of anything anymore.

I TOWELED off my hair as I sat in my robe, Ruby lounging next to me, flipping through the channels and slurping on the wine she'd brought. She'd arrived early and been on my porch when I'd gotten home. One of the first things she said to me was how my hair needed a wash.

"You smell better now," Ruby mumbled.

"Hey! I've showered almost every day."

"Yeah, well don't put that on your resume. It's like telling people you've given up eating children. People generally have a higher bar."

"Not showering is the same as eating children?" Ruby could be ridiculous at times, but that was exactly why I loved her.

"In this metaphor, yes. You want ice cream?"

Sugar had been my staple diet these last few weeks. "Actually, I don't."

Ruby snapped her head up at me. "Wow. That's progress."

I nodded. "I really think it is. I'm feeling a little better. But then again, I haven't been online today."

"There's been nothing new for a week," Ruby said as she reached for my laptop. "And there won't be now. You're all clear."

She seemed so certain, but my heart still sped as she logged on.

"Look, nothing." She spun the computer toward me. "Told you."

I exhaled. Thank God. "It doesn't even seem to be on the original site. I can't find it anywhere."

Ruby rolled her eyes. "I'm not trying to be mean, but you know you're not Elizabeth Taylor back from the dead, right? The press really isn't that interested in you."

I tipped my head back on the headboard. I hoped she was right.

"Have you heard from Matt?" she asked.

I shrugged. He'd called me every day, but I hadn't answered.

"He obviously really cares about you," Ruby said, staring up at me.

"I cared about him, too."

"Past tense?" she asked.

My insides twisted in pain at the thought I'd never see him again.

Even if he hadn't lied to me, if we were going to have any kind of future together we couldn't be sneaking around the whole time. But going public led to misery. "I think so. I mean, how can this possibly work between us? He lied to me and went behind my back and even if he hadn't, you know I can't deal with the attention."

"This is different from New York though, isn't it?"

I frowned and set down my damp towel and began to brush through my tangles. "If you mean worse, then I guess so."

Ruby scooted up the bed and sat up, crossing her legs. "I don't think so. New York was so ugly because Bobby betrayed your trust. Matt hasn't done that."

"Are you kidding me? He kept important things from me. And now so many more people have seen that picture."

"But no one that you care about, so who gives a shit? None of the people who matter are judging you."

"So, you're telling me that you'd be okay that thousands of people had seen you naked?"

She sucked in a breath. "It doesn't matter how I'd feel. It matters how you feel about it."

"I think I could have handled it, you know. I think I could have weathered that storm. But knowing that Bobby contacted Matt for money and Matt didn't tell me? He lied, even if only by omission. He treated me like I was a thing, not a person."

"I really think he was trying to do the right thing."

"Hey, you're supposed to be on my side."

"I *am* on your side. But I like you and Matt together. You deserve someone like him."

"Someone who has paparazzi following him around the whole time? Someone who lies?"

"Someone who cares about you. Treats you well. Understands how special you are. He made a mistake. He was trying to protect you and he got it wrong. He knows that. The easier thing to do is to shut him out and run back to Worthington and pretend you never met him. But I don't think that will make you happy."

I closed my eyes to try to stop the tears. He had treated me as if I was special. Right up until he'd covered up Bobby's blackmail attempt. "Ruuuby. Don't." My best friend might act tough, but she was a total romantic at heart. "I need you to tell me what a shit he is and how I'm going to be so much better off without him."

"Well, if that's what you're looking for, you've got yourself the wrong friend. I'm not going to tell you something I don't believe. I think he made a bad choice and you ran before you had a chance to work things through. His intentions were good."

I didn't think Matt had deliberately hurt me. I'd believed him when he said he was trying to save me the worry and pain. But he'd got it wrong. Made it worse.

"I think you're mixing up being embarrassed by the photographs going public and being mad at Matt. Have you forgotten that he didn't release the photos? That was all Bobby. Matt tried to stop him."

Was I being too hard on Matt? Was I blaming him for things that were Bobby's fault?

"I'm also going to say that you need to get your ass out of bed before it gets even flabbier than it already is."

Reluctantly, I laughed. "You can't tell me I'm getting fat while I'm going through the breakup blues."

"I totally can." She reached under my bed where I normally kept my workout gear. "Where are your sneakers? We need to get you running along the beach, not away from gorgeous, kind movie stars who are crazy for you."

Before I could respond, she blurted out, "What are you doing with this trash?" She pulled out the tabloids I'd bought earlier that day.

She threw them on the bed and tore one open. "Oh God. He hated doing this."

"How would you know?"

She didn't say anything, just kept turning the pages, scanning the interview. Then she moved on to the next magazine.

Suddenly she snapped them all shut and gathered them up, hugging them to her chest then shifting to face me, her teeth worrying her bottom lip. She sighed and said, "I have a confession to make."

The room swayed and I turned my whole body toward her. What could she possibly have to confess? We told each other everything.

"I don't want you to freak out. Promise me?"

I crossed my fingers in front of her, making sure she knew that whatever I promised was bullshit. "Sure, I won't get mad. Just tell me."

"Matt called me."

I jerked back as if she'd hit me. "What for?"

"He wanted my opinion on a few things."

"What things?"

Her mouth opened and closed a couple of times as if she was struggling to find the right words. "I can't keep this from you."

More secrets? I sat down, staring up at her. What had Matt done now?

"He explained that he and his publicist were working on a deal with some of the gossip sites and tabloids to stop them from running the pictures of you." She took a seat opposite me.

"What do you mean, a deal?"

"A trade. Inane interviews in exchange for the rights to the photo." She tipped the tabloids onto the bed.

I spread the magazines out, his beautiful smile beaming up at me. I had no idea that he'd been working to protect me like this.

"I think he contacted Bobby again. Paid him off. Made sure any other photos were destroyed."

I covered my face, relief washing through my body. He'd gone further than I'd ever thought possible.

"I think he felt really guilty. But you wouldn't answer his calls, so he came to me for permission to fix this. He didn't want you to think this was about him or his career, or that he was doing it behind your back. He just wanted to protect you. I told him to do whatever it took. And if you hate me for not telling you, then . . ." She shook her head. "I'm going to toss you out of the window."

"Of course I don't hate you," I replied. She'd just been trying to do the right thing and keep me from worrying. A lot like Matt had.

Ruby took my hairbrush from me and finished brushing out my hair. "Whatever happens, it's a really nice thing that he did. And even before, I know he should have told you that Bobby was blackmailing him, but he was trying to save you pain."

Matt was sheltering me from the storm, proving he was worth getting rained on for.

"And there's another thing." She dropped the hairbrush and began to scan through the articles. "Take a look at this."

Ruby handed me the tabloid. I squinted at the paragraph she pointed at, trying to skim what was written. "He turned down Anthony Scott," I said, almost to myself. "Shit, you don't think he did it to punish himself, do you?" I asked but continued to read. No, the article made his motivations clear. He'd met someone who'd helped him find himself. Focus on what mattered.

Me. He was talking about *me*.

My heart swooped.

"I think he's a really good guy, Lana." Ruby rested her head on my shoulder.

"I'm in love with him." I tilted my head, resting it on hers.

"Of course you are. He just made a mistake. You need to decide whether he deserves another chance. In case you were wondering what I think? He absolutely does."

"I'm going to top up our wine," I said, then stood and

headed into the kitchen. I gazed out onto the deck as I unscrewed the bottle. That was where I'd first kissed Matt Easton. Where we'd watched the thunderstorms together. My insides ached. I missed him. I could find a thousand pictures of him on the internet and as handsome as he was in each one of them, none of them showed how beautiful he was on the inside. Or what it felt like to be loved by him.

He'd listened to me. Heard me. Tried his best to honor my wishes.

He deserved a second chance, didn't he?

And so did I.

TWENTY-SEVEN

Lana

I slipped my sunglasses over my eyes just before exiting baggage claim. The flight from Portland to LAX had been uneventful, but it had felt as if it lasted weeks. Once I'd decided to give Matt a second chance, every second was too long away from him.

There were no photographers as I turned right toward the taxi stand. Hopefully Ruby was right. I was yesterday's news. I wasn't the movie star, after all.

I wanted to be able to talk to Matt face-to-face. I didn't want to tell him the things I had to say over the phone. He'd accused me of running away from him. And I wanted to show him that I was back if he'd have me.

I slid into the back of the cab and tried to relax, to tell myself I was doing the right thing. I really didn't know how Matt would react when I showed up. Thanks to social media, I knew where I'd find him this afternoon, and I'd managed to get a ticket to the same charity lunch. It had cost me a month's profit from the shop, but he was worth it.

It seemed fitting that it was a big public event. Perfect to prove to him that not only was I not running anymore, but also I'd forgiven him about Bobby and accepted the attention from the press was a part of him that couldn't be changed. I wanted him to understand all that mattered to me was that we were together.

Sooner than I expected, we pulled up to the Beverly Hills Hotel. My stomach twisted with anxiety. I'd thought this would be the perfect setting for a reunion. But now that I was here, I realized I hadn't considered what it would do to me if I had to bear a very public rejection.

A red carpet had been laid outside and photographers were snapping away, shouting questions and requests as guests made their way toward the entrance.

The cab came to a standstill a little way down from the start of the step and repeat and I got out, craning my neck to try to find Matt.

I turned to the driver and gave him a huge tip in return for him delivering my overnight bag to reception.

I had a red carpet to walk.

Trying to muster the courage to take that step toward Matt, I took a deep breath, hovering at the velvet rope. My knees almost gave way as I caught sight of Matt's bright-blue eyes and too-long hair further along the line of guests slowly making their way up the red carpet. I wanted to push past everyone and launch myself at him, but that would attract a little too much attention.

Carefully, I stepped inside the velvet rope, never taking my eyes off him. I willed him to look over at me. He was smiling, chatting to photographers as he made his way along the carpet. There were about eight or ten people between us but the walkway wasn't wide enough for me to overtake anyone.

"What's your name, please?" one of the photographers in front of me asked. My attention was pulled from Matt.

"Me?" I asked, half relieved that he didn't know and surprised that he cared. When he nodded, I took a breath and replied, "Lana Kelly."

I heard people ahead of me mutter and they turned to glance in my direction. I didn't care. As Ruby said, I didn't know them and their opinion of me was none of my business. I kept my gaze on Matt as I took a few steps forward.

Someone whispered in Matt's ear and he lifted his head up and our eyes met.

I couldn't help but smile at him. I'd missed him so much and even being this close to him made me feel better.

Matt looked like he'd been turned to stone. His expression wasn't fierce, but it wasn't joyful either.

People were looking from him to me and back again. And I didn't care one bit. I just wished he was close enough to touch, to pull into a hug.

The line kept moving forward except Matt stayed still. I inched closer and closer to him until finally he was right in front of me.

"Hi," I said, my voice trembling.

"Hi," he replied, then froze as if he didn't know how to greet me. What I wanted him to do was pull me into his arms. "You're here."

I nodded. "I've stopped running."

His eyes widened. "Does this mean that . . ."

"I know what you did. Ruby told me everything." I sucked in a breath. "It proved you were the kind of man who would do his best to shelter me from any storm. But no more secrets, right? I feel like I can handle anything if we're together, side by side."

"I promise," he said. "And I'm so sorry."

"And I promise I'm done running. When I'm with you, I'm where I need to be."

His face burst into a grin and then he glanced around at the photographers taking picture after picture.

I reached up and stroked his jaw, bringing his attention back to me. "As long as I have you, I can handle whatever strangers have to say about me. Or whatever pictures. I didn't understand how if I let myself love you, the other stuff just dissolves into noise."

He frowned. Had it been the wrong thing to say? It was a risk to tell him I loved him, but he deserved to know. And if he didn't love me back? Well, that was what ice cream and reality show reruns were for.

"You love me?" he asked, his voice a low rumble.

"I do," I admitted. "I'm sorry if that's too much, but we agreed no more secrets. I am *in love* with you, Matt Easton."

"Thank God," he gasped as his gaze dipped to my mouth, then back to my eyes. "I've loved you since the moment you rescued me from the Worthington bandstand," he said. "And I thought I'd lost you."

Relief burst through my body and he pulled me toward him and cupped my face.

He wiped a tear from my cheek with his thumb. "Don't cry. I only want to make you happy."

"You do. I've never been so happy."

He pressed his lips to mine and I sank against him. No matter where in the world I was, I was home if I was with Matt.

The snap of cameras drifted out of my hearing. Nothing mattered. Not if I was with this man.

He snaked his tongue into my mouth and I set my palms against his shoulders. I might not care that everyone knew

Matt and I were together, but my views on PDAs hadn't changed.

He pulled back. "Did I hear someone suggest we get a room?" His hands circled my waist.

"Nope, but I think that's an excellent idea. As much as I don't mind being in public with you, I like being in private with you even more."

He might be one of the world's most famous movie stars, but no one knew the Matt Easton I did. No one knew quite how sexy he was. Or how kind, generous and thoughtful. Because when the cameras were gone, it was just him and me. Boy and girl. Two people in love.

Forever.

TWENTY-EIGHT

Matt

I pulled Lana inside the suite and pinned her to the door with my hips. I couldn't believe she was actually here. I'd missed her scent—the ocean breeze mixed with summer flowers. Missed the way she looked at me as if I were her everything. How had I survived without her for so long?

Seeing her today was the last thing I expected. I was a guy who normally took things in his stride, but the sight of her sent a bolt of shock through me that almost had me paralyzed. I'd been terrified that she'd come to end things.

Before things went any further, I needed to tell her everything. Something I hadn't told Ruby. I put my arms around her and held her body against mine as I moved us away from the door. "I have to tell you about Bobby."

She nodded. "Ruby told me you paid him off. Thank you."

"We could have called the police but that would have just attracted more attention." I dropped a kiss on her forehead.

"I agree. You were protecting me. I wouldn't want to go through a court case." She swept her fingers over my lips.

"There's more."

Her eyes narrowed as she looked up at me.

"Sinclair told me that he would handle it, that I shouldn't go with him to hand over the cash." I focused on the dining table across the room. I couldn't bear to see disappointment in her face. "I told him I'd stay in the car. I just wanted to see the fucking weasel—to see if he'd have the nerve to show up. When he arrived, I couldn't help myself. I ended up punching him. In the face. I think I might have broken his nose." I winced. "I'm sorry, I just lost it."

When she didn't respond I glanced down. She was rolling her lips together as if she was trying to stop herself from smiling.

"You're not in trouble are you?" she asked.

I shook my head. "He knows he can't go to the police—he'd be charged with extortion."

She pushed her fingers through my hair. "I think I love you even more." Lifting up on her tiptoes she pulled me down to meet her mouth and I sighed, so relieved she wasn't mad.

"I LOVE YOU," I whispered as I dipped my head and placed a kiss under her ear. I enjoyed the way that sounded.

"I love you so much," she replied, and my cock jumped in my pants as if she was talking dirty. I'd never thought those words could be a turn-on.

I reached down for the bottom of her skirt and slid my hand up to cup her ass. "You wore a skirt," I said.

"I know you like it."

I groaned. There was nothing I didn't like about Lana.

Her heart, her soul. She inspired me to be a better person. And the fact that she was headstrong, determined and desperate to please me in bed—what more could I want? I hooked my thumb through her underwear and pulled them off. "You still wore panties. I don't like those."

She fumbled with the buttons of my shirt. "I wanted to make sure you were the only man to see what I had under my skirt."

"Such a good girl," I replied, biting her neck then across the tops of her breasts. I'd almost forgotten how soft her skin was, how easy it was to leave a mark. I straightened and pulled her from the door. I wanted her lying down and naked so I could study every inch of her to make sure she was all mine.

We fell onto the couch and I grabbed at her blouse, lifting it out of her waistband. I pressed my lips to hers, desperate to feel her desire on my tongue. She fumbled with my zipper and the tips of her fingers brushed cool against my hot skin. We went together perfectly.

"This is it. You get that, right?" I asked. "I need you to understand that there are no more breakups. Whatever happens, we're in this side by side. Okay?"

She nodded frantically as she pulled at my shirt. But I was serious. All I'd done the past few weeks was hope for her to come back. I was never going to go through that again. I stilled and she looked up at me.

"I know," she said. "We're together now."

"Now and always," I replied, and the sober look she gave me in response told me she understood. There was no going back after this. I dipped to press my lips against hers, taking any opportunity to taste her. "We're talking about weddings, kids, the whole nine yards before we leave this room."

She laughed and we tugged at our clothes until we were naked. I turned her over so she was kneeling on the seat cushions with her hands braced on the back. I took a step back to admire her, her alabaster skin luminous in the glow of the hazy sun through the blinds.

"Matt," she called, snapping her head around to look at me, her hair sweeping over her body. "Please."

I wasn't trying to torture her, but watching her was like foreplay. I fisted my dick, pulling up and groaning at the thought that I'd soon be inside her, coated in her need for me.

I grabbed a condom and rolled it over my straining cock. Standing behind her, I swept my hands over her skin and raised my palm, then brought it down on her ass, my hand tingling. The sound our flesh made as it connected smashed through the air like a crack of thunder. It was a starting pistol, an announcement of who was in charge.

Nothing got her wetter. I reached down and slid my fingers into her slippery folds. I always checked, but there was never a time she wasn't ready for my dick. It was the biggest compliment she could give me.

"Ready, baby?" I asked, trying to give myself a few more seconds of anticipation before the main event.

In response, she dropped her head and lifted her hips. I curled my hand over her hip and nudged my cock toward her wetness.

"Don't stop," she cried. "More."

I couldn't resist any longer and pushed all the way in to the root. I'd never felt so fucking privileged as I did sliding my dick into my beautiful girl. Her fingers grasped the velvet pillows as she panted. She wouldn't last long, but I'd make her come again and again and again until her body was weak and her soul was mine.

I gathered her hair in my hand, pulling so her face tipped back. I didn't want to waste the pleasure rippling across her face. I picked up my rhythm, holding her still, making sure she felt every thrust, every inch of me. I wanted her to have no room to think, to worry, to speculate about the future. I wanted her here with me, totally focused on how I made her feel.

Her cries grew stronger, and her body tried to jerk away as her muscles tightened around my cock. It hadn't taken long to get her to the point of no return.

Thank God. I wanted her to come again before I found my own release, and I wasn't going to be able to hold out for as long as I usually did.

Her thighs began to tremble, and she cried out as her orgasm passed through her. I stilled, concentrating on the curve of her shoulder, the dip of her lower back. Every part of her drew me in.

I pressed my chest against her back, skin against skin, and circled her clit with my fingers, pressing and pushing. She began to whimper. The control I had over her body was phenomenal. I knew exactly what she needed and how to give it to her. But it wasn't one way. My body responded to hers as if it was made for her.

I pulled out and brought her up, turning her around and pressing her body against mine.

"I need more," she said.

"I know you do." I dipped my head to kiss her. "And you'll get everything I can give you."

Her hands drifted down my back and made me shiver as I took another kiss from her before lifting her up and walking through to the bedroom.

"Lie down," I said as I lifted my chin toward the

mattress. "Let me see that perfect body that belongs to me now."

She sat on the bed, her legs dangling over the side as she splayed her arms, lowering herself down as if she were offering herself to me. I sucked in a breath—I'd never seen anything so beautiful in my life.

I stepped toward the bed. "Lift your legs."

She bent her knees and her thighs fell open, revealing her still-swollen pussy.

"I'm going to fuck you hard. Now. For hours. Forever."

She pulled her knees apart, telling me she was ready. Gripping both of her legs, I pushed into her. She was tighter than before if that was even possible. I stilled to catch my breath as my balls hit her ass.

Impatient, she dipped her fingers down to her clit, and I batted them away. "No. You have me to give you your pleasure now."

I circled my thumb around her clit as I began to push in and out of her. Her breasts moved with the rhythm, reminding me of the first time I saw her, her wet clothes clinging to this incredible body in front of me.

Unable to resist, I leaned forward, taking a dusty pink nipple in my mouth, sucking just before my bite went too deep. She screamed and she thrust her fingers into my hair —not to pull me back but to urge me on. She was greedy for sensation. She wanted everything I could give her, and I'd give her everything—at least I'd spend my whole life trying.

I moved in and out of her slowly and surely, allowing her to enjoy the drag of my dick. Pulling back to look at her, I knew what she wanted. She wanted to come again. I pushed harder and faster, her hips rose to meet mine, and our bodies slammed together again and again.

She gripped my shoulders, her fingernails digging into

my skin, and I had to fight against the vibration in my spine telling me I needed to empty myself into her.

Just before I gave in, she arched her back and screamed my name.

I couldn't hold back any longer—I pushed into her again and exploded along with any notion of a future without Lana. My body covered hers as if I were sheltering her. I wanted to feel this close to her forever, share every experience and thought I had. I'd finally found my place in the world. Nothing else mattered. Not Hollywood, not scandals and not movies.

As long as it was the two of us, I had everything I could ever want.

EPILOGUE

Matt

"I thought we were going to the dunes?" Lana asked when I pulled off the coastal road just on the outskirts of Worthington and headed down a track toward the ocean.

"Don't be mad, okay? I just wanted to take a little detour first." Since the publication of the photos, I hated keeping anything from her, but I was hoping she'd give me a pass on this one surprise.

"Why would I be mad?"

"I hope you won't be," I replied.

"Matt. Seriously."

I stopped the car and turned off the engine. "Look at that view," I said as we faced the cloudless sky, the bright blue water and the almost-white sand.

"What have you done? You know I don't like secrets."

"That's what makes you so infuriating." Before Lana could reply I opened the car door and rounded the hood.

"Why are we here?" she asked, stepping out of the car as I held the door open.

I took her hand and led her to the middle of the plot on which we were standing. "Because I wanted you to see this. The land goes right down to the ocean."

She shielded her eyes from the sun and looked out across the field that petered down to the beach. "I've lived here my whole life. You don't need to convince me of how beautiful it is. Now answer my questions. Why are we here and why am I going to be mad?"

I took a breath. "Because I've been doing a bit of research that I haven't told you about."

She narrowed her eyes. "What kind of research? For a film?"

I shook my head. "As much as I love your cottage, I'm not sure it's our forever home. When we have our family—"

"Our what now?" She furrowed her brow. We'd talked about kids. We knew we both wanted them. At some point. But we'd never gotten specific.

"I figure three kids is a good number, but you could convince me to have four. But the cottage just isn't big enough for all of us."

"It's plenty big enough for me, which is all it needs to be if you want four kids."

I wrapped my arms around her and pulled her against me. "We can negotiate the final number."

She pushed at my arms, creating a little distance between us. "We're not trying for a baby here and now, and you know how I feel about PDAs." She glanced around as if anyone would see us.

I chuckled. "How do you like the spot? The peace, the view, the ocean breeze? We can still walk into town from here."

She relaxed in my arms. "What are you saying?"

I hoped she'd love this idea as much as I did. "This lot is

for sale. I want us to buy it, build a house big enough to raise four boys, with a huge wraparound porch where we can watch the thunderstorms, read to each other and grow old."

Her eyelids flickered as if she was trying to find focus. "You want to be based in Worthington?"

We'd been splitting time between Los Angeles and Maine, but the more time I spent on the East Coast, the more I realized I didn't have to be in LA to have a career. "I thought we could buy a place in Malibu for when I need to be there for work, but spend most of our time right here, just like we've been doing these last six months. I don't want to raise kids in Hollywood."

She grinned up at me, her arms slipping through mine and circling my waist. "You sound pretty enthusiastic about the kids thing."

"I'm enthusiastic about everything in my life. Most of all you."

"Even my yoga pants?"

The first time I'd mentioned getting married had been in a suite at the Beverly Hills Hotel the night Lana first told me she loved me. She'd said we'd talk about it again in six months when I was sick of her yoga pants. I'd always love her —yoga pants and all—and today was six months exactly since that night when our lives together began. I wasn't about to let her go. I wanted her bound to me in every way possible.

"So, you've bought the land?" she asked, looking up at me.

I shook my head. "I'd never make a decision like that without you." The wind caught a strand of her hair and I tucked it behind her ear. "We're a team."

"You couldn't have said anything better. And I think you might have found the perfect spot. I love it here."

"We can work with architects and design the house ourselves. You can have a studio. We can build a privacy wall if you want."

She sighed. "No walls. Not here. It will be our home and I want people to feel welcome when they come here. I don't want our kids to think they're locked in. I loved the freedom of growing up in small-town Maine."

I raised my eyebrows. "Kids, huh?"

She grinned.

"Six months ago, I told you I loved you in yoga pants and always would."

"Has it been that long?" She glanced over at the ocean. "It feels like nothing and everything has changed."

"Some things should change. It's time."

"Time?" she asked.

"For me to ask. For you to say yes."

The corners of her mouth twitched. "Here? Now?"

I released her, took a step back and dropped to one knee. "Lana Kelly, will you do me the honor of becoming my wife?"

She kneeled in front of me on the grass. "Of course," she said, flinging her arms around my neck. "I didn't really think you were going to wait a whole six months."

I chuckled. "It's been killing me."

"What about my ring?"

I shook my head. "No way. As if I'd make a decision like that without you. And anyway, I didn't know if you'd want one. Or if you might want to make it yourself."

She pressed her palms to my cheeks and swiped her thumbs along my cheekbones. "I'd really like to wear my mom's ring, if that would be okay with you. Does that sound weird?"

I leaned and dropped a kiss on her lips. "I think that's a beautiful idea."

She pulled back. "I can't wait for you to be Mr. Kelly." A huge smile lit up her face.

I chuckled. "Life with you will be a constant challenge. I'm looking forward to every moment."

THERE WERE NO GUARANTEES, but the sky was such a bright blue that I felt sure that any rain would hold off during the ceremony. It was my job to provide shelter from the storm, and today, of all days, I wanted to make sure everything was perfect.

Most of the guests were already seated, but there were a few still finding their way in. "Hi, Mrs. Wells," I said. "Polly. Welcome." I looked down to find Molly, Polly's cat, with a big pink bow around her neck.

"Hello, handsome," Mrs. Wells said with a wink.

I winked back. "I'm glad all three of you could make it."

"The flowers look perfect," Polly said. Displays of lilacs and white roses surrounded the chairs, giving the air a perfume that was unmistakably Maine.

"Lana chose them," I said. "I can't take any credit."

"You had the good sense to marry our girl. You deserve a lot of credit for that," Mrs. Wells said.

"I'm very lucky." I grinned. Thank God, she hadn't slipped through my fingers. "My brother will show you to your seats."

I turned to James, who was looking at Molly and rubbing his brow as if he might be hallucinating. "Sure, follow me," he replied.

Lana and I had both wanted to get married in Worthington. Lucky for us the mayor had agreed to close off the park for the ceremony, and then the reception would be held back at the new house as a kind of a combination wedding celebration and housewarming.

"Mr. Easton, you're looking very handsome," a man said from behind me. I turned to find Mr. Butcher and his fluffy dog dressed in matching tuxes. He lifted Posey slightly. "She's doing the androgynous look today. And that," he said, hooking his finger under my lapel, "is Tom Ford, if I'm not mistaken."

I straightened up my bowtie as I chuckled. "Yeah, you're right."

He shrugged. "I'll never lose my eye for beautiful things."

"I hope you don't. I know how much Lana values your opinion." Mr. Butcher often got to see Lana's designs before I did, and I liked that she had someone in Worthington who understood how talented she was other than me. "Let me show you to your seat. It's on my way." We began to make our way down the aisle.

"I hope you're going to convince her to hire more help for the store. She needs to be focusing on cultivating her talent." He leaned in closer and whispered, "I heard about *Vogue*."

I placed my finger over my lips. We were all sworn to secrecy, but *Vogue* had confirmed this week that they were going to be using her jewelry in an upcoming photoshoot featuring young, independent designers.

"I think she wants to concentrate on designing for Barneys, but she'll still make some very exclusive pieces." Lana and I had talked about her spending less time in the shop. She had reduced her days, but as more orders came in, the balancing act was becoming too much.

"I knew that girl had something special," he said.

"You'll get no argument from me there." The violins started up and I indicated for Mr. Butcher to take a seat. I nodded as I passed Brian and Sinclair on one side of the aisle and Audrey and her husband on the other. Maine was seeing a slice of Hollywood this afternoon.

I hugged my father, the best man, as I took my spot in front of my friends and family. My three brothers sat in the first row. I was the one who'd wanted a big wedding. Lana would have been happy to go to Vegas. She'd teased me that it was because I liked to be in the spotlight. But really, I wanted to share my happiness and joy with everyone in my life who mattered.

Murmurings at the back of the audience caught my attention, and I turned to find my beautiful fiancée coming toward me, her smile lighting up my world as it always did.

Lana had refused Sinclair's offer to walk her down the aisle, maintaining that she didn't need anyone other than her father's memory to accompany her. I couldn't take my eyes off her as she approached, greeting our guests with nods and smiles on her way. My heart always sped up when she was near and this moment was no different. I was lucky to know this woman. Honored that today she would become my wife.

As she drew nearer, I reached out and guided her up the steps of the bandstand. It seemed fitting that we'd marry where we'd first laid eyes on each other. Life had a funny way of delivering just what I needed, when I needed it. If she'd been a different woman, she might not have come to my rescue that day, called me an idiot, or looked quite so alluring, soaking wet and screaming at me. She looked just as beautiful then as now.

I'd still start a war for this woman. Now and forever.

Lana

There was never a time when my husband looked like anything less than the hottest man on the planet, but as I watched him on stage, holding the Golden Globe for Best TV Mini-Series, I'd never seen him look so handsome. The whole world knew how good-looking he was, but few knew how decent, kind and smart he was. No one but me knew how hard he loved me.

I clapped as ferociously as I could, trying not to cry and ruin my makeup with millions watching.

He swept his hands through his hair, then leaned toward the mic. "Thank you, Audrey. Producing this series with you was the most fulfilling thing I've ever done in my career. You are always a great partner in crime." He glanced back at Audrey, who had just given her speech as co-producer, and nodded.

She'd asked me to make her jewelry for the evening, and seeing her up there wearing the earrings and bracelet I'd crafted felt as if I were up there collecting an award myself.

"This award is a tribute to the magnificent cast and crew I was completely privileged to work with. Thank you to everyone who worked on this series and to the studio for taking the chance on some kid from Indiana."

I held my breath, hoping he'd get to say what he wanted before the music drowned him out.

"I can't leave the stage before thanking my parents, who taught me what hard work really looks like."

I grabbed Matt's father's hand and squeezed.

"And my brothers, who still keep my feet firmly on the ground." He took a breath and found me in the crowd. "And finally, thanks to my incredible wife. She sat next to me as I read this book, made me believe I was capable of getting the story of these kids made. She is the brightest star here tonight, and I hope one day I deserve her." He blew me a kiss and his eyes never left mine as he strode right back to his seat, leaving the organizers confused, as everyone else went backstage to greet the press. But I knew my husband, and I knew he'd want to share every moment of this with me.

He sat and I grabbed his hand as he cupped my face and pressed his lips against mine. Seeing him happy was all I wanted.

"How about we skip these parties and take a plane back to Maine tonight?" he whispered in my ear.

I grinned and shook my head. "Your entire family is in town. They want to celebrate with you," I said as quietly as I could.

"But I want to celebrate with *you*," he said. "I'm so lucky to have you."

"You have the rest of your life to celebrate with me. I'm not going anywhere. Remember, we're in that same suite in the Beverly Hills Hotel tonight as we were when I came to see you almost two years ago. We've got some memories to relive."

"You're very convincing, Mrs. Easton."

"I know, Mr. Kelly."

He chuckled and turned his attention back to the stage. "We're going to have to agree on a surname when we have kids," he said, squeezing my hand.

"Then that gives us about eight months to come to a decision." I placed his hand on my belly.

His eyes went wide and he shifted in his seat so his whole body turned toward me. "You took a test?"

I shook my head. "I have one in my bag that we can do when we get back to the hotel. But I'm three weeks late and want to eat nothing but ice cream."

He cupped my face and pressed his lips to mine. "Fuck the Golden Globe. You just gave me the best prize of all."

OTHER BOOKS BY LOUISE BAY

Sign up to the Louise Bay mailing list to see more on all my books. www.louisebay.com/newsletter

Duke of Manhattan

I was born into British aristocracy, but I've made my fortune in Manhattan. New York is now my kingdom.

Back in Britain my family are fighting over who's the next Duke of Fairfax. The rules say it's me--if I'm married. It's not a trade-off worth making. I could never limit myself to just one woman.

Or so I thought until my world is turned upside down. Now, the only way I can save the empire I built is to inherit the title I've never wanted-- so I need a wife.

To take my mind off business I need a night that's all pleasure. I need to bury myself in a stranger.

The skim of Scarlett King's hair over my body as she bends over . . .

The scrape of her nails across my chest as she screams my name . . .

The bite of her teeth on my shoulder just as we both reach the edge . . .

It all helps me forget.

I just didn't bargain on finding my one night stand across the boardroom table the next day.

She might be my latest conquest but I have a feeling Scarlett King might just conquer me.

A stand-alone novel.

Park Avenue Prince

THE PRINCE OF PARK AVENUE FINALLY MEETS HIS MATCH IN A FEISTY MANHATTAN PRINCESS.

I've made every one of my billions of dollars myself—I'm calculating, astute and the best at what I do. It takes drive and dedication to build what I have. And it leaves no time for love or girlfriends or relationships.

But don't get me wrong, I'm not a monk.

I understand the attention and focus it takes to seduce a beautiful woman. They're the same skills I use to close business deals. But one night is where it begins and ends. I'm not the guy who sends flowers. I'm not the guy who calls the next day.

Or so I thought before an impatient, smart-talking, beyond beautiful heiress bursts into my world.

When Grace Astor rolls her eyes at me—I want to hold her against me and show her what she's been missing.

When she makes a joke at my expense—I want to silence her sassy mouth with my tongue.

And when she leaves straight after we f*ck with barely a goodbye—it makes me want to pin her down and remind her of the three orgasms she just had.

She might be a princess but I'm going to show her who rules in this Park Avenue bedroom.

A stand-alone novel.

King of Wall Street

THE KING OF WALL STREET IS BROUGHT TO HIS KNEES BY AN AMBITIOUS BOMBSHELL.

I keep my two worlds separate.

At work, I'm King of Wall Street. The heaviest hitters in Manhattan come to me to make money. They do whatever I say because I'm always right. I'm shrewd. Exacting. Some say ruthless.

At home, I'm a single dad trying to keep his fourteen year old daughter a kid for as long as possible. If my daughter does what I say, somewhere there's a snowball surviving in hell. And nothing I say is ever right.

When Harper Jayne starts as a junior researcher at my firm, the barriers between my worlds begin to dissolve. She's the most infuriating woman I've ever worked with.

I don't like the way she bends over the photocopier—it makes my mouth water.

I hate the way she's so eager to do a good job—it makes my dick twitch.

And I can't stand the way she wears her hair up exposing her long neck. It makes me want to strip her naked, bend her over my desk and trail my tongue all over her body.

If my two worlds are going to collide, Harper Jayne will have to learn that I don't just rule the boardroom. I'm in charge of the bedroom, too.

A stand-alone novel.

Parisian Nights

The moment I laid eyes on the new photographer at work, I had his number. Cocky, arrogant and super wealthy—women were eating out of his hand as soon as his tight ass crossed the threshold of our office.

When we were forced to go to Paris together for an assignment, I wasn't interested in his seductive smile, his sexy accent or his dirty laugh. I wasn't falling for his charms.

Until I did.

Until Paris.

Until he was kissing me and I was wondering how it happened. Until he was dragging his lips across my skin and I was hoping for more. Paris does funny things to a girl and he might have gotten me naked.

But Paris couldn't last forever.

Previously called What the Lightning Sees

A stand-alone novel.

Promised Nights

I've been in love with Luke Daniels since, well, forever. As his sister's best friend, I've spent over a decade living in the friend zone, watching from the sidelines hoping he would notice me, pick me, love me.

I want the fairy tale and Luke is my Prince Charming. He's tall, with shoulders so broad he blocks out the sun. He's kind with a smile so dazzling he makes me forget every-thing that's wrong in the world. And he's the only man that can make me laugh until my cheeks hurt and my stomach cramps.

But he'll never be mine.

So I've decided to get on with my life and find the next best thing.

Until a Wonder Woman costume, a bottle of tequila and a game of truth or dare happened.

Then Luke's licking salt from my wrist and telling me I'm beautiful.

Then he's peeling off my clothes and pressing his lips against mine.

Then what? Is this the start of my happily ever after or the beginning of a tragedy?

Previously called Calling Me

A stand-alone novel.

Indigo Nights

The only thing better than cake is cake with a side of orgasms.

Dylan James has no expectations when it comes to relationships. He uses women for sex and they use him for his money and power. It's quid pro quo and he's good with that. It works.

Beth Harrison has been burned. She's tired of the lies and the game playing that men bring and has buried herself in her passion—baking which keeps her out of the reach of heartbreak. As she begins her career as a TV baker, a new world opens up to her.

Dylan and Beth both know that casual sex is all about giving what you need to get what you want.

Except that sometimes you give more than you need to and get everything you ever wanted.

A stand-alone novel.

The Empire State Series

Anna Kirby is sick of dating. She's tired of heartbreak. Despite being smart, sexy, and funny, she's a magnet for men who don't deserve her.

A week's vacation in New York is the ultimate distraction from her most recent break-up, as well as a great place to meet a stranger and have some summer fun. But to protect her still-bruised heart, fun comes with rules. There will be no sharing stories, no swapping numbers, and no real names. Just one night of uncomplicated fun.

Super-successful serial seducer Ethan Scott has some rules of his own. He doesn't date, he doesn't stay the night, and he doesn't make any promises.

It should be a match made in heaven. But rules are made to be broken.

The Empire State Series is a series of three novellas.

Hopeful

Guys like Joel Wentworth weren't supposed to fall in love with girls like me. He could have had his pick of girls, but somehow the laws of nature were defied and we fell crazy in love.

After graduation, Joel left for New York. And, despite him wanting me to go with him, I'd refused, unwilling to disappoint my parents and risk the judgment of my friends. I hadn't seen him again. Never even spoken to him.

I've spent the last eight years working hard to put my career front and center in my life, dodging any personal complications. I have a strict no-dating policy. I've managed to piece together a reality that works for me.

Until now.

Now, Joel's coming back to London.

And I need to get over him before he gets over here.

A stand-alone novel.

Love Unexpected

When the fierce redhead with the beautiful ass walks into the local bar, I can tell she's passing through. And I'm looking for distraction while I'm in town—a hot hook-up and nothing more before I head back to the city.

If she has secrets, I don't want to know them.

If she feels good underneath me, I don't want to think about it too hard.

If she's my future, I don't want to see it.

I'm Blake McKenna and I'm about to teach this Boston socialite how to forget every man who came before me.

When the future I had always imagined crumbles before my very eyes. I grab my two best friends and take a much needed vacation to the country.

My plan of swearing off men gets railroaded when on my first night of my vacation, I meet the hottest guy on the planet.

I'm not going to consider that he could be a gorgeous distraction.

I'm certainly not going to reveal my deepest secrets to him as we steal away each night hoping no one will notice.

And the last thing I'm going to do is fall in love for the first time in my life.

My name is Mackenzie Locke and I haven't got a handle on men. Not even a little bit.

Not until Blake.

A stand-alone novel.

Faithful

Leah Thompson's life in London is everything she's supposed to want: a successful career, the best girlfriends a bottle of sauvignon blanc can buy, and a wealthy boyfriend who has just proposed. But something doesn't feel right. Is it simply a case of 'be careful what you wish for'?

Uncertain about her future, Leah looks to her past, where she finds her high school crush, Daniel Armitage, online. Daniel is one of London's most eligible bachelors. He knows what and who he wants, and he wants Leah. Leah resists Daniel's advances as she concentrates on being the perfect fiancé.

She soon finds that she should have trusted her instincts when she realises she's been betrayed by the men and women in her life.

Leah's heart has been crushed. Will ever be able to trust again? And will Daniel be there when she is?

A stand-alone novel.

KEEP IN TOUCH!

Sign up for my mailing list to get the latest news and gossip
www.louisebay.com/newsletter

ACKNOWLEDGMENTS

A huge thank you to everyone who read this book. I love creeping into your lives for a few moments here or there and hopefully into your imaginations for a little longer. I loved living in Worthington while I wrote this book. I think I might move there. I want a porch and a swing and to eat lobster roll. Maybe when I'm old enough to not care about putting a lead on a cat it will happen.

Thank you comma Elizabeth. I don't care what you say, I'm still smarting from this one. I haven't forgotten yet. When does it get easier? It's you next! So excited for Defenseless. I really hope you knock it out of the park. You deserve to.

Neeeeeeena. Thank you for all your support. I hope we have many more What Is Happening?!?! moments together. And remember, Valentine will never stop needing you.

To all those amazing authors who offer incredible advice and support. I just hope that I

Najla, you are THE most patient person in the universe. You're awesome and your covers are awesome. Thank you.

Jules, Megan you gals are the best. Sally, Charity, Peggy and Davina thank you for finding all my mistakes!

Thank you mummy for everything. 100 bags.

Thank you to everyone who tells their friend about one of my books, blogs about it or retweets something or likes a post. I don't take you for granted and I am so very grateful!

69362904R00171

Made in the USA
Lexington, KY
30 October 2017